NO GOING BACK

Book 7 of the Lily Harper Series

H.P. Mallory

NO GOING BACK

Book 7 of the LILY HARPER Series

Copyright ©2019 by HP Mallory

Acknowledgements:

To my son, Finn: I love seeing the world through your eyes.

To my mother for always being there for me.

To my editor, Teri, at www.editingfairy.com: thank you for an excellent job, as always.

"... the wish of so impure a blotch possess'd thee..."
- Dante's Inferno

ONE
TALLIS

It seemed like forever since the angel and I had stepped outside the Asylum's gates. Not that getting beyond them offered much comfort. The endless cold penetrated every crevice of the Underground City's Ninth Circle, sinking its icy fangs into every part of me body.

Even with the Druid magic warming me bones, the chill 'round us tore into me bare chest like a thousand needles. Worse yet, me pants and boots were sae rotted from weeks—mayhap months—of captivity they couldnae provide protection whatsoever. Every step forward became a mighty struggle worthy of a skald's song.

Even so, I still hoped we were coming closer to the Circle's edge. That hope died when I recognized the frozen electric vehicle ahead of us. This modern vehicle had carried me and the stookie angel as we'd made our way down to this frozen wasteland. Now it could go nae further without repairs. However brutal the Ninth Circle was on living things, it was downright merciless to machinery what overstays its welcome.

Fool that he was, the squat angel waddled up to the driver's side door and grabbed the handle. He tried pulling it with his stubby hand but couldnae even budge it a hair. After a minute of failing, he released it then yelped when the layer of ice took skin from his

1

palm as retribution. He balled his other hand into a fist before impotently pounding the frozen door.

"C'mon, ya hunk o' junk! Lemme in already!"

Me eyes started scanning the chilly terrain 'round us on the off-chance someone might have overheard his loud protest. "Wha'ever gave ye the idear the vehicle would be obligin', ye bleedin' dunderheid?"

The angel slammed his fist into the door one more time and held it there. Another layer of skin ripped off his knuckles when he pulled away. Rubbing his destroyed palm with the hand sporting the raw knuckles, his expression reminded me of a whipped dog.

"Ah shut it, Conan," the dunderheid muttered. Then he faced the vehicle again. "Come on, you fuck!" he glared at the vehicle and kicked it with his toes. "Angel Bill needs ta get hisself outta this frozone, yo," he continued, addressing the vehicle. Then he turned back 'round to face me. "I don't see how ya managed ta stand it down here this long. My balls are nearly froze all the way off!"

I shrugged. "Needs must, stookie angel, needs must."

"What must?"

"Ye do what ye must tae survive," I grumbled. "Boot whinin' 'bout it 'tis as useless as askin' how we survived the torture an' starvation in Alaire's dungeons."

The angel grunted as he continued rubbing his sore palm. "Yeah, well, gotta say, yo, this spot makes *Tall, Blonde an' Evil's* place look like a Hilton!"

I rubbed the window of the vehicle with me forearm. The extra heat from me magic barely prevented me arm from being frozen to the glass. As expected, icicles were forming all over the interior and the seats. "Ye didnae leave anything important in there, did ye?"

2

The little angel shivered and started rubbing his arms when he should have been rubbing his chest. "Only thing in there you could call vitalitical was the navigation system, Tido. An' that ain't doin' us much good without the rest workin', is it?"

I put me arm back down and sighed. "Aye... an' more's the pity on both accounts."

A faint glow began highlighting the stookie angel. At first, it was sae faint, I thought it a mere trick of the light. But it brightened to the point that it was soon shining like a distant beacon.

Even in the thick, icy fog surrounding us, the blindest imp could have seen the lightshow from a distance. I had nae idea why the fool angel thought a burst of illumination would help us, but it most assuredly wouldnae.

"Lleu's sake, man, douse it!"

The light went out immediately, leaving me in the darkness yet again. This time with an annoyed angel.

"Well, excuuuuuuse the fuck outta me, Conan! All I'm tryin' to do is get somewhere closer ta room temperature! Don't forget I lost all my man-blubber that was keepin' me warm back at Hell-tel California! Now I ain't even chubby fit no more! I'm just fit!" His voice cracked. "I used to be all warm an' cuddly with my six pack o' puddin' cups an' now look at me!" His cracking voice gave way to sobbing which yielded to a shriek. "Look at me!"

In that regard, he had a point.

Before our most recent and unfortunate trip to the Underground City, the angel's overindulgences made him more resemble a stout, little gnome than an angel. A short, stubby ball of fat, piss and vinegar, he had always been more interested in wine, women and food than being a proper angel.

But becoming a prisoner in Alaire's castle took a heavy toll on him. While there was still a bit of meat upon his bones, the fat was trimmed away to almost nothing. Being unable to die, he could surely feel the pain of his trials just as much as I had.

As befits a creature who speaks in such a bizarre and disjointed manner, it took me a moment to figure out what he was trying to say as regards his angel light. "So yer light can warm as well as blind?"

The wee angel became downright indignant. "Helloooo! Divine Fire for all yer lightin' an' heatin' needs! I tell ya, yo, there ain't a single iceberg I can't meltinate if I put my angel light on full blast."

I did me best to keep me temper.

Sure, the dunderheid was a bumbling, careless, irresponsible excuse for an angel, but he'd also saved me life back at the Asylum. An' now he was the only person I could call an ally. "Aye, an' if Alaire's lackeys see yer light, they might jist come 'meltinate' us too. It's nae what I call a good tradeoff."

He rubbed his saggy cheeks then slapped them hard as though he were trying to ward the cold away. "Cool story bro." Then he sighed, long and hard. "Look, Tido, my braincase is gettin' as popsicled as that car. So if you gots a better idea—"

When I reached down to put both me hands on the angel's forehead, I did something I didnae think possible: I shut him up. Shoving that small victory aside, I focused on me inner fire. I felt it begin flowing out from me chest like a free-running river. It went through me until finally, it entered the stookie angel himself. Just to make sure me warmth stayed within the idiot bampot, I held me hand on him for another few seconds before pulling back.

The angel's mouth opened and closed for the span of a heartbeat, but nae words came out. He looked a bit like a cod just yanked from a stream. Finally, as I resumed me trek towards the Circle's edge, he began blathering on about what? I didnae know. Meanwhile, he began running after me as fast as his stubby legs would allow him.

"Damn, yo! What was that Harry Potter shit?" He didnae wait for me to respond. "I didn't think that Druid, dark arts shit worked on people of my divinitage."

I looked over me shoulder at him and slowed me pace so he could catch up. "Well, now ye know. Feelin' warm enough tae make it the rest o' the way?"

The angel finally reached me side and did his best to match me pace. "Depends how far we gotta go..."

"The distance Ah know not." I peered into the chilly mist ahead. "By all the shapes o' the Morrigan, may it nae be far."

***

Our trek became nae easier as the vehicle faded into the frozen distance. Despite me Druid magic, the angel and I were moving far too slowly for our own good.

For the first time ever, I found meself missing Donnchadh. Aye! That beast of a spirit I had to hold in check every waking moment. Aye! that damned spirit that near defiled me dear Besom twice.

But me old companion also possessed two abilities I now sorely needed: the power to keep the cold at bay and the strength to fight whatever the Underground City had to offer.

Funny... After centuries of wishing I were rid of the bothersome reaver inside me, now me wish had been granted but at the worst possible moment.

To add insult to injury, me Besom, the fair Lily, had allowed that murderous bastard to lodge within her just sae she could destroy an even nastier spirit that preyed upon her soul.

If I'd thought they'd listen, I'd pray to me old gods and ask them to grant Besom the fortitude to contain Donnchadh good and proper. Given I could only barely manage to control Donnchadh meself, I wasnae hopeful me prayer would be answered.

Large lumps of ice began to appear in the mist. By squinting hard, ye could tell each of these mini-ice boulders held automobiles within them.

The angel grunted in surprise. "That a Model T, yo?"

I nodded and pointed at the vehicle behind it. "An' that one 'tis a Humvee... an' that o'er there's a Jeep. 'Tis a veritable Sargasso Sea fer dead vehicles."

The little angel gave me a funny look. "Sar-gatso what? An' since when did you become a car-oisseur?"

We passed the Model T as I replied. "Needs must, Walloper, needs must."

The angel pursed his lips. "What are all these cars doin' out here in the dead endzone anyways?"

A grim, irrepressible smile appeared on me face when we trod between the Humvee and the Jeep. "Me best guess?"

"Yeah, an' what the hell's a *walloper* again?"

"Alaire's got a fool idear that an automobile should be able tae withstand the Asylum's cold … clearly such isnae the case."

A crackle and hissing pierced the gloom, making me halt. I held up me hand for the angel to do the same. The hissing went on and I barely managed to make out the sound of voices. Voices which were a wee bit softer than the noise.

Near as I could tell, the volume of the sounds indicated someone was directly in our path. Seeing another frozen vehicle to our right—judging by the massive gun barrel on top—I pegged it as a Sherman tank and made a chopping gesture towards it for the stookie angel. He had the rare good sense to stay quiet for once and followed me lead to the front of the massive death machine.

A quick glance 'round the right corner of the tank showed me we were alone. Better yet, there were nae tracks to indicate anyone had been by in a while. I crouched low as I could—roughly the angel's height—and duck-walked me way towards the other end of the tank. I cautiously poked me head 'round the side of the Sherman and saw the sources of the noise.

A dozen creatures were huddled 'round a set of crates, most of the crates filled with greater imps. The heavy hair and claws identified them as natives of the Ninth Circle. But one of them, huddling near a laptop computer on top of one of the crates, had narrower features and he wasnae quite so giant and grotesque.

Instead, he was quite beautiful. His features revealed he could only have hailed from the City of Dis. I imagined him the war leader of this not-so-merry band.

The laptop screen made the hissing and crackling sounds I had heard earlier. I spotted a few humans who also possessed remarkably good looks, but naethin' compared to the Dis imp.

The angel leaned his head out to get a better look, taking in a sharp breath that turned into a hiss. "We got us a problem here, Tido."

"Ye can say that agin, stookie angel," I muttered back.

The little one's whisper became harsher. "No, Tido, you ain't gettin' my gist!" I looked back at him in question and he motioned to the humans. "That pair of Abercrombie and Bitch models with the Dis Dope? They're Soul Retrievers!"

"The rest was serpent all..."
- Dante's Inferno

TWO
TALLIS

I gave the angel a sharp look. "Ya cannae be serious, man."

"Major heart attack serious, Conan," the angel insisted. "Got me an eye fer auras an' those two got the look of a couple o' dead dum-dums who went rogue-sane."

I didnae want to believe it.

Me Lily was a Soul Retriever, after all. And thanks to Alaire infiltrating the Underground City with his monsters, many of Besom's colleagues were sent out on what turned into suicide missions.

To think they'd join Alaire willingly? The thought was near impossible.

"Mayhap the soul retrievers are prisoners?" I asked with a shrug.

The stookie angel looked like he wanted to yell at me. "Prisoners?" He shook his head. "Dude, the Asylum's just down the road. Get real, yo! They ain't prisoners! They're traitor-bastards!"

I rubbed me shaggy beard (courtesy of me long incarceration in Alaire's dungeon) in frustration for I knew the angel was correct. These soul retrievers were nae escaped prisoners. They were in cahoots with the imps.

8

Having apparently seen enough, the angel pulled his head back. "So what's the plan, Conan?"

I took a closer look. "Road's nae good. Even if we could git past 'em, they outnoomber oos an' we're weak. Catchin' oop to oos would take nae time."

The fool angel growled, "Christ, I coulda toldja that!" He took a deep breath. "So if we ain't doin' the hundred-meter dash-and-die, what are we doin', yo?"

I squinted harder. "Let me think."

A sharp jab hit me ribs, making me damn near yelp. I regarded the stookie angel with annoyance. "That's your cue to blow my mind with your next brilliantastic idea, Tido."

I waved a dismissive hand at him and returned to watching the scene. I wanted to escape too but his distractions couldnae make that happen any faster.

'Twas then that I saw something to be hopeful about. It was naethin' but a faint boxcar shape in the fog, big enough to hold every vehicle we might pass on our way. It was good to know the old girl was still in one piece.

I kept me eyes on the answer to our quandary as I finally answered the wee one's unspoken question.

"Ah jist spotted our way outta the Circle, stookie angel."

"What, d'ya mean?" he asked with a furrowed brow. "You see a road? I thought ya just said—"

I grabbed him by the back of the neck and practically shoved him 'round the corner. "Nae... look, man!"

He squirmed against my grip. "How many times I gotta remind you that whiles I might be prime man meat, I ain't interested in no bromance..." His fool thought died upon his lips as he cocked his head in the direction of the box. "Izzat what I think it is?"

"If ye think 'tis a freight elevator that'll take oos straight oop tae the morgue, then aye. If we're loocky, she's jist as foonctional as ever."

I pulled him back 'round and released his neck. The angel rubbed it with his skinned palm. "Okay, fine, we gots us a goal. But I'm still waitin' on the plan to git us there, yo."

I glanced at our surroundings, feigning one more cautious look at the situation. But I was just stalling. Even under the best of circumstances, defeating so many greater imps was near impossible.

The angel barely suppressed a groan behind me. "You don't gots a plan, do ya?"

Curse me bastard luck that he saw through me! I whirled 'round, glaring me own frustration his way. "Ah'd have thought ye angels had a wee bit more faith that things would work out fer the best."

The angel rolled his eyes hard enough to resemble a slot machine. "We're stuck down here an' the bastard responsible has posted his demon shits everywhere. You see anythin' to be faith-filled about?!"

While he indulged in his grousing, the hissing was interrupted by a fresh series of loud crackles. The latter became more deafening until a deep hum replaced it. The angel and I looked 'round again to see a familiar, hated face appear on the laptop's screen. I fought me urge to rush from our cover and smash me fist through the laptop.

"It's been precisely six hours since your last report, Captain," Alaire's smooth, menacing voice announced over the tinny speakers. "Why am I calling you instead of the other way around?"

The captain, who did happen to be the handsome one, turned to face one of the soul retrievers. The human immediately backed away in fear.

"Shit! I'm sorry," he started. "I just—"

One of the Greater Imps cut off anything more the human had to say when it drove its massive fist into the poor sod's stomach. The blow was hard enough to lift the turncoat off the ground and he landed upon his knees. The captain followed that bit of brutality with a series of kicks into the Retriever's chest and face.

When the imp had tired himself, he pointed a finger at the battered Soul Retriever. "Make another mistake and you lose a limb."

"Speaking of losing," the onscreen Alaire prompted, "I am rapidly losing patience over the delay of the progress report."

The captain turned his full attention to the screen. "As you suspected, Sire, the vehicle used to transport Tallis Black *did* pass this way once again."

The blonde bastard stroked his chin. "Pass? As in it did not return?"

The captain gave Alaire a curt wobble of his head, barely indicating a shake. "No, Sire. Given the unfinished nature of the vehicle's repair, I can only speculate that—"

Anger edged into me hated foe's voice. "You're in the Ninth Circle! That means you must do far more than merely speculate, Captain. I want that vehicle found and searched immediately... as in an hour ago!"

The captain took his boss's audacious demands in stride. "I'll send over six of the imps right—"

"Send nine, just to make sure."

The captain retreated at hearing the order. "But, Sire, in Black's currently weakened state, we can—"

Alaire's voice grew so loud, he nearly blew out the speakers of the laptop. "Do I need to remind you there's also an angel on the loose? You may be prepared to take needless chances but I assure you that I am not. Now do as you're told or *you'll* be the one receiving a severe beating upon your return!"

Before the captain could reply, the screen quickly degenerated to hissing static. The captain nervously cleared his throat and started pointing at his troops.

"You, you, you, you, you, you, you and you... go find that car at once!" That order was followed by a kick to the beaten man's back, making him bark out in pain. "And take this moron with you."

The nearest walking hairball started grabbing the man's broken arm when the angel and I pulled back. The angel seemed to be in awe. "Wow... Blondie actually thinks I'm a threatanator."

"Ah didnae recall Alaire referrin' tae ye as sooch."

The angel waddled 'round me to look at the three remaining troops on watch: the captain, the other Soul Retriever, and the last remaining Asylum imp. "Just 'cause you didn't hear it, don't mean it didn't happen. Anyhoo... you gotta plan yet, Tido?"

I couldnae conceal the grin on me face as I stood up. "Aye... sneak o'er to the elevator an' mind ye dinnae get caught."

I gestured for him to follow me lead and we scampered away from the relative safety of the tank. While the chilly fog made it difficult for us to see more than a few feet ahead, Alaire's troops had the same problem. As long as we kept our footsteps slow and careful, we could slip past them with nae trouble. Still, I kept me eyes on the lot of 'em, just in case.

Their eyes were fastened on the stretch of road their comrades had taken only a few moments ago.

We were just about past them when *it* happened. A headache pounded the inside of me skull like a blacksmith's hammer. Right behind it, I heard the soft lilt of a familiar voice, one I'd been yearning to hear since I landed in this frozen wasteland... me besom, Lily.

Tallis, I'm coming for you. Go to the morgue.

12

I didnae know if I were just imagining her lovely voice in my head but I decided to trust her words, all the same. Besom and I shared a connection that allowed us to communicate in the visionary world. How such was happening now, I couldnae say.

I stumbled. I was just loud enough to make the guards' heads turn 'round.

"Ah, what the hell, Tido?!" the angel roared, making me headache even worse with another of his poxy, bright lights.

I barely shut me eyes and turned me head to ward off the worst of the flash. The howls I heard behind us indicated Alaire's bully boys werenae quite so quick nor lucky.

But as surprising as the angel's trick was for its intended audience, it couldnae compare to the surprise the commander gave us afterwards. He ran right at the angel and scooped him up by the throat.

"Did you actually think someone who stared into the hottest fires of Dis could be blinded by your pitiful illumination?" he demanded as he shook the stookie angel.

Poor wee fellow beat the bastard's wrists in vain while choking in his grip. I yanked out me sword and ran the blade across the greater imp's calves in one motion. As expected, the sudden pain dropped him to his knees and he released the angel on his way down.

"Git tae the elevator!" I shouted at the angel while turning me attention to the laptop. The native greater imp and turncoat Retriever were too stunned by the light burst to stop me from cleaving the damned machine in two with a trio of quick, hard strokes. True, the laptop was most likely not the only means they had to reach Alaire. But damned if I could leave it be! Not as long as it allowed them to easily call for reinforcements.

All at once, the captain recovered enough of his wits to whip out a pistol from his side. I once again found meself wishing for Donnchadh's speed and strength when the imp opened fire on the angel. Judging from the metal ricochet of the shots, he hit everything but his target. But again, I saw nae reason to take chances. Me blade pierced the gun barrel just before I spun 'round to whack its owner in the face with the flat of me sword.

That knocked him to the ground and I ran past. If time were nae an issue, I'd have buried the sharp blade into his neck. But the patrol he sent out couldnae have failed to hear or see the ruckus by now. We had to depart before they arrived.

Without missing a hitch, the captain dropped his broken gun and paused, pulling another one from the small of his back. At this range, there was nae way he could miss his target and I could scarce afford another crippling injury. Calling on the magic I'd been using to heat meself, I cast another spell to prepare for the shooting.

Everything 'round me began moving slower, like 'twas underwater, including the captain. I saw the extended plume of flame as the gun fired. More importantly, I saw the spinning bullet lazily coming right toward me. Ignoring the nasty cold, I deflected the slug with the center of me blade. As the bullet hit the snowy ground to me left, a second shot was fired, aimed at me head.

While I ducked it, a third bullet sliced the air where me chest had previously been but me face now was. I quickly executed a horizontal slice, cutting the lead slug in half, sending one part into the air while the other drove into the ground between me legs.

After that, I started back-pedaling as fast as I could. Even with time slowed, I barely warded off the bullets as I hastily made me way to the elevator. The iciness I'd been avoiding started to bother me again, slowing me down.

Me heels touched the metal floor of the elevator at the same moment that I slipped on the ice above it. I landed hard and flat on me back. One of the bullets whizzed over me face before leaving a shower of sparks on the elevator's back wall. While me eyes took in the sight, I heard the angel shout out.

"Coooooooooonaaaaaaaaaaaaaaan…"

When time resumed its natural speed, the magic I'd been using had run its course. The stookie angel began talking and I could understand him again.

"Hey, Conan, if you're done showin' off your tricks, I could use a little o' yer bearawn here!"

The last bit of magical assistance took the wind out me sails. All I wanted to do was remain lying upon the floor, especially with so many bullets aimed at us. Upon hearing the distinct click of an empty gun before the captain began cursing, I finally got off me duff.

The angel was pulling the lever in order to move us upward but the hoarfrost upon it suggested he was attempting the impossible. I was out of breath by the time I reached him. I leaned against the lever like an old man leans upon a cane. The angel looked at me and began shaking his head as if he had a piece of meat caught 'tween his jaws.

"No, no, no, no! Don'tcha lose conk-ness on me, Sasquatch!"

I used the last of me strength to pull meself upright, placing me hands on the lever and pulling hard. I might as well have been trying to fell a great oak with me bare hands. When both of us released the lever, the angel shone his light again as he kicked the stubborn machine.

"Whit are ye…?"

"Fuck it, Tido! I'm already cold an' those ugly fuckers and the real perty one know we're here anyways!"

My body responded to the angel's heat immediately. Me skin felt so relieved that I was ready to sing his praises. But hearing rapid footsteps, there was little time for either of us to enjoy this brief reprieve. Then I realized we werenae the only thing the angel's aura was heating up—so was the lever. That realization gave me enough energy and strength to grab it again. "One more time, stookie angel! Keep all the light comin' in!"

This time, I felt the lever begin to budge in the right direction but it still got nae further than halfway. I shut me eyes and yelled at him, "Put all ye got intae that furnace, man!"

The heat radiating from him changed in an instant, going from comfortable to blistering. Me whole body reacted like a roast lamb cooking over a spit. We both shouted a final cry of agony when the lever loosened and returned to its proper position.

With a heavy lurch, the big, old, metal box began rising, knocking us both off our feet just as the angel's lightshow ended. I could hear shots behind us but none of them were close to hitting home. For just a brief second, me body was grateful for the bone-chilling cold that still surrounded us. Then me body went back to feeling as frozen as the hunks of ice we were leaving behind.

Me eyes hadnae quite cleared away the brightness before I was jarred by a couple of slaps on me face.

"Don'tcha die on me, Tido! I still need ta beat yer ass fer damn near makin' us the latest victimartyrs o' demon-o-cide!"

I felt a crooked grin on me face. "With yer constant yappin', I'd say dyin's damn near impossible."

By then, I could see his emaciated face, and he did his best to hide his relief. "Yeah, well, flatteraise won't git ya off my shit list, Conan."

I sighed and allowed me muscles tae relax. "Well... will it git me a bit o' warmth tae guard 'gainst this cold?"

He rolled his eyes in mock disgust. "Yeah, I guess ya done enough fer that."

A bit of his light shone again, and this one was much easier on me eyes than the last few flashes. I absorbed the heat like a plant reaching for sunlight. The climb up to the morgue would take a few hours, allowing us plenty of time to recover from our ordeal. A wee bit of food could have sped things along but just escaping from the belly of the Underground City was a decent enough start.

Me mind drifted back to me Lily and the situation she was facing. Could she really be on her way to us? I surely hoped sae because 'twould mean she had escaped Alaire.

Basking in the warm, welcome glow of her guardian angel, I once again vowed nae to stop until we were reunited with Besom. This time, I *did* say a prayer. And I prayed to any powers that were listening that I could succeed.

"His ill-strain'd nerves he left."
-Dante's Inferno

THREE
LILY

The skies began to change from dark to gray as I was finally leaving the Seventh Circle of The Underground City.

The euphoria of escaping from Alaire's castle was long gone though. Now that I was flying on the back of the winged shrew I'd tamed—er, Donnchadh had actually done the taming—I was plagued by a hundred questions floating around my mind like a hurricane.

Were the other Furies just as loyal to me as this one appeared to be?

What would I do when I actually got to the morgue?

Did Alaire command some kind of machine or flying monster that could take us out of the sky? And if so, when would that creature show up because I had to imagine Alaire was in the process of alerting any and every one of his foul minions that I'd escaped.

That last thought had been haunting me for quite a few miles now. But lacking any other signs of pursuit or interference, I thought maybe, just maybe I was on my way to escaping?

I lacked the words to describe what a relief that possibility was. Ever since Alaire had introduced himself to me over the phone while I was in the Dark Wood, the Master of the Underground City always seemed to stay two or three steps ahead of me. No matter how hard I tried to prevent him, he knew exactly how to manipulate me to get what he wanted.

And that was precisely the reason why my body had become a sock puppet for the spirit of an evil, little bitch named Persephone. Luckily, I'd been able to rid myself of Persephone and funny enough, Alaire was glad in the end. Be careful what you wish for...

Even so, the price of my freedom was now calculated in the memories of everything Persephone and Alaire did to me while she was at the helm of my body. The ways Alaire had defiled me were memories I couldn't shake...

His lips all over me.
His fingers inside me.
Alaire inside me...

Every time I remembered the particulars, my stomach dropped and I felt ill. But as terrible as those memories were, they paled in comparison to the things Alaire had done to my guardian angel and to the man I... *loved.*

I'd thought the day we escaped from the castle would also be the day our current troubles vanished. But no! Our troubles seemed to multiply like rabbits. And now those troubles included the fact that Tallis had been exiled to the worst part of the Underground City. Meanwhile Bill had pulled off some kind of escape caper that landed him in parts unknown. Now, I assumed Alaire was actively hunting both Bill and me and maybe even Tallis.

God, why couldn't anything about the afterlife ever be as simple as the AE offices pretended?

My ears suddenly developed a harsh ringing that was swiftly followed by a killer headache. All that cranial pain made me tighten my grip on my flying steed's bare, feminine shoulders. The Fury turned her human head to look at me in a perfect *Exorcist*-style, one-eighty just so she could growl at me. Seeing the look on her face pissed me off and I growled right back. Or Donnchadh did.

She whipped her head back around in a hurry after that. But my anger toward her remained riled. I suddenly wanted to rip her head off for *daring* to defy me. Then I would start on the rest of her limbs...

None of these feelings were mine. They belonged to Donnchadh, the spirit within me. And he was angry. As per usual.

I shoved the impulses back down with vehemence and purpose, like a sledgehammer hitting a railroad spike. After my temper finally cooled off, I thought, *How did Tallis stand living with this asshole inside him for all these centuries?* It was only the thousandth time that thought had crossed my mind since I'd allowed Donnchadh to take domicile inside me.

Yes, I was now suffering the after-effects of another new problem: replacing Persephone with the fierce spirit of Donnchadh. Having witnessed the effect of Donnchadh's presence in Tallis, I already knew he was a hopelessly mad beast. But nothing could have prepared me for the experience of being pushed into ultra-violence at the drop of a hat by the nasty spirit. His anger constantly burned. Like a fire, he burned with ferocity eternally, sacrificing all sanity and reason in exchange for a never-ending rage-a-thon. If a better alternative to exiling Persephone once and for all had existed, I'd have taken it in a heartbeat.

I was so busy thinking about the asshole spirit, it took me a second to realize the incessant ringing and headache had already passed, just as quickly as they came. I wanted to blame them on Donnchadh too but somehow I didn't think he was the culprit. This time.

On a hunch, I placed my hand on my sword's hilt. I caught the faintest echo of the ringing I'd already experienced, which made me quickly pull my hand away.

I glanced down at the blade and couldn't help my smile. I thought of the blade as an extension of Tallis, himself. He'd artfully crafted it and in doing so, he'd either intentionally or unintentionally created a link between the two of us. I was more than sure this sword had actually protected me from certain harm.

Now it had apparently developed a mind of its own. And I called that mind the *Self.* I didn't exactly know what the *Self* was but it seemed to be something deep within me that reflected itself in my sword. And this self hadn't led me astray yet, which was the reason why I continued following its instructions. And when it told me to go to the morgue and the information came in Tallis' voice, I was only happy to do so.

Strangely enough, this deep piece of my soul had led me to some personal breakthroughs that all my countless self-help books never managed to accomplish.

But, as pretty as that piece of information was, the fact still remained: I had a freaking sword *that talked to me.* I previously expected objects to be just that... objects. But I was starting to understand that since the moment of my death and my subsequent revival, things were never as they appeared.

Yes, I had died.

And yes, I was brought back to life and yes, there had been lots of small print.

Quick rundown: The hereafter was run by Afterlife Enterprises, an amoral conglomerate that made Enron look like a responsible corporate citizen. Worse still, there seemed to be a conspiracy going on between the office manager, Jason Streethorn, who'd recruited me and Alaire, the current master of the Underground City.

I couldn't speak to Jason's goals in all of this or if he was just stupidly trusting. But I knew Alaire well

21

enough to know that his sole intention was to consolidate his power. Having spent more facetime with Alaire than I cared to think about, I knew he wouldn't stop at ruling just the Underground City. Only total domination over the great beyond would suit Alaire.

Swallowing my fear, I touched the sword one more time and then I closed my eyes, asking my *self* to guide me.

When I released the blade this time, I came away with the conviction that both Tallis and Bill were okay.

***

At any other time or place, the gray, cloud-covered skies would have made me nervous. But after the endless night surrounding Alaire's castle, this charcoal sky was as pleasant to view as a sunrise.

The grayish light filtered through the puffy clouds ahead of me, making everything around them much easier to see. I noticed an occasional flash running through the clouds like lightning, although I never heard the traditional roll of thunder afterwards.

When we finally reached the clouds proper, the Fury leaned her head back and took a deep breath through her nose. I did the same. It was the closest thing to fresh air since I'd been relegated down here.

A droning filled my ears. At first, I guessed it was another Self-created internal sound effect. But no, the more I listened, the more I realized the sound was coming from around me rather than within me. I could hear it crossing the sky, from my right to my left at a respectable speed. When the Fury growled at it, it confirmed the sound was definitely not coming from inside my head.

The droning noise seemed familiar enough but I couldn't place it. It reminded me of a dragonfly I'd seen once during a memorable summer at my grandma's house... Now increase that dragonfly up to Godzilla's size, and you can imagine the buzz.

The fear that this could be some kind of Underground City version of *Mothra* made my hackles rise as the droning came ever closer to us. That's when the true source of the noise finally burst from the clouds: a fire-engine-red, World War I-style propellor plane. Its front-mounted machine guns were firing right at us.

Son of a bitch! I yelled at myself.

My Fury was already responding before our attacker ever came into sight. She kept twisting and turning her body into a serpentine pattern of evasive maneuvers.

It took all the strength in my hands and legs to stay on top of her while she turned upside down and dashed sideways.

Only when the plane flew past us did my winged steed return to an even keel. But by then I was sick to my stomach and barely able to think about anything other than trying not to heave.

My nausea was all the opening Donnchadh needed. He slid into my conscious thoughts, carving his way with a burning feeling deep inside me. I knew his ignorant hatred would do a serious number on my ability to think clearly, and I glanced at the protective runes encircling my right arm. The runes were meant to help me keep Donnchadh in check but I wondered if this bloodthirsty barbarian could break free of them.

As I heard the plane coming in for another pass, I debated the wisdom of setting Donnchadh loose. Sure, we were being attacked. And I had no doubt our pilot would try to finish the job he'd started. But this wasn't a Roman arena where one gladiator could just rip the other guy apart. If I made the smallest error up here, I could get injuries that even *Donnchadh* would have a hard time healing.

23

But heal them he would because when one was possessed by Donnchadh, they not only benefitted from his extreme strength and power, but they were also blessed with his gift of immortality.

And there was no denying that Donnchadh was the main reason why no one had ever defeated Tallis in a fight. If I could manage to get close enough to our flying ace, Donnchadh might be able to end this very quickly.

I tapped the Fury's shoulder, making her turn her head around again. "Take out that spinny thing in front of the plane," I told her, circling my finger to better communicate my meaning. Even with the dumbed-down English, I wasn't sure she had a clue as to what I wanted her to do.

She turned her head back around, leaving me to hope for the best.

I touched the runes with my left hand. "Donnchadh, I free you to take control of my body and defend us from this attacker," I said aloud. Right after the runes flashed, a surge of anger and power flooded into me from top to bottom.

The first thing my heightened senses detected was our flier adopting a higher altitude. Donnchadh wanted to leap at him straightaway but he didn't. Like a truly skilled hunter, he waited for just the right moment.

The second the plane emerged from the clouds, Donnchadh launched himself and me from the Fury's back, vaulting us right over the plane's spinning blades.

The pilot had just enough time to look startled before both my feet slammed into his chest like twin battering rams. I felt the soft cushion of his leather jacket absorb some of the blow.

Most of the pilot's face was covered by his leather helmet and his big goggles but his jaw and throat were

24

completely exposed. Donnchadh drove my right fist straight through his helmet until I made contact with his jaw, spilling blood onto the silk scarf around his neck. The leather strap of his helmet came undone and I slapped the thing off him entirely, watching as it fell out of the plane and disappeared into the dark sky.

The sloppy punch made the lower knuckles of my hand throb. The pilot wasn't too wild about the punch either, if the stubby pistol he pulled from his belt was any indicator. My resident psycho spirit slapped the gun out of his gloved hand, dropping it back into the cockpit. That was followed by another set of punches to the pilot's face.

After that, my hands wrapped around the pilot's throat and started choking the life out of him. That roused him damn near instantly, making him pull my hands away as he struggled to break Donnchadh's grip. But Tallis's former companion refused to be denied.

I felt the pilot weakening with each passing second, his tongue bulging out of his mouth at an odd angle. His face went completely red.

A harsh shriek of metal behind us broke Donnchadh's concentration. We turned around to see pieces of the propeller flying right at us. Donnchadh barely ducked the metal carnage in time before some of it hit the tail of the plane with a sickening crunch.

When I looked up again, I caught a glimpse of my Fury making a hairpin turn to catch up with the plane from behind. My fear of imminent death surged and I felt the warrior spirit getting pushed back into his cage. No matter how much he raged over the indignity, the power created by the runes held firm.

"*Nein!*" the pilot shrieked in a heavy German accent, reaching around my slim form to grab the control stick.

25

My ample breasts, however, impeded his progress, which made the situation awkward in more ways than one. My pet flying monster started dive-bombing after us but quickly vanished in the cloud cover while the plane picked up speed on its way down.

The pilot looked up at me in a controlled panic. "I beg you, *fraulein*, give me leave to land this plane. It is doubtful either of us will survive otherwise."

Scrunching myself as close against him as I could, I put my head to his right side and hissed, "Do it!"

I ignored my discomfort when my breasts were unceremoniously flattened as the pilot struggled to pull the control stick upward.

We gradually leveled off right before hitting the ground with a hard jolt. That was followed by several more bone-wracking thrusts forward and back while the wheels rolled across the uneven terrain. We abruptly came to a slamming stop when we hit something and then both of us were pitched into either side of the cockpit. The pilot flew right into me, his head ramming into my chest. Pain enveloped me and I had to wonder if he'd crushed my lungs because I was finding it near impossible to breathe.

As to the pilot, I couldn't say if he was alive or dead. All we could do for the next few seconds was just lie there motionless.

I don't know if it was Donnchadh or the Self, but I managed to shake off my shock first. Taking a deep breath, I sat up and tried to ignore the burning in my lungs. After another few seconds, though, the burning subsided and I could stand.

Doing so, I unsheathed my sword and placed it directly under the pilot's chin. The tip of the blade was sharp enough to make him lift his head and look at me.

So he wasn't dead. Good for him. Of course, seeing as how he was in The Underground City, it probably followed that he wasn't alive to begin with.

Not so good for him.

"If you want some advice," I started. "It's in your best interest to cooperate with me."

The pilot raised his hands without hesitation. "I could not agree more, *fraulein*. Please accept my unconditional surrender."

I raised an eyebrow at him and carefully crouched down in the cockpit, my sword still under his jawline. I'd expected more of a fight and I told him as much.

Keeping his hands raised, the flying ace shrugged. "And what purpose would such a struggle serve? You have proven yourself my superior in hand-to-hand combat. You are also armed while I am not. I have no allies I can call upon at this time. And, most importantly, you allowed me the trust and time to land my *Fokker* safely. When I consider all these things, surrender is the only logical conclusion."

I squinted as I felt around the cockpit floor. "*Fokker*?" I repeated, subduing the desire to make a crack about milking a cat. But, I held the desire in check. Yay me.

A sheepish smile cropped up on the pilot's face. "*Entschuldigung, fraulein.* We are currently occupying a *Fokker DR-I triplane*, my personal flying machine of choice."

My fingers finally located the pistol he'd dropped and I stood back, pointing it at his head while keeping my sword in place. "For whatever it's worth, sorry about wrecking it."

The smile turned from apologetic to understanding. "I assure you no apologies are necessary. If a pilot and his passengers are able to walk away from a landing, I deem it a successful one."

I couldn't help smiling at that. "So this isn't the first plane you've wrecked?"

He gave me a knowing chuckle. "Nor the second... but may I make a small request?"

"As long as you don't ask me to set you free, I'll consider it."

"*Nein, nein, nein*, nothing so obvious. I merely ask that we exit this plane so that we can carry on this conversation in a slightly more comfortable location."

I pulled the sword back but kept the pistol aimed at his head. "You first... and exit slowly, keeping your hands clasped behind your head."

He nodded and did as he was told. With his hands atop his head, he had a hard time exiting the plane using just his legs but he managed it. Even as he jumped to the ground, his hands never left his head for an instant. When I reached the ground, I sheathed my sword and jabbed the gun into his side so he wouldn't get any ideas. In the meantime, I took a quick glance at our surroundings.

The gray skies were accented by the outline of wrecked buildings around us. This had once been a city like Dis, albeit with more European-styled architecture. But now most of it was no more than smashed rubble and teetering walls. Distant and not-so-distant fires dotted the landscape like incompetent mockeries of street lights. While nothing in the Underground City could ever be classified as "safe," this area screamed *war zone*.

The pilot noticed me surveying our immediate area. "The morgue is not a very comforting sight, I know. I much prefer to see it from the air whenever possible."

I put my back against his plane as I listened for imminent threats. Then I faced the pilot again. He seemed to be familiar enough with this place that I figured he might be able to answer a question. "How dangerous is it down here?"

He opened his mouth to answer but a sudden cry from the sky cut him off. My Fury landed in front of us with suprising grace. A few seconds later, a flock of her sisters did the same, surrounding us on all sides. The Furies turned as one towards my prisoner and made threatening noises, snapping their teeth in his direction like overly famished dogs.

I yelled at them, "Knock it off!"

To their credit, every one of the birdbrains backed off in a hurry. None of them made a move as I walked around the pilot to face him. I gestured at his head with the pistol. "Take off the googles."

"Of course," he replied, slowly lowering his hands from his head. He moved just as slowly when it came to peeling off his headgear. Maybe he didn't want to spook me?

When he removed the goggles, I was pleasantly surprised by the look of his face. It had a certain appeal to it. Rounded to the point of appearing as though he were in his thirties, his features included a large pair of pale eyes whose color I couldn't make out, a nicely shaped nose and broad lips. His nondescript dark hair was cropped as close to his skull as possible without appearing shaved. He was handsome.

He slowly allowed his goggles to slip through his leather-clad fingers until they hit the ground. All the while, he stared at me with the same expression I was probably giving him. After another few seconds, he cleared his throat.

"My apologies for gawking, *fraulein*, but you are... quite attractive."

My Fury tried snapping at him from behind me. I leaned against her and scolded her loudly.

"What did I just say?!"

29

She growled unhappily with the dressing down but backed off.

I faced the pilot. "No more flattery. You're my prisoner and that's the extent of our acquaintance."

The pilot nodded in appreciation and smiled down at me. He was quite tall. "Apparently, I have just incurred another disadvantage, *fraulein*."

"Which is?"

"Might I have the privilege of knowing the name of my captor?" With manners like that, you'd think he'd just asked me out for coffee.

"Lily... Lily Harper. And you are...?"

The pilot's posture straightened a little at the question. "*Kapitan* Manfred Albrecht Freiherr Von Richtofen, of the Flying Circus under the command of *Kaiser* Wilhelm."

I thought I'd heard something familiar in the jumble of names and titles he'd just rattled off. "Can you repeat that?"

He smiled and the smile turned into a quick laugh before he responded.

"Perhaps it would be easier to call me by another name." He cleared his throat. "The Red Baron at your service, *fraulein*."

"For yonder I behold a mist new-risen on the sandy
plain."
- Dante's Inferno

FOUR
BILL

The elevator ride up seemed ta go on foreverly. It
didn't take me no time at all ta git bored.

It reminded me of this one time like three years
ago when I was datenapping. That's when you're out
on a date with some chick who's yammering on and
on about tampons or cats or some shit and you're like
so bored outta your head that you find yourself asleep
with your eyes open.

This time I was even more bored 'cause I didn't
have no girl to look at, just Conan. An' it ain't like you
wanna hear more 'bout Tido's cats.

Lookin' at Tido sucked a big hairy ball so I turned
my attention to the cliff face of the rock we was
elevatin' up.

Now I get that there's a good gap between the
Underground City's Circles but in the name of Ozzy,
the Prince of Darkness, why did an ascent-spirational
escape like this feel more like we was waitin' in line at
the DMV and we was number 654?

Still, one good thing I could say is that about
halfway up—at least I think it was halfway up—the
Freon-frozone of the Asylum finally calmed the fuck
down. That allowed me to reducify the heat I was
radiatin' fer both me and the Yeti. One thing I never

told nobody was how much of an exer-strain it was to serve as a master blaster furnace for the Divine Fire.

Maybe the archangels could pull it off with more grace. But yours truly could only channel that kind of holy-smokes wattage fer so long. Mainly 'cause I was like super beyond tired and I also had to poo.

Conan was still lying on the heavy metal floor like it was a feather bed, with his eyes shutightedly and his breathing steady-Eddy. I couldn't blame him. After what we'd just escaped from, he'd earned some down time.

I felt a fart come zippin' out an' it sounded like Dracula opening up his coffin. I looked over at Tido to see if he'd heard it but his eyes was still closed. I figured I had me a minute of fart lapse before Tido smelled it.

Not wantin' to get all embarrassed, I pulled out my cell phone and hit the phone icon. Then I scrolled through my shit tons of contacts until I found the one for Polly and Sally. I hit the phone icon again and glanced over at Tido to see if he'd smelled Essence D' Bill yet but he was still passed the fuck out.

Soze I paid attention to the dialing of the phone and that was when I realized I couldn't hear no dialing of the phone. There weren't no message, no dial tone, not even a freakin' busy signal. I tried it again, but got the same results. That's when the bright-bulb idea dawned on me to check the screen. Sure enough, the bars were completely x-ed out, which meant Verizon weren't gonna hear me this deep down in hell.

I slammed my fist into the base o' the lever and shouted, "Dammit!" And another fart zipped out.

I forgot how badly I'd tenderized my knuckles on the door earlier but the painage from the impact did a great job o' reminding me. While I shook my hand in distractification, the universe's hairiest Scotsman finally spoke up.

32

"Nae service, not this far down."

I turned around to look at him but didn't notice him sniffin' the air all suspicious like. Shit, maybe Tido had allergies and his nose was all stuffed up. Lucky fer him 'cause that one had been ripe.

"How long you been awake?" I asked.

He used his elbows to prop hisself up. "Ne'er went tae sleep."

"You looked asleep."

He shook his head and his nappy ass, long hair echoed the movement.
"There's a place halfway twixt wakin' an' dreamin' where ye can git the rest ye need without slippin' into the oonconscious."

"Can you get you some wet dreams in that place too?"

The yeti eyed me with an expression that said he weren't sure what the hell's I was going on about. Nevermind. I didn't have the interest to go splainin' the importance of beat time.

"If my phone don't work, then how come those imp-tastic ass-wipes got ahold o' Blondie on that laptop?"

He grunted a little, reminding me of a big ol' hairy bear with a bad attitude an' a stopped-up rear end. "Alaire would have made sure an internet connection existed 'tween his minions an' himself."

I was surprised to hear the words "internet connection" comin' from Tido's mouth 'cause Tido was like as old as the Dinosaurs I think.

"How d'ya even know what the internet is?"

His grunt this time was more alphatic. "Ah live in the Dark Wood, ye bloody dunderheid, nae in a cave."

"Same damn thing."

He rose up the rest of the way, stretching out his back and lifting his huge fists in the air. Once he set those extra-large mitts o' his back down, he started scratching the rainforest o' hair on his face. "Are... ye tryin' tae reach Besom?"

I gestulated at the lever. "Uh, I thought we was on our way to findin' Besom? Ain't that why we're in this contraption in the first place? You forget you heard her voice tellin' you to head to the Morgue?" I eyed him for another second. "You got you some old-timer's now or what?"

"Alzheimers, ye bloody scrote."

"What's a scrote?"

"Ah scrotum."

I started laughing 'cause that shit was downright funny. I couldn't see past all the foliage on his face but I think he might have frowned.

"Ah meant the mobile phone, ye Jessie. Does Besom carry one wif her?"

"What the hell's a *Jessie* again?" I demanded, eyeing him. Tido seems to think he's like aces at comin' up with names to call me but he really ain't good at it 'cause he ain't got no sense of humor.

"An effeminate man," he said real disinterested like. "Does Besom have a mobile, man?"

I started scratching my cheek. "Nah, at least, not last time I saw her."

"Then who were ye callin'?"

"The animal shelter."

"Och aye," he said and frowned at me. "The whit?"

"I was reportin' the fact that I was stuck inside a slow-ass elevator with some kinda feral man-dog that looked more like the missin' link."

Tido glanced around hisself like he wasn't sure where the man-dog was. Then he looked back at me with a frown.

"You, Conan, you're the man-dog."

He frowned. "Shut yer geggie, ye bloody lavvy head. Ye arenae foonny, ye howlin' roaster."

34

"Well, if you were speakin' you some English, maybe I could make me a comment."

"Ah called ye a toilet head an' a smelly idiot."

"Sticks an' stones, Cro-Magnon Man, sticks an' stones." Then I took me a big breath an' wondered if maybe Tido had smelled my fart yet? I mean, he did call me a *smelly* idiot. "I'm actually tryin' ta reach a couple o' babes I got an in with over at AE."

Tido's eyebrows rose, pushing up the shelf of hair above them. "Ye mean tae say that someone can actually stand tae listen tae ye?"

"Ha, ha, fucking ha... if it weren't fer their inside info, you fugly nutsack, I'd never have found you at all."

Conan raised up his hands like he was submittin' to a pat-down from the po-po. "A bit o' bad taste on me part. An' fer that, Ah'm truly sorry, ye dobber. Ah sincerely am."

I glared at him. "Was that a punchpology or was it a true one?"

"Ah what?"

"A punchpology. Like when you say you're sorry for some lame shit you did but then you combine it with like a verbal punch so the person on the other end ain't fully sure whether yer apology's sincere or what."

"Och, aye, 'tis a sincere apology, ye baw."

"Okay, well thanks then, Tido. Apology accepted." I held out my fist so we could bro-fist bump an' show that we was good with each other but then Tido couldn't stop from laughing. "What's so funny?" I asked as I eyed him real narrow like.

"Ah jist called ye a testicle!" he said and then slapped his hairy thigh like he thought he was Dave Chapelle as R. Kelly singin' *I wanna piss on you.*

Finally Tido cleared his throat. "Ah'm assumin' these fair ladies hae proper names?"

I wouldn't look at him and just pretended like I was super interested in my shirt. And this time when the fart came up, I didn't do nothing to restrain it. I even turned around so Tido was in the direct line of destructination.

"Angel," he repeated.

"What?" I asked without botherin' to turn 'round.

"Who were ye callin'?"

I turned around finally and glared at him. "Not that it's any o' your business, but the gals I was callin,' they're two of the Muse sisters, Polyhymnia or Polly and Thalia who goes by Sally."

"The muses?"

"They're VPs of Requisitions but—"

"Requisitions coverin' everthing what comes down tae the OOnderground City?"

I kicked his shin and he made a face like it hurt. The pansy. "Yo, did I interrupt *you* when *you* was talkin'?! Goddamn, you'd think you'd have picked up some manners by now, even if you is just a cave man!"

"Go oan."

"Polly an' Sally are like my eyes an' ears in AE."

"Eyes an' ears?" he repeated and looked like he didn't believe a word ol' Bill was saying. That got me pretty smokin' annoyed.

"Yeah, they've told me some pretty tit-tit-illating dope."

"Like?"

"Like they said somethin' about a lot o' shipmentals headin' this way that keep changin' the cargo contents on the paperwork. And Polly bein' such a tight ass, one period out o' place sends her into a hystericidal rage."

The big man's eyes started burnin' with a new kind of fury. "Alaire..."

"Skeletorhorn too," I added while I nodded my head real important like. "Neither o' my girls wanted ta come out an' say it, but I gots a bad feelin' that Skeleterhorn is Blondie's inside man."

Tido stood up and started pacing around, makin' the elevator wobble somethin' real bad that made my stomach upset. "It takes more than jist one man in the right spot tae pull off somethin' that big," he said. "If that 'tis sae, we're lookin' at ah whole nest o' traitors in the mix."

I stowed my phone in my pocket. "Well, since that call ain't gittin' through anyway, you can go back ta yer nap now."

He shook his big, dumb head. "Nae. Ah couldnae sleep anyway with all ye've told me in me head."

"Speaking o' which, what *was* runnin' through yer head when we was tryin' ta slip-slide past them uglies at the Asylum?"

It was hard to see under the excesspit of fur but it looked like he was opening his mouth to answer. Before a single sound could come out—grunting included—the elevator came to a halt. Tido yanked out his sword, pointing the tip at the double doors. When they slid open, though, it was nothing but us an' the elevator and the clouds outside.

The light poking its way through them clouds puzzlated me. "Yo, this thing take us farther up than we wanted ta go?"

Tido gave me a shake of his head. "Nae. Welcome tae the outskirts o' the morgue."

Good news was that the light through them clouds was a step up from all that frozone fog. Bad news was that what it showed us didn't exactly make me slap-happy. The ground outside the box was just as rocky as the cliff and as flat as Conan's version of home cooking. Conan squatted down on the ground so he could wipe away some of the dust. A couple seconds later, he found a cobblestone path under all the grime.

37

"There we are, me beauty."

I took a better look at the path. It wasn't nothin' special. "I'm guessin' there's somethin' I don't know 'bout this road?"

He stood back up, using his floppy boot sole to clear off more cobblestones ahead. "We follow this road—an' *only* this road—an' it'll lead oos tae the morgue proper." He looked at me real sharp like. "Ye moost step where I step an' naewhere else."

I shrugged. "Always been yer part o' the show, yo. I'm down with that."

Tido used his foot to wipe off the dust on the road as we walked. I admit I got a little mor-badly curigross about what might happen to us if we mewandered off the path. But if Tido said it weren't safe, I wasn't about to test my luck. Still, can't say I was loving the pace. By my estimath, we were traveling roughly seven inches an hour.

Much as it irkolized me, I did my best to put up with it. When you're as low on the angelic toe-the-line pole as I am, dealing with bullshit and tedi-dumb is something ya get used to. Still, this wasn't my home office and Tido sure as shit wasn't my boss. So I opened my mouth up to tell him to acceleraise the travel speed. What I saw just beyond him, however, sealed my words and they stayed in my mouth.

One second, there weren't nothing in front of us. The next, a bunch of lumpy-ass rock towers started playing Ring-Around-The-Horizon for as far as the eye could see. The tops o' them were so high, they extenulated right up into the cloud cover. Nothin' I could think of explanatated why they all had big chains wrapped 'round 'em. "Where'd those big ass rocks come from?" I asked Tido.

Conan waved me off like the mega-sized rock towers popped in front of him every day! "The Titans."

"The Titans?" I repeated, soundin' real freaked out like 'cause I remembered me some show about Titans an' they was like eatin' people I think. Hopefully it weren't no documentary.

"Aye, the Titans."

"Where'd they come from?"

"They've always been there. It's jist we're finally close enough tae see 'em." Tido didn't seem overly concerned 'bout the man-eating Titans. He just wiped down the next step ahead of him, which exposiated a right bend on the path.

"It's only when ye see the Titans that ye know ye've entered the morgue good an' proper," he continued.

I squinted hard at the nearest big rock er Titan. My natural telenoculars kicked in, giving the Hubble a run for its money on zoom footage. This way, I got me a way better look at this monstrocitower.

One of the few perks of being an angel is knowin' some subjectives firsthand. I've seen every rock known to man, demon, angel and lawyer. And the texture on this thing? It didn't look like no rock I'd ever seen befores. So I was bettin' them Titans weren't made outta rock. Insteads, this thing looked lots closer to fine Koran-theon leather after it's been bake-ovened out in the sun for too long. But there wasn't any sun down here. And who'd make anything outta leather that's a million miles tall? The chainmail on the oversized bondage gear was definitely a special mix of alloy-cations. But I still had no clue what this thing really was.

"Ach, whatcha standin' there fer, man?!"

Tido's voice made me yank my eyeballs and my mind back to the present tension, which nearly made me fall over. I had to blink real fast and hard ta get my head back in the game. I saw Sasquatch taking

39

about six steps aheadlong of me. It took me a few to catch up to him.

"Hey, I *know* those things ain't rocks."

Tido shrugged and took the next step he cleared off. "Ne'er said they were."

"Right, you said they was Titans."

"Aye."

I put my hands on my starvaciated hips and tapped my foot. "So what the hell are Tit—"

Movement on top of one o' them giant things cut me off. A couple of big holes split open on its rocky skin with a rumble. Just below them holes was a longer, bigger split, one that comparicized to the Grand Canyon in its depth. When that one finished opening, something started to scream.

"I commend my TREASURE to thee, wherein I yet
survive; my sole request."
- Dante's Inferno

FIVE
BILL

"Jesus!" I yelled as I stuffed my hands into my
ears to protectorate my eardrums.

Even that didn't stop the Too-Loud-Around-
Sound from inunderating my ears like a busted water
main. Tido wasn't havin' any easier time with it, forced
down on his knees from the shrieking that echoed
around us like it was comin' from everywheres.

Conan shut his eyes real tight and shielded his
ears with his hands. The frown on his face told me
how much he wished this monster would do an open
sesa-cease. I kept my eyes peeled, which is how I
spotted a big, winged something when it landed on the
shriekerating Titan.

This new Thing From Another Nightmare was a
regular Birdzilla. Like a giant buzzard, it was
terrifinating enough to be in its own special class of
uglory. Its moon-sized beak pierced the rock skin of
the Titan as it started ripping into the enormous
thing. I didn't think the huge chasm's screams could
get any louder, but did they ever... and ever... and
ever.

Big, black drops flew down from above us, lookin'
like huge drops of messed up rain. Each one of them
blobs was at least three times Tido's size and he
weren't exactly what you'd call a dwarflet.

41

But the weird thing was: none of them bucket drops stuck around. And the other weird thing was that none o' them black drops landed on the path we was on. Instead, they kept rainin' down 'round us, but on the dirt. An' once the drops hit the ground, they got sucked into the dirt faster than I get off on a Playboy centerfold. All that insuctionation got me to thinking what could happen if I lifted so much as a pinky toe off the cobblestones.

After a minute of agonoise, Big Bird Deluxe left the Titan and flapped its big wings back up into the clouds. I didn't think my ears would ever stop ring-a-dinging from all the abuse they'd endurated. And I was so freaking scared, the poo that'd been knocking at my door got sucked right back up my intestine.

When the lower hole opened up again, I was *sure* that horrible screaming wasn't never gonna stop. But all the hole wounded up doing was sighing.

This whole episodomy made me take another hard look at the enormous thing. This time, I looked for something unusuary. Even though I'd never seen one like it, that massively mauled monolith definitely had an aura over it. From that realization, I was able to determinate that the lower hole was actually a mouth and the pair of holes on top were eyes.

The Titan's eyes found me an' the still-kneeling Tido PDQ. The mouth grinned before it started speaking in a voice that like bounced all around us 'cause it were so loud.

"Tallis Black, how singularly rare for the former Master of the Underground City to grace us with his presence."

Conan got on his feet and tossed his head way back so he could meet our host eyeball-to-moonball. "Aye, no denyin' it, *Prometheus Fire-Thief.* But we live in 'interesting times'."

Even if my Scottish sherpa hadn't mentioned they was Titans before, I would've recognized the name he called the big galoot. "Yo, wait… you're *the* Prometheus? The same guy who nabbed a bit o' the Divine Fire before handin' it off ta humans?"

The mountain's deep chuckulation sounded like it started from somewhere down in his legs. "The one and only, little angel… and as you can see, my liver still suffers for that crime every day." I figured he was talkin' 'bout the fact that the big-ass crow seemed ta think his liver was some kinda delicassey.

The giant on Prometheus' left started saying somethin' that didn't make a hell of a lot of sense. One of the subjectives all angels are good at is mastering foreign languages. An' most o' my lessons came to me through passive learnin'—the art of sittin' one's ass on the couch an' watchin' TV an' lettin' the knowledge come to you.

But even with my library o' knowledge, I'd be damned if I could figure out what the actual fuck this guy was spouting off.

Apparently, Promethius didn't have that langua-pedia neithers 'cause he gave Huge Rock Dude #2 a look like #2 had been hittin' too much o' the ganja and was like Highlingual or somethin'.

"Really, that's no way to address the first true visitors we've had in—"

Pro got cut off by the articulaudable words of the other big guy on his right. "Too long, brother, it's been far too long." Every sylla-bull throbbed with the kind of pain you feel deep inside your gut after you drink too many beers an' eat too much cheese.

Pro exhalitosissed another sigh that sounded as down as the other guy's voice. "Yes, Epimetheus, it has been far too long."

43

Tido's shoulders straightened out like he was in some damn Army review. "We are glad tae be o' service tae ye."

Pro's big, old boulder eyes nailed me with a hard stare. "I must say, little angel, I am a bit surprised to see the Druid traveling with your kind."

I found me a good spot behind my ear to scratch. "Yeah, well, we ain't like best bros or nothin'. We just got us what ya'd call a mule-tual interest in findin' our Lils an' gittin' the hell outta here, yo."

Conan picked that moment to decide I needed an interpretator. "Lils, o' course, bein' one Lily Harper, a Soul Retriever."

Pro didn't look like that was ringin' no bells.

"We became separated an' we've been tryin' tae find her ever since," Conan continued esplainin'.

Seekinating a better look at our host an' his two fugly bros, I pushed my way in front of Tido. Tido's eyes bugged out just before he grabbed my shoulder and shucked his all-bliterated boot off his foot. It landed near the spot I would've stepped on.

An' good thing too 'cause the ground made his footwear into *foot-where?* As in, it sucked Tido's shoe into itself until there weren't no shoe left no more. Not even the laces was left behind.

"Thanks for the solid, man," I said to Conan with a little nod.

While Tido pushed me back behind him, Pro said, "You should be more cautious, William. Your kind may never die but being trapped within this ground is a terrible fate and one that would be considered much worse than death."

Time for my eyes to bug out. "How you know my name, Pro-man?"

"Let us just agree that I know information I should not know and leave it at that."

44

While we was talkin', Tido pulled off his other boot and tossed it. The ground sucked it down just as quickly as the last one. Guess he didn't see no point in only wearin' one boot. That was just as well 'cause I figured Tido had a case of Flinstone Feet where's he could walk on anything barefoot just like Fred Flinstone who didn't wear no shoes or nothing.

I cleared my throat to change the subjective. "I'm kinda shock-a-prised that none o' Blondie's boys were out here waitin' fer us."

Conan rolled his eyes before giving me a mangry look. "Lleu's sake, man, can't ye talk plain an' simple?"

Pro came to my rescue this time. "We know of whom the angel speaks, Tallis Black."

Brother Epi wheezed for a second 'fore speaking again. "Alaire's minions *were* here... but they did not stay."

"I got no idea why!" I said, lookin' round myself. "This place is like Club Med!"

Tido gave me a real irritated expression but Pro didn't seem ta mind a little angel humor. Clearly, Conan's a total bore.

"Then Alaire finds fault with you and yours?" Pro asked Tido.

"They hate us 'cause they anus," I answered with a nod.

"Aye," Conan said.

"Until my brother's tormentor appeared, Alaire's reinforcements were determined to stand their ground as long as necessary. Yet, hearing the sounds that both the cursed bird and Prometheus made were more than enough to drive them down to the dubious safety of the Ninth Circle," Epi continued.

When he started making a mad-dog noise in his throat, I was gratefulfilled to see he was chained up.

45

Last thing I wanted was some enormous rock dude fallin' over an' landin' on me.

"I have listened to my dear sibling crying out in agony for countless eons," Epi started up again, shaking his massive head which caused a major wind to come blastin' into us. "And yet, none of Alaire's weaklings could withstand the screams."

Conan's head and shoulders slumped like the averageous Mr. Happy after all the Viagra wears off. "Aye."

Right about then, the other rock dude who was spoutin' off some weird-ass language terminulated the intelligentle conversation with more of his gobbledy-gook.

Pro took it in stridation and deciperated for us. "Brother Nimrod wishes to know if either of you have seen the Spites?"

An' yeah, I lost my shit.

Like Lost.My.Shit.

"Brother Nimrod?" I asked an' then started laughin' real hard—the kinda laugh that makes snot come rippin' out your nose an' I think I prolly farted a few times too. But, shit, I couldn't remember the last time I laugherated so damn hard.

"Is there something you find funny, angel?" Pro asked.

"Funny?" I couldn't stop my laughing even if the rock dudes was gettin' upsets with me. "His name is Nimrod!" I said an' started laugh-fartin' again.

"Dinnae mind the angel," Tido said, lookin' as annoyed-like as Pro sounded. "The bloody bampot is off his heid."

"Perhaps I should ask Nimrod's question again?" Pro said an' this time I really tried to keep the shit-giggles in but damn-it-to-hell, it weren't easy. I turned me around and bent over, tryin' ta hide my laughin'

46

but all that did me was get a swift kick to the ass from Conan.

"Pull yerself together, man!" he whisper-railed.

"Dude, when the hell's you ever heard o' someone named Nimrod?" I whispered back to him with a shrug like I seriously couldn't help it. "Nimrod! Come on!"

"It doesnae matter!" Tido whisper-railed me again and then gave me a real mean look.

"Fine," I said an' all my good mood vanished just like that. Fuckin' Tido's about as much fun as a can full of dog shit. "What the hell's a Spite?" I asked as I looked up at the monoliths in front of us.

"Nae, we have nae seen the spites," Tido answered in a big voice as he addressed the mountains.

Epi started rattling his chains like an economy-sized Jacob—or Bob(?)—Marley. "How can something so disruptive to the Underground City remain so elusive, brother?"

Pro rattled his chains too but only 'cause he was shrugging his shoulders. "All I know is that our lost Spite remains so, Epimetheus. And we are in no position to find it, which is why we—"

 For the first time while conversating, Epi interrupted his bro, and even added some chain rattling. "The lost Spite *must* be found! So long as it roams outside the borders of Tartarus, it will bring ruin and disaster to all who cross its path!"

"Who the fuck's Tartar?" I asked, shaking my head 'cause whatever the hell's they was goin' on about, I weren't following.

Conan leaned in and gave me a quick whisper. "Tartarus is the ol' name fer the morgue."

"Can this Spite thing cause some permanent damage?" I asked, gettin' worried like 'cause if these rock dudes was afraid of some spite, I figured good ol' Bill oughtta be scared of it too.

47

Tido's face had the kind of bleakness you see on guys that are about to die. "None o' the Spites are anythin' tae trifle with."

Nimrod started freaking the fuck out again. And, 'course he made as little sense as ever but his tone sounded like he was two seconds from a deadpanic attack. Pro looked at him with a firm set of his mammoth jaw.

"I am aware of what I said before, Nimrod. But apparently, things have changed."

Tido did another bench-pressive lift of his hair using just his eyebrows. "Whit things have changed?"

I could've sworn I saw Pro smirking at the Druid. "You may certainly ask, Tallis Black. But surely you realize the answers you seek are not always forthcoming."

I did my best imposteration of a pogostick and hopped right over that one. "What the hell does that mean?!"

The smirk I saw straightened into a line. "It means, William, that I have told you all I am willing to divulge at this time."

It felt like the same kind of admonication I got from Uriel when I was still in training. It sounded like Pro was being a big ol' dick.

Then the smirk popped back on Pro's face. "Besides, I believe the location of Lily Harper is of far greater importance to the both of you, is it not?"

Conan attemptried his best to concealiate it, but his body language told all. I'd absolutely kick his ass at poker.

"Then ye *have* seen her?"

Epi started makin' a whole bunch of awful noises, but Pro just gave him the side-eye. "Epimetheus, being blind, has not seen anything in centuries. But I believe he has a tale to tell; don't you, brother?"

48

Epi didn't cut to the chase. He was too busy making some weird-ass noise. It sounded like a laugh, a sob and a cough blended together into a smoothie. After two minutes of that racket hangin' around like a wet fart, I couldn't take it no more.

"Well, spit it out already, Epi!" Tido nailed me with his stink-eye and a snake hiss but I was long past giving a shit. If he had something to say, I wanted to hear it. If he didn't, I wanted to find somebody who did.

Epi seemed to get the hint. He settled down and leaned his head forward. That's when I got a good look at his eye-boulders. What truly captivacated my attention was all the gunk I saw ringed around them. It looked like his eyes had been leaking out the funky stuff forever, and whatever it was, it sure as hell weren't tears.

He pulled a deep breath into his mouth before he finally talked. "Someone showed up recently... a sweet child. She has visited us for several nights now..." He grunted as he looked over at Pro. "Did the child actually appear to us, brother, or am I—"

Pro spoke with authority. "Unless I shared the same dream, Epimetheus, the one you speak of has come more than thrice to visit you."

The next words from Epi sounded like he was barely holding off an epic man-cry. "Then I am doubly grateful. The thought that this slip of a girl, who climbed onto my body to wipe my eyes... the fear that she may have never been real..."

Conan buried his right hand into his beard. I wondered how many fingers lost their way in the overgrowth. "This sounds like Besom," he said, mostly to hisself.

As Besom's personal guardian angel, I could agree. Still, it sounded a little too good to be true. "I dunno, Tido. Helpin' folks out? Yeah, Nips has been

49

doin' that since forever. But this mountainursin' shit? Be nice if we got us a genuwhine eyewitness account from somebody who actually saw her."

Pro looked kind of embarrassed. "You have to understand, William. While personages like yourself and the Druid are notable enough to warrant our full attention, the same is not true of the dead. They are no more than tiny motes to us, indistinguishable from dust."

"But Lily ain't dead," I argued.

"Regardless, Epimetheus's caregiver never once uttered a word while attending to him. So none of us can truly say that she is indeed the one you seek," Pro finished.

The idea of givin' this man-mountain the benefit of the doubt didn't sit well in my crawdaddy. At that moment, I was convincified he knew a lot more than what he was telling us. "Yeah, I get that. I mean, how many o' the recently deceased come by an' see you guys anyways?"

That casual line got me some info I never saw coming. "Now that you inquire, there have been quite a few such beings to come by of late. We were advised that a civil war is currently being waged within the Circle beyond us."

I saw the way Tido subcutaneously stiffened up until he was standin' there, like super straight, like he was trying to hold in a huge ass fart. Little did he know that the key ain't in holding it in. Key's in letting it rip real slow like so it don't make no sound. The smell you can't do nothing 'bout though.

"A civil war?" he repeated. "An' who's fightin' who?"

Epi sighed like a parent giving an explanationary to some kid who couldn't understand the answer. "We do not know."

Conan started wiping off more pieces on the path so he could pace.

"What disturbs you so, Tallis Black?" Pro asked.

Tido kept on pacing but his eyes were paddle-locked on Pro's face like heat-seeking missiles. He didn't answer so Pro kept on talking.

"You believe that I am less than forthcoming, Tallis Black." The big eyes on Pro narrow-margined on Conan as if he was barely two steps from crossing a line. And his comment weren't no question. The way he said the words made me once again gratefulfilled for the chains holdin' the three of 'em in place.

I wondered what the big, dumb Scottish hick was trying to do. Arguing with the guy guarding the door was seriously ill-bad-vibesable. "C'mon, Tido, how do it matter? Outside o' Nips' location, there's not much else we wanna know anyways."

That managed to stop Conan dead in his tracks. But he didn't look any less mangry at me or Pro. "If'n a man lies aboot one thing, stookie angel, he'll lie aboot another... like knowin' the whereaboots o' Lily." He looked back at Pro an' his eyes narrowed. "An' Ah know ye've got the seer's gift. Yer damned name means 'forethought'! So Ah'd say ye know quite a bit more than yer tellin' oos."

Pro's expression turned as stony as the path beneath us. "Be that as it may, Lord of Fergus Castle, neither I nor my brothers have anything further to share with you this day. Make of that what you will."

I elbowed Tido in frustration. "Nice going, dumbass! Now he's never gonna let us through."

Pro chuckled like I made a pretty good joke. "On the contrary, William, we are perfectly willing to allow both of you pass... for a small price."

"Uhh, no disrespect, Pro," I started. "But we ain't got nothin' more than the clothes on our backs." I

51

glanced down at Tido's ugly feet. "Well, minus a pair of shoes."

Pro opened his mouth when Epi wheezed out a few words. "The price is this: find the girl... the one who took such good care of me. Lead her to the world above. She does not belong here."

Even with his back to me, I knew Tido was eyeing Pro something fierce. "Epimetheus speaks fer ye, Fire-Thief?"

Pro gave his bro the stink-eye but nodded. "He does. The duty of extracting tolls falls upon his shoulders." He continued nodding. "And regardless of the girl's true identity, Epimetheus is correct. She does not belong in this place."

"Do you accept our terms?" Epi asked.

I didn't think Epi's caregiver would be Lils. Still, it wasn't an unreasonable demandate an' it meant Tido an' me didn't have to continue on our quest naked. So there was that.

"Aye, ye have me word," Tido said.

Pro smiled like he just got hisself a brand new Playstation. "Very good... Nimrod, if you please?"

I controlled myself this time. Swear.

Nim-wha sucked up the air so hard, he swallowed some of the clouds with it.

"Ah, shit," I muttered while grabbing Tido's leg. Sure enough, when Nim-wha blew all that wind out, every one of them clouds flew right back into our faces. I hung onto Conan's leg for dear life. Tido was steady as an oak and didn't even budge... I figured he'd prolly summonated that freaky Druid magic and made his feet grow roots or something.

When the clouds passed, there was good news and bad news. The good news? All that sucking an' blowing uncovated the path for us. The bad news? The same trick exposasized the ground all around the path. It was pulserating in waves like the ocean, if the ocean was fulfilled with sand instead of water. Every once in a while, a glob of red stuff that looked anything but good popped out from underneath the sand. I had ta wonder what happened to Tido's boots. Then I decided I really didn't want to know.

I notarized that the path went right under Pro's feet when he lifted one of them gargantuan things up. "Our unpleasant conversation aside, we wish both of you abundant good fortune in the tasks that lie ahead."

I releasified Tido's leg and started walking. "You know, I'd offer all o' you man-mountains the same sentimentalments but, well..."

Pro's big, booming laugh pushed back the clouds a little more. "Well spoken, William. Do take care of yourself as well as your companion."

I looked up at him and nodded. "LLAP, yo."

"I am not familiar..." Pro started.

"Live Long and Prosper," I filled in for him.

It took a lot less time to pass under Pro's foot than I thought it would. Conan seemed a little tense while we was walking. I configured he could use something to take his mind off whatever was givin' him brain constipation.

"So... Lord o' Fergus Castle?"

"It's nae oop fer discussion."

I held up my hands. "All right, all right, I just find it kinda hard ta believe that you ever had anything more than that Lincoln Log cabin you coinhabitate out there in the Dark Wood, yo."

"Nae as hard as believin' anyone e'er called ye 'William'."

"Only other guy that ever called me that was Uriel."

That tasty morsel hit me hard, harder than all the torture I'd suffered in Blondie's personal dungeon. But that were somethin' I wanted to talk about even less than Tido wanted to talk about his castle.

A lot of wrecked buildings were visibearable just past Pro's shoe. I watched the tube of black smoke snaking its way towards the sky and my empty guts monkey-wrenched. "Ever git the feelin' we really put our feet in it this time, yo?"

Conan sucked in a breath through his teeth before answering. "Ah cannae disagree, stookie angel. But, then again, fer the likes o' oos, whit's new?"

"Not he who loses but who gains the prize."
-Dante's Inferno

SIX
LILY

I was doing my best not to fangirl out.

Yeah, I was still stuck in the Underground City. And I'd barely survived a plane crash. But! I was flying on the back of a bird woman with the freaking Red Baron! How many girls could say that?

The rest of the Fury flock swarmed around us like a living force field. Originally I had believed there were three furies in the Underground City who were duty-bound to protect the crown that had once housed the soul of Persephone but upon Donnchadh asserting his control, the rest of the furies had come and joined our cause.

Before we'd taken off, one of them brought me some rope to tie up my prisoner's hands... hands which were now securely restrained behind him. Not wanting to take any chances, I still held his pistol to his back.

But, really, between my security measures plus the distance between us and the ground below, the Red Baron had no incentive to misbehave. To his credit, he didn't try. He did exactly what he was told, and spoke only when spoken to. He was so blasé about it, you'd think getting captured was part of his daily routine.

Despite being surrounded by—well, maybe not *friendly* faces but certainly, less hostile ones—I started feeling lonely. If Bill were here, he'd be complaining about something in his usual word salad. If Tallis were here, he wouldn't say much but... he wouldn't need to. Just having Tallis around made me feel... safe. Even without Donnchadh, Tallis was a survivor and he knew The Underground City like the back of his hand. I guess that made sense considering he'd been the Master of the Underground City at one point.

But instead of Bill and Tallis, I had a bunch of literal man-eaters at my side. Their idea of a conversation sounded more like the squabbling of chickens, pecking at each other. Every now and then one of them would erupt into a loud squawking that was beyond nervewracking.

Being in the presence of an actual human—and a celebrity to boot—was actually pretty exciting. Too bad none of my old self-help books offered any useful pointers on starting a conversation with a flying ace who'd been dead for over a hundred years.

I cleared my throat. "Do you mind if I ask you a question, Captain Von Richtofen?"

A ghost of a smile appeared as he looked over his shoulder at me. "If I may point out a pertinent fact, *Fraulein* Harper, being your prisoner, I am hardly in a position to refuse such a request."

Feeling a little flustered, I decided to press on. "Yeah, true but... compared to some of the demons I've encountered in the Underground City, you've been very polite, at least, so far."

The smile on his lips became wider. "Dare one say I've been a model baron?"

I really didn't know what to say after that. On the one hand, I wanted to talk to him but on the other hand, he *was* my prisoner. And I didn't want to get too chummy with him. For all I knew, he would use my kindness against me.

He cleared his throat and wet his lips. "I believe you wished to ask a question of me...?"

Shaking my head to clear out the mental cobwebs, I replied, "Why did you attack us back there?"

Just the mention of our previous aerial battle was enough to rouse Donnchadh. Interrupting him with my fear of crashing to the ground left him with a bad case of unsated bloodlust. Now he was straining against the magic of the runes like a water reservoir stressing the restraints of a dam. And Self or no Self, I had serious doubts on this dam's ability to hold back that red deluge.

"My standing orders and duty are to secure this Circle's outer perimeter," my prisoner answered. "Supplies that are vital to our ongoing efforts come through this area on a regular schedule. As such, my commanding officers fear intruders could either take or destroy said supplies."

Okay, that made a lot of sense but I was still a little pissed at being targeted. "And you thought *we* were those intruders?"

"When one is a soldier, one's duty precludes all independent thoughts on matters beyond one's control. Thus, when I am instructed that any outsiders should be considered enemy combatants, I do not question. In our current struggle, there can be no neutral positions."

I was about to ask him exactly what this struggle was about when I heard another plane buzzing through the clouds. I started to get nervous and looked around myself, seeking any signs of an attack. As testament to their own paranoia, my flock of Furies began doing the same.

My prisoner, on the other hand, remained as calm as ever, gently shaking his head. "Let me reassure you, *Fraulein* Harper, we are quite safe at the moment. Judging from the acoustics, that particular plane is following a heading that will carry him well out of our own flight path."

I jammed the gun a little deeper into his ribs. "Now you wouldn't be saying that just to make me drop my guard, even a little, would you?"

He seemed upset with me and turned around to face me with a frown. "Have I been anything less than truthful since I became your prisoner? My word is literally all I have left to call my own. Without that, I am nothing."

I eased the pressure of the gun barrel, my cheeks burning again. "I'm just... accustomed to dealing with demons."

He nodded sympathetically. "Your distrust is the natural outcome of the nature of our acquaintance."

A distant explosion on the ground caused me to look away. Donnchadh snarled at me internally because I'd just given the captain the perfect opportunity to attack me. I shoved my spiritual misanthrope back down in his hole so I could concentrate on the hellscape below us. Even by Underground City standards, what existed below us was much worse than grim.

Near as I could tell, two big armies were battling on the streets of a cityscape. There was enough open space in the middle of the street for a pair of soldier columns to face off, each of them a mile long.

Both sides kept firing at each other when they weren't hacking away with their blades. Sometimes it looked like a fair fight—guns versus guns, swords versus swords. But other parts of the battlefield revealed some seriously lopsided matchups. Sword-wielding soldiers were getting massacred by rifle and machine gun fire, artillery shells pelting down on them like explosive raindrops.

Some areas generated enough smoke to completely obscure the clashing forces. But the clanking of steel-on-steel and the incessant chatter of gunfire left no question as to what was actually going on behind the smoke.

I looked at my prisoner. "Care to explain what this battle is about?"

The captain had a sad, wistful look on his face as he glanced down at the violence. "Some time ago, a number of the local condemned souls broke free of their bonds. Together with the support of discontented demons who once were their tormentors, they rose up in rebellion against the Malebranche. What you see below are the ongoing results of that rebellion."

I did my best to ignore the fighting while I responded. "The Malebranche?"

"Yes."

"What, exactly, is that?"

His eyes stayed fixed on the combat. "*The Malebranche* refers to the thirteen demon dukes who dominate this Circle. After losing their third *Bolgia* to the rebels, the demon dukes began pressing some of the other condemned prisoners into service."

"You mean, people like you?"

"*Jawohl...* myself and many, many others. We have been bleeding for them ever since."

I had a hard time understanding such an arrangement. "Okay, why would any of you fight for the guys who kept you locked up and tortured all those years?"

"Do not underestimate the power of freedom from pain," he answered sadly. "Even though we still inhabit the Underground City, we now do so as a somewhat free people." A shadow darkened his face. "But we also know that such freedom will not be ours forever. When the struggle is over and we are no longer needed, we shall return to our previous indentured state."

I frowned at him. "There's another thing I don't get... you're probably the most honorable person I've met down here." Actually, I thought Tallis had the edge on Manfred in that department but no point in hurting his feelings.

"*Danke schoen...* for your kind words."

"Well... you just don't seem like the type who belongs down here." Of course, if my memory served me correctly, the Red Baron had been a fighter pilot in World War 1 and he'd been an enemy to the U.S.

He pointed to his collar. "If I may direct your attention to the clothing underneath my jacket, it will prove how mistaken you are."

Donnchadh acted up again, screaming internally that this was a trick. I ignored him—as best I could—and pulled down the collar of Manfred's coat. What I saw underneath made no sense to me. It looked like a glittering, gold robe that reflected the very faint light around us.

I ran my fingertips over it. It felt hard, made from a heavy material that could have been used as armor plating on a tank. It didn't feel at all like the gold weave it appeared to be.

The flying ace gave me a rueful look as I pulled my fingers away. "Do you see now, *fraulein*?"

"I see a gold-painted, heavy robe of some kind. But I still have no idea what it is or why you're wearing it."

He hummed and told me, "It is the mark of the hypocrite, a stigma for those who dare to compare themselves to gold when they are actually nothing but lead beneath."

I glanced down at my gun dubiously. "So... is your robe thick enough to stop a bullet?"

Disgust crossed Manfred's face. "Would that the Malebranche were so considerate. *Nein, fraulein...*"

"Look... I know you're being respectful because you're my prisoner, but could you just call me 'Lily' instead of *fraulein* from now on?"

He raised his eyebrows in genuine surprise. "The term is the German way of addressing young, unmarried ladies such as yourself. Under the circumstances, I cannot, in good conscience, call you by your Christian name." He didn't wait for me to argue but continued talking. "To return to your previous question... the heavy weight is the only resemblance to lead this clothing possesses. Were you to shoot me directly in the back, it would do nothing to reduce the momentum of the bullet by so much as a mere nanosecond."

A big explosion suddenly burst out of nowhere beside us. One of my Furies was annihilated in the blast, leaving nothing but a trail of feathers. I glanced down and watched her body as it plummeted down to the ground. That was right before a series of booms started exploding all around us.

Not again, I thought as my Fury performed evasive maneuvers around the airborne bombs that rent the air.

Manfred spoke and the tension in his tone was as heavy as his robes. "Anti-aircraft cannons... not particularly accurate, but as you can see, one direct hit could end all of us."

I ignored my lurching stomach and answered him. "Guess you're not the only one who thinks my Furies are enemy combatants." As if to underscore my point, another Fury flew right into one of the blasts. She didn't even leave a feather in her wake.

I shook my head. "We've got to get on the ground fast!"

Manfred reacted like I'd just said we should jump off the fury's back without any parachutes. "*Nein*! However terrible things may be in the skies, they are a hundred times worse below!"

"We're dangerously close to getting shot down!" I screamed back at him. Then not waiting for further argument, I slapped the shoulder of my Fury twice. "Land!"

My not-so-trusty steed took a direct nosedive, heading straight for the ground. Her sisters followed her lead. The anti-aircraft guns kept shooting but we were too fast for any of them to touch us. The bursts followed, popping up wherever we'd just been two seconds before. You'd think that a place with access to that kind of hardware could have used more accurate guns. That was one oversight I couldn't complain about.

We landed in the middle of one of the columns of soldiers, comprised mostly of humans with a few demons mixed in. Considering the enemy was at their backs, I guessed they were in retreat. Nobody wore anything even close to a consistent uniform, so I wondered if *maybe* these were the rebels? But, rebels or not, we had bigger fish to fry.

The nearest human shouted at the other soldiers before he came running towards us, his sword brandished high in the air as if to cut off my Fury's head.

My bird woman leapt off the ground, knocking Manfred and me off her in the process. When I looked up again, she'd already torn the human into pieces, pieces that were scattered on the ground, looking like beef jerky. The rest of the furies surrounded us in a protective circle while they hissed and squawked at anyone who came too close. After a minute, the rest of the troops had the good sense to retreat, this time from us.

For the duration of the battle, I kept my gun out in case any of them tried to make a play for us. Manfred got down on his knees while the Furies launched their victory squawks at the fleeing idiots who tried to kill them.

I looked over at the flying ace. "You were saying something about the ground being worse, Captain?"

He shrugged. "You have yet to see the worst this place has to offer."

A plane, possibly the one we'd heard earlier, returned to hearing range. Even with my utter lack of aeronautical experience, I knew something was wrong. The engine was sputtering and could barely keep going. When the plane emerged from the clouds, I could see the nose was on a direct collision course with the ground. A cloud of black smoke was trailing directly behind it, and devouring everything from the tail forward. Then I realized the smoke wasn't drifting away from the plane like it should have been. No, it was fastened onto the plane like an oil slick or a sticky blob.

The sight of that black stuff caused my Fury flock to cry out their dismay. Likewise, Manfred threw himself flat on the ground from which he'd just picked himself up.

"Down, *fraulein, schnell, schnell!*"

I didn't have any idea what a "*schnell*" was but the terror in his tone made me dive for the ground and hug it for all it was worth. I didn't dare lift my head even when I raised my eyes to see our incoming aerial visitors. The misty, black cloud blob managed to cover half the plane by the time both passed over our heads. Judging by their trajectory and speed, there was no way the pilot could manage even the rough landing we'd experienced earlier.

I heard a crash in the distance, followed by a strange, buzzing noise. It reminded me of the sound of a beehive full of angry bees. A chorus of shouts and screams, probably from the victorious army, was audible above the buzzing. While I'd seen and heard a lot of ugly things when I was in the Underground City, that cacophony definitely qualified as one of the worst.

I expected Donnchadh to get so hot and bothered by the incoming hoard of soldiers that I'd have a hard time subduing him. Instead, he seemed unusually chill in the face of this latest horror. I could sense his approval of the wholesale slaughter we thankfully couldn't see, laced with a little regret that he wasn't participating in it. That reaction scared me more than his usual angry outbursts.

The brutality was over as quickly as it started. The black, misty cloud suddenly detached itself from the plane and flew back up into the air, disappearing into the true cloud cover above. I didn't move for several long minutes before picking myself up. Only then did Manfred and the Furies follow suit.

"Quite wise, *fraulein*. Many have been slain by foolishly assuming safety where it was absent."

While I helped him back to his feet, I looked across at the now quiet battlefield. A lot of bleached white bones lay on the other side. Most of them were still clutching the weapons that failed to save them. I gestured at my Furies and then towards the newly dead. They flew ahead of Manfred and me while we proceeded on foot.

We walked down to the line of anti-aircraft guns, my heart in my throat the entire time. Not a single fighter on the field had survived. Humans and demons alike were picked clean, leaving their equipment in virtually pristine condition. Beside one of the guns, a sat phone lay next to a human skeleton. The voice on the other end was yelling loud enough to blow out the receiver.

"By the Eternal Flame, you will give me a sit rep, soldier, or be immediately re-imprisoned for insubordination!"

Yeah, insubordination was no longer a concern for whoever had been manning the phone. I hung it up and went back to looking around. Some of my Furies scavenged the bones but ultimately, there wasn't enough meat on them to be interesting.

And that was when it struck me that whatever I'd just witnessed didn't make any sense. "What the hell happened?"

Manfred took a slow breath before answering. "The Spites happened, *fraulein*..."

"The Spites?" I repeated, clearly lost.

The Red Baron nodded. "In other words, the worst possible thing this Circle has to offer."

"Resounding like the hum of swarming bees..."
- Dante's Inferno

SEVEN
TALLIS

The scarcity of food was affecting me worse than I dared admit.

Of course, seeing how badly the morgue had been wrecked and ruined in sae short a time didnae help. I had nae idea how long it had been since me last visit here. It had to have been before Besom took her first swordplay lesson from me. But not very long before, which made the destruction of the familiar buildings that much more shocking.

The angel prattled on and on about the destruction, calling it "a Disneyland version of Dresden." Talking out his arse as usual. I could understand why he felt such a way. In the midst of such obliteration, what hope did either of us have of finding Lily?

I wish I could say 'twas the angel's nonstop blathering that caused me nae to hear what was waiting for us. But between the wreckage of the Morgue and me belly moaning its emptiness, there was nae way I could have prepared meself for the ambush.

A pack of lesser imps emerged from between the building cracks, coming at us like a horde of land piranha. The memory of one of those little bastards lifting me sword made me see red. In two breaths, I cleaved three of the bastards in half and was ready to kill the rest. The angel had taken it upon himself to fight against them too though his tactics left much to be desired.

I ran toward the thickest cluster of the imps, thrusting me sword straight into them. Half a dozen of the infernal pests were speared on me blade like a shish kabob. The rest returned to the tight places from whence they'd come.

I waved me blade through the air to shake their dead passengers free, causing the angel to smirk.

"Need a hand with that, Tido?"

Before I could answer, a pack of dogs suddenly scrambled around the corner, barking at the top of their lungs. They moved sae fast, I couldnae get a good look at them. What I was able to see, though, was that they were grey, and roughly the size of horses. Horses with gleaming fangs that longed to bite.

"Oh, no! Not this shit again," the stookie angel muttered right before one of them snatched him off the ground as though to make a fast snack of him.

I swung me sword at the ones what were coming at me, imps and all. 'Twas enough to knock the mutts backwards but the imps stuck to the blade, giving me no edge to cut them with. One of the dogs snapped at me blade, taking a couple of the imps into its mouth.

I yanked the sword sideways, cutting the fellow beside him. A heavy weight hit me from behind, pushing me to the ground. The barking in me ear moved left to right, telling me that one of the pack was circling me. One look at the snarling faces staring down at me revealed my error. These grey canines were nae dogs at all, but savage wolves.

The pack suddenly all looked up as one. I heard the sound of a bullet being chambered. The sound appeared to come from the top of one of the destroyed buildings surrounding us. Then a gleaming rifle came into me view and I stared down the barrel of it. I could make out a duster coat and heavy boots before a deep voice spake to me.

"Hand off the sword."

I released me blade and he kicked it behind him. The barrel aimed at me head never wavered. One of the wolves walked over, dragging the angel by his shirt. He looked up at our captor with clear defiance stamped about his face.

"Who the fuck are you? Head o' the local hell-spitality committee?"

The boot found a new home on the back of the angel's neck which caused a snapping noise and the angel screamed.

"One more word, little man, and I will bury a bullet in you."

I looked at the stookie angel with a quick shake of me head. When a man talks like that, he's beyond idle threats. I peeked up at the stranger and could barely make out his face: broad, flat features framed by a square haircut. His face was dark olive, as though he'd been left out in the sun too long. His eyes were as flat and pitiless as the rifle he held.

"Found ye," he said in a deep, accented voice as though he hailed from the American Deep South.

I growled at him. "Ye know who Ah am?"

The barrel moved a bit to the left and the man fired. The heavy round entered me left arm, causing me to bite my lip from the searing pain. He flicked the lever on the rifle back and forth before aiming it at me head again.

"You are my bounty, Tallis Black, no different from the slaves I used to hunt in my former life." He pressed the now-hot barrel into me forehead, and it seared me skin. "And if you give me reason, I'll gladly plant a round straight through your head, bounty or no bounty."

His point made, he stepped back and whistled. His pack peeled away from us, one picking up me blade in its jaws. They surrounded all three of us like a protective guard. He stepped back and gestured upward with the rifle. "Both of you, on your feet."

We rose as best we could. I was lightheaded from the blood loss caused by the bounty hunter's bullet. He gestured with the barrel again towards the rubble ahead of us. I put me hands up and started walking in that direction. I could hear the steps of the stookie angel behind me while the pack scattered to encircle us on all sides. The one in the lead continued carrying me sword.

I got me a chance to look at the bullet wound in me left arm. The bullet had gone clean through but not without tearing a nasty gash through me bicep. I had little strength left and nae food. But none of that mattered if I died of blood loss. I focused the last of me magic on the task of staunching me wound. The flesh quietly mended, and the unrestrained bleeding ended. A bandage would have been nice but such had to wait for now. If I healed too quickly, this bounty hunter might decide to test the limits of me abilities.

The bastard gunman's pack finally steered us to a building that was mostly intact. Judging from the outside, it could have been an office building. But I knew better. Nothing in the Underground City was ever as benign as it might appear.

The presence of the two door guards only furthered me discomfort. These particular demons had pale, hairless skin, mostly covered by fancy three-piece suits. Their beady eyes refused to blink, their noses merely a couple of slits above their mouths, and their mouths were nae more than round holes ringed from the outer edge to the inner with sharp teeth. They resembled snakes with their leathery skin and oblong heads. This breed could only have originated from the morgue, pasty nightmares that fed off both living and dead flesh. They were called Mephits.

The one on the left saw our caravan first. "Returned."

The hunter stepped in front of us to acknowledge the greeting with a nod. "Has the cardinal returned as well?"

Both guards shook their heads.

"What about Avernus?"

The monster on the right pointed toward the open doorway. "Waiting."

A flick of the rifle towards the door got us moving again. The entrance hallway was so tight, all of our captor's beasties could barely fit two-by-two. The walls were made of some sort of heavy metal—steel or lead mayhap. The only other doorway was the open one ahead.

The room beyond was roughly the size of Fergus Castle's main hall, and the fluorescent lights dimly flickered over our heads. More of the Mephits were walking about with the look of an army prepping for battle. That image didnae exactly fit with the maze of cubicles they wound through.

I noticed humans chained to the desks inside the cubicles, all of them working at the computers on their desks at a furious pace. Whenever they slowed down, one of the monsters would pull a whip from under its coat and strike their backs. In the far left corner, I heard the heavy rumble of an engine, mayhap a generator to supply power.

The bounty hunter called out the name "Avernus" over the din of the engine while his wolves herded me and the stookie angel towards the wall on the left. A perfectly proportioned woman in a dark blue business suit with long tresses, came out from behind one of the nearer cubicles ahead of us. Her skin was reddish but paled next to her flaming red hair and the red horns that poked through either side of her forehead. Huge black wings expanded from her back and with her pointed red tail, 'twas quite obvious she was a Succubus demon.

The bounty hunter appeared uncomfortable upon seeing her but stood at attention all the same.

The woman glanced at both of us with bright, flashing eyes before smiling at our captor. "I knew I could count on you, Jedidiah. With all due respect to the cardinal, it would have taken his army a full week to accomplish what you just did in a day."

Jedidiah looked like he was anything but comfortable with the praise. "Just doing my duty, Avernus."

The woman pressed against him, putting a delicate hand between his legs. "And you do it so well, my loyal hunter. Yet you still choose to reject the standing offer I gave you?"

"N-n-not at this time," he sputtered out.

"Are you certain?"

"Yes, I am certain," his face became more and more tense with her fondling of his crotch.

Avernus pouted her lips but removed her hand and body from his side. "As you please... but I shall look forward to the day or night when you finally surrender."

She slunk past him to get a closer look at us. Her bright red eyes were now all business, looking us over as though we were fresh cuts of beef. Finally, she pointed at me. "You, I know."

I grunted. "Ah dinnae know how."

I didnae recognize her but I knew well enough to know she was nae friend. Not an unattractive woman, she was shapely but she was also hard. Her features were long and angular, chiseled. There was naethin' soft about her.

"We crossed paths once, but it was many centuries ago so I doubt you'd remember me," she said. "We're both a long way from my original stomping grounds in Dis." She moved her finger over to the angel. "You, I don't know."

Naturally, the angel took that as an invitation to open his mouth. "Yeah? Well, toots, if yer chief zookeeper over there hadn't dragged us in, I might actually want—"

A shot from the rifle cut the dunderheid off, throwing him against the opposite metal wall. The shot echoed in the enclosed space like a cannon, making human and Mephit alike jump. I was damn near deafened from the racket meself, worse than poor Prometheus's yelling.

Avernus marched up to her subordinate with considerable less flirtation. "What do you think you're doing?"

Jedidiah flicked the lever on his rifle, unfazed by the racket and fuss he'd just caused. "Keeping a promise I made to the little man outside. Besides, he's a spy and the cardinal's orders are to shoot them on sight."

The angel groaned as he got to his feet, the bullet hole leaving a large gap in his chest. "Okay... fine... mission accomp-blessed. Now can we get back ta the part where the hot chick was checkin' me out like she was ready to experience angel sausage?"

The hunter put the rifle onto his shoulder only for Avernus to slap it back down again. "He's an angel, you idiot! Empty your whole rifle on him and it won't make a bit of difference."

The stookie angel managed a cheeky grin while he spread his arms wide. "Hey, don't listen ta her, Daniel Boone. Hit me with a few more rounds. Maybe you'll eventually pull it off."

The hate pouring out the bounty hunter's eyes told me he wished to oblige the fool angel. Regardless, Avernus's grip on the bounty hunter's rifle remained firm until he finally lowered it. The situation back under control, Avernus looked at me sword at his side.

"That looks like a fine weapon."

I did me best to keep the smirk off me face. She touched the hilt then pulled her scalded hand back and screamed. I couldnae keep from laughing long and hard.

"Did ye really think Ah'd craft a blade that a demon could wield? Yer little cousins can steal it but, by Lleu, no demon'll ever wield it."

The hateful look she gave me was bloody priceless. It almost compensated for the dire straits in which we'd found ourselves. Avernus waved her hand through the air while Jedidiah stood at attention.

I glanced over at the wolf pack before saying, "Ah'm surprised ye managed ta git a pack o' *Fenrir* oonder yer control."

That observation resulted in the hunter giving me a hard, disbelieving blink. "Most refer to them as hellhounds."

"An' wrongly so. Nae mistakin' the wolf in these beasties when ye've had a chance tae look at 'em oop close."

What I didnae add was that I was sure the bounty hunter had placed runes on the wolves to keep them under his control.

One of the humans poked his head above his cubicle. "M-M-Mistress Avernus?"

Giving her injured palm one last shake, she barked at the sheepish creature, "What?!"

"The cardinal r-r-requests your presence shortly."

Jedidiah raised an eyebrow at his boss. "Do you believe the cardinal's hunt was as successful as mine?"

Avernus blew out a breath of visible irritation. "Without any allies, his prey is practically helpless on her own. So what does it matter if he catches her or not?"

I felt me heart skip a beat. Could they be speaking of Lily? That thought went nae further as the wolf pack began herding us back towards the door. I felt the barrel of Jedidiah's rifle on me the whole way down the corridor.

Once we were outside again, I noticed a flickering light coming from around the corner. True, this shell of a city had plenty of such freestanding fires that emitted such light. But none of them, so far as I knew, could move.

A few moments later, the source appeared at the head of a squad of humans and Mephits, a strolling figure engulfed in bright blue flames. The closer it came, the more I could see the man inside it. Though the fire burned at a constant, steady rate, his flesh remained whole and unblemished. Me eyes widened as he came close enough that I recognized him.

"What wounds I mark'd upon their limbs..."
- Dante's Inferno

EIGHT
TALLIS

"Cardinal Cauchon," I breathed out as he and his troops stopped in front of us. I made a discreet glance at me sword. It wasnae more than a few feet from where I stood, but nae way could I make a move for it with the pack 'round me. 'Twas nae the right moment.

The cardinal's eyes lit up with recognition. "Tallis Black... No words can express how much I have been looking forward to this moment."

Me eyes locked onto his, and I wanted to lock me hands 'round his neck. "Would that Ah could say the same."

The angel looked between us. "You know each other?"

Cauchon's eyes burned hotter than the fire upon his flesh. "Quite well, angel... I am not likely to forget the one who dared to pass sentence upon me for merely doing my duties in life."

"Dinnae pass yer vices off as virtues tae me, inquisitor," I spat back at him. "Every century o' flame ye've endured was still tae good fer the likes o' ye."

He stalked up to me with quick steps. The wolf pack parted like the Red Sea at his approach. He came sae close, I could feel the heat from his fire. "The same can be said of the fate for which I am about to condemn you."

He gestured at one of the Mephits. The creature shoved someone out from behind him, throwing her forward. The girl, who stumbled before landing on her knees, turned out to be a wee slip of a girl with short, dark hair. She was wearing battered men's clothes and looked as though she couldnae be more than twenty.

She looked up at me with calm, sad eyes, asking—nae begging, but *asking*—for understanding. Something about her manner made me heart go out to her at first sight. Sure, she was nae me Besom. But I knew with certainty that she didnae belong in this place.

Matter of fact, she looked like someone who could have selflessly tended to a Titan's eyes for many days....

"Place her alongside the others," Cauchon ordered Jedidiah. The pack's master obeyed, coming close enough for me to grab me blade. But too many others were watching... The moment had yet to arrive.

The girl was dragged alongside us before the hunter kicked me knees out from under me and then did the same to the angel sae that we all knelt together.

Avernus picked that moment to speak. "With all due respect, Your Grace, why are we performing the executions here?"

Cauchon took the question calmly enough. "Actually, *Mademoiselle* Avernus, *we* are not performing executions at all."

"Explain."

Cauchon nodded. "Within a few moments, the swarm shall make its appearance." He raised an eyebrow. "That is, unless your machines have miscalculated its pattern of flight...?"

Avernus paled at the implied accusation and she held up her hands. "No, no, nothing has been miscalculated."

The guards began shutting the heavy doors with trembling hands. As I looked upon each of them, fear was clearly evident in their expressions. Even the Fenrir seemed to think it was a daft idea to be caught in the swarm's path. Clearly, this swarm was something to be feared.

Cauchon gestured again at one of his lackeys, who tossed him something bright and shiny. It wasnae until Cauchon caught it that I could tell what it was: a perfectly crafted diamond with a blue tinge to its sheen.

The fool angel picked this moment to open his mouth. "Hey, yo, last I checked, diamonds were only a *girl's* best friend..."

The cardinal shoved the diamond right into the stookie's angel's face, making him scream out as the superheated stone branded him. Any ideas I had about assisting the fool angel died when Jedidiah pointed his rifle right at me head. The angel kept yelling before Cauchon pulled the stone away. An ugly red wound was burned into the angel's cheek. The bleedin' dunderheid only made the pain worse by rubbing it with his bare hand.

"Clearly the stone is no friend to you, you disgrace to the Celestial Choir," the cardinal said as he spat upon the angel's burned face.

The glare in the angel's eyes told me he heard the cardinal loud and clear. He spat an impressive-sized glob of phlegm right at his torturer's face. The blue flames surrounding the cardinal burned the mucus to naught before it could even touch Cauchon. Even so, the cardinal clearly didnae appreciate such blatant disrespect.

Just as I thought this ribald bastard weren't worth the divine firmament used to create him, the angel did something that reminded me he was still an angel at his core.

When Cauchon turned his back to us, the girl began whispering to me traveling companion in what sounded like French. And damn me if the angel didnae speak back to her in the same language near perfectly. Aye, the walloper's French sounded better than his English.

Jedidiah turned his gun on the girl, which made me sneer. "What, ye think words are a match tae yer weapon?"

The hunter ignored me, keeping his eyes and rifle trained on the girl. "English from now on... unless you want to suffer the consequences."

"Jedidiah..." The cardinal's voice boomed with massive disapproval. It cut through me captor's anger enough to make him blink. But his gun remained on its target.

Turning to the man taking aim at her, the girl bowed her head. "Apologies, *monsieur*. I shall speak English from this moment forward."

The way she looked at Jedidiah made his anger waver. He pulled the weapon back and looked away, his lip trembling ever so slightly as if he were restraining grief. Clearly, the girl had an effect on him.

Meanwhile, Cauchon faced us again. The hand that was holding the diamond had turned chalk-white, and he slowly squeezed the stone as if it were a sponge. Me concentration was interrupted by the girl's quiet whisper in me ear.

"Bless you, *monsieur*, for speaking on my behalf."

Though she meant well, the grip of failure lodged in me throat. "Fer all the good it did either o' oos, lass."

"But you tried all the same. No wonder you travel in the company of an angel."

Were it anyone else—say, Besom in the early days—I would have railed against her for being sae naïve as to think the situation were sae simple. But, in the company of this girl, words failed me. I felt nae anger and nae need for remonstration. She was simply a girl completely at peace with whatever fate awaited her.

The stookie angel spoke up but had the rare good sense to keep his voice as low as ours. "He might be my travelin' partner, but Tido's got a lotta work ta do before he reaches my level."

Her lips twitched into an amused smile. Naïve though she might be on some subjects, she could smell the stench of the stookie angel's falsehood clearly as anyone.

She whispered to him, "Bless you likewise, sweet angel, for also standing up for me."

The angel's voice sounded a bit choked when he answered. "Hey, no sweat, sweets. I mean, yo... it's in the job descriptation, right?"

A sudden cracking sound caused us to look at Cauchon. Somehow, the damned cardinal had managed to squeeze the diamond hard enough to make it shatter. The cracks inside its perfect façade began spiderwebbing and within seconds, the whole thing fell apart. He put his hands over the fragments and crushed them between his palms.

When he opened his hand again, the diamond was thoroughly ground into dust. Over his head, on the distant horizon, a black cloud burst through the grey, dipping low and heading in our direction. That simple sight was enough to make Cauchon's lackeys nervous again. They took turns examining each other, licking their lips and taking the odd step back.

Cauchon gave them what he mayhap thought was a reassuring smile. "Have no fear, *mes amis.* The remains of the true Hope Diamond shall protect us from all the ravages that await our prisoners."

"*The* Hope Diamond?" the angel asked nervously.

"Yes, my divine friend," Cauchon replied, a smile perverting his ugly face. "The very same."

He began walking in front of his troops, distributing the diamond's dust in front of them like granules of sand. Looking back at the descending black cloud, I finally understood what was coming our way. "Sae it be the Spites then, Cauchon?"

The chuckle he gave me was as unsettling as his smile, making the closest of his Mephits shiver. "*Mais oui, Monsieur* Black. From what I understand, death at the hands of the Spites is a death unlike any other."

The angel swallowed hard but did his best to put on a brave front if only in his voice. "Hey, yo, Catch-On... I think ya mighta missed the part where I told yer hench-assholes I can't die, yo. Remember the whole immortal part?"

The cardinal didnae appear disturbed by his words. "A fortnight past, the swarm slew one of the Malebranche. He was driven to the location of his death where we arranged a perfectly placed ambush. He was the second of his brethren to fall prey to these hateful spirits."

"Did you hear a word I just said?" the angel demanded. Then he faced me and shrugged. "Guess not." He paused for a moment. "Hey, Tido, what's the word you're always callin' me that means testicle?"

"Baw," I replied.

The fool angel nodded and faced Cauchon again. "You're a dumb bawhead."

Cauchon was so busy making his speech that he failed to hear the angel or notice the girl when she clasped her hands together and began muttering a prayer in perfect French.

Jedidiah only had eyes for the Spites coming towards us, thus he didnae notice either.

The Fenrir inched back from the diamond dust Cauchon continued to sprinkle. "And considering the Spites are no more than fallen archangels themselves, well, do you still believe your chances of survival are ultimately any better?" Cauchon continued.

The girl's prayer grew more fervent and more intense. She began swaying back and forth in perfect synchronization with the rhythm of her words. It made me think of the priestesses of the Morrigan in me breathing days, fervently communing with the great powers they served.

When the cardinal finished spreading the diamond dust, Jedidiah finally noticed the girl and her prayer. Cauchon caught the hunter's expression and waved him off.

"Oh, let her be, Jedidiah. The girl is simply reciting her last rites, something I know for a fact she was denied while she breathed."

The cloud was now close enough that I could see the individual specks comprising it, each one as black as the next. A buzzing sounded, as angry as any beehive disturbed by a bear.

Mayhap the angel would survive the mist of darkness but I wouldnae. Seeing as how I'd had Donnchadh stripped from me, I was naethin' but a sitting duck. Me end was near and I could feel the truth in it as easily as I could see the vehicle of me destruction as it closed in upon us.

And all I could think of was me Lily.

How would she survive the horrors of the Underground City and Alaire without me? I was meant to be her protector and I had failed her.

It was a truth for which I would never forgive meself.

If only I could have held her one last time and kissed her goodbye… If only I'd been given the opportunity to tell her how I felt—that I loved her. Aye, I had told her before but that didnae change that fact that I wished sorely I could tell her again.

If only I could have apologized for my inability to keep her safe.

If only…

The Spites were nearly upon us when the girl ceased her praying and threw her arms wide. I turned me face into the direction of the black mist. If I were to go out now, I would do so with the honor of facing my enemy front on.

"*Les anges nous protegent!*" the girl yelled and I understood the words to mean: *Angels, protect us!*

As if she had spoken a direct command, the Spites gave us wide berth, separating around us as though their black mist were averse to our beings. And yet, they swarmed everyone else, enveloping them in amorpheous blackness that evaporated their bodies until they were naethin' but white bones that dropped to the ground with hollow echoes.

The diamond dust proved to be terribly inadequate. Horrified screams ripped up and down the ranks of our enemies, including Jedidiah, who stumbled close enough for me to reach him. I yanked out me blade from the sheath at his side, rose to me feet and brained him with the pommel in one swift motion. He fell to the ground senseless, still clutching his useless rifle.

The girl's voice rent the din of buzzing and screams with crystal clarity. "*Suivez moi, mes amis!*"

Follow me, my friends, she said.

Looking over at our captors, I had to be sure none of them were in any condition to track us. I felt a tiny hand grab me by the wrist and I looked down upon the small girl.

She said, "Come please, Tido!"

"That's what I'm sayin'!" the angel called out with a quick nod.

"Bloody hell," I grumbled, but I didnae have the time nor the wherewithal to correct her. Aye, there was nae denying the good sense of a retreat. While keeping a wary eye on Cauchon's embattled soldiers, the angel and I followed the girl's lead as we weaved our way through the chaos.

Strangely enough, wherever she stepped, no Spite came within four feet of her. The angel began to fall behind, having trouble keeping up the pace. I grabbed him by the scruff of the neck, making him yelp. He wriggled like a worm impaled on a hook.

"Hey, Conan, go easy you fucktard!"

I lifted him up to me eye level. "Ye dinnae wanna git left behind, ye blatherin' fool! Git goin'!"

I couldnae support the angel's full load but I assisted him all the same, draping me arm 'round his back and supportin' a good percent of his body weight. He limped beside me, muttering all the way.

Soon enough, we were on the other side of the swarm, running deeper into the morgue's ruins. I dropped me hold on the angel and watched him fall to the ground when a loud whistle pierced the air.

The girl held up her arms again, this time to stop us from continuing forward. Her eyes were filled with unmitigated fear.

"Malebranche!"

The useless angel and I exchanged a concerned look for the demon dukes would have near as much mercy towards us as the cardinal we'd just left behind. A quick glance 'round the landscape gave me me bearings.

"This way!" I yelled.

Now 'twas the girl and the stookie angel's turn to follow me. I only hoped the direction I took them would prove safe. We heard the unmistakable steps of a professional army closing in behind us.

When the sounds of battle became too loud to ignore, I risked a glance behind us. The Spites were once more parting the skies, now fully sated with their prey.

As I returned to the business of figuring out a locale in which to hide, I found meself praying to whoever would listen that me Besom was okay.

"Who in his lifetime many a noble act achiev'd, both
by his wisdom and his sword."
- Dante's Inferno

NINE
LILY

For the third time since becoming airborne, my
stomach rumbled. I'd managed to ignore it before
since I'd been preoccupied by all the crazy shit that
seemed to happen every other minute. But my tummy
finally hit its limit. Now it wanted me to know I hadn't
eaten in God only knew how long.

That didn't change the fact that I didn't have any
food on me and it wasn't like we could make a quick
stop at the Burger King drive-through.

Ha! Funny, Lils, I said to myself.

I decided to distract my mind by paying attention
to my surroundings instead. I hoped to trick my
stomach, but I was also actively sweeping the scene
for any signs of trouble.

The Spites' swift decimation of the army had
definitely shaken me to the core. All my previous trips
to the Underground City left me face-to-face with
calculated, cruel, and what the Dungeons & Dragons
enthusiasts in my old medieval group liked to call
"chaotic" evil.

The Spites were a ferocious, malicious,
unstoppable force of nature. There was no talking to
them, no bargaining with them, and no escaping
them. Based on what I'd witnessed, my best strategy
was to make sure they didn't notice us, and after they

moved on, to put as much distance between us as was possible.

So that's exactly what we were doing—flying the opposite direction of the Spite cloud. My Furies were busily soaring above the morgue at a lower altitude to monitor the ground activity. I had no plans to land unless we had no other choice. Manfred wasn't exaggerating how dangerous the land was.

Speaking of my prisoner, he was sitting in front of me, squirming and pulling against his bonds like he had an itch. He heaved out a sigh before turning to look at me.

"While I have no right to ask anything of you, *fraulein*, I nonetheless feel compelled to make a small request."

I raised an eyebrow at him. "And that is...?"

"Please free me of these bonds. If we are unfortunate enough to be attacked again by forces unfriendly to us both, I would very much prefer to have at least a fleeting chance to defend myself."

Donnchadh reacted to this idea exactly as I expected. He began filling me with an anger that was deep and powerful. Clearly, he didn't advocate the idea of releasing the Red Baron. "A suspicious person might argue that your true motive is to escape."

He frowned. "If you are such a person, I can hardly blame you for your distrust. Nonetheless, I give you my word as a gentleman that I shall not take advantage of any mercies offered to me."

My stomach picked that moment to growl again, making it easier for Donnchadh to shove his way into my consciousness. Seeing through my eyes, I could read Donnchadh's thoughts as though they were my own. The first thing he noted was that a fall from this height wouldn't be pleasant but it also wouldn't be fatal, and that was something Manfred had, no doubt, taken into consideration.

We were close enough to the tops of some of the ruined buildings that Manfred could easily jump without breaking any limbs. And if he did manage to get away, how long before he reported the mysterious woman with the flock of angry furies to his superiors?

Even taking all of that into consideration, I reached for and pulled out my blade. I was surprised when Donnchadh quieted down and backed off. If we had been somewhere safer and my belly were full, I might have wondered why. But I wanted to take care of my next task before my harrassenger acted up again.

Harrassenger? I thought to myself with a smile. *Bill would be proud.*

Placing the blade against the rope, I sawed away at it. It took all of two seconds to cut clean through. The captain sighed with relief as he rubbed his sore wrists. Then he put his hands on the Fury's shoulders, which made her turn her head a full one-hundred-and-eighty degrees.

After a warning hiss, she tried taking a chomp of Manfred's face. He barely withdrew far enough to save his nose. When I saw her rearing back for another strike, I decided to step in.

"Down, girl!"

She hissed at me like a cat just denied a juicy mouse.

"I mean it! Back off!" I said.

Her expression read "Fine!" and she turned her head back. My flying ace held his hands up, now uncertain as to where to put them. After resheathing my sword, I gently lowered his hands onto the bird woman's flanks. A bolt of electricity shot through me once our skin made contact and I immediately pulled away.

I didn't understand what had just happened but it didn't seem as though Manfred had experienced it. He continued facing forward.

"So how does it feel to be the most renowned war pilot of all time?" I asked, deciding to make conversation so I wouldn't have to listen to my stomach continuing to growl.

The Red Baron slowly nodded his head. "I used to care about such things."

"And now?"

"Being in this place changes the importance you place on silly things such as fame." He grew quiet for a few seconds. "There have been plenty of moments I have wished for a time before the war. Had I the opportunity, I would go back and rethink many of my decisions." He was silent again before he turned around to face me. "The Great War truly cost too much."

I cringed at the guilt I saw on his face. "But from what I know of your history, you didn't commit any atrocities. Being the best pilot, you earned the respect of all sides. So maybe you were sent here by mistake? You wouldn't be the only one."

The gloominess remained on his handsome face. "While you are very kind to say such things, *Fraulein* Harper, I believe I have earned my place here. I long ago made peace with it."

I still wasn't sure I believed him. "But why?"

His eyes hardened all of a sudden and then he turned back around again. "A series of misdeeds that I have no interest in expanding upon, *Fraulein* Harper..."

"Misdeeds?"

"I must ask that you please respect my privacy on this matter."

Silently, I reviewed the historical facts I knew about him. While he'd had the undying admiration of his fellow pilots, he'd also been a bit of a showman. The plane my fury had taken down wasn't the only one he'd painted red but it was the reason he'd earned his nickname of *The Red Baron.* He may not have been evil, but he must have done *something* to warrant his being here.

Donnchadh poked his head out of his spiritual foxhole again. I did everything I could to push him back inside it but lacked the necessary strength. Right on cue, my stomach chose that exact moment to remind me I was starving by inflicting another ripping sensation in my guts.

Of course, my prisoner didn't fail to notice me struggling. "You appear distressed, *fraulein.*"

I waved him off, hoping I was convincing. "It's nothing. I just haven't eaten since I esca—"

I stopped myself way too late for it to matter but the truth was that I didn't want him to know I'd just escaped Alaire. Maybe the Red Baron would attempt to return me?

He glanced back at me and his eyes brimmed with sympathy at my accidental confession. "So you have also been a prisoner of the Malebolge?"

I frowned at him again. "The what?"

His expression spoke volumes. "An old name for the Circle beneath us, one that I understand is no longer used."

I nodded but didn't reply. I was worried I'd already said too much. His voice went from crisp and professional to gentle and caring. "With all due respect, *fraulein*, it is obvious to anyone who has been here for longer than a day that you do not belong here. That piques my curiosity... How did you manage to arrive here?"

I didn't doubt his sincerity, but for safety's sake, I was reluctant to tell him anything. So I decided to go with the bare minimum. "I'm being hunted right now…"

"Hunted?"

"I was taken without my consent," I said simply. "And now I've rectified that situation."

His eyes widened in shock before narrowing down into slits of anger. "You were taken by the Master of the Underground City?"

I was surprised but didn't respond.

"I will take your silence as agreement," Manfred said.

"Take it however you want to take it but I didn't admit to anything." I took a breath. "I was separated from my friends and I was advised I'd find them down here in this Circle."

He gave the landscape below a rueful glance. "Then *Gott* help them. As you have seen, survival in this place is no guarantee."

Donnchadh roared his defiance inside me while I nodded. That's when Manfred asked another question I wasn't comfortable answering. "Would I be pressing this matter too far by asking who you were in life?"

I fully intended to keep my mouth closed when I heard ringing in my ears again. I closed my eyes…

…only to see my Self staring back at me. Before, she was just a reflection in my blade. Now, she was standing before me on the grounds of Fergus Castle, Tallis's ancestral home that had become an intermittent psychic safe house. She wasn't physically perfect, as I was in this current body, but she looked and felt more real. *I saw a blend of the old me and the new post-AE me in her smile and the light of her eyes. She put her hands on my shoulders, kissed my forehead and whispered, "You can trust him…"*

My eyes snapped opened again. Manfred looked at me with visible concern, so I decided to cover up the episode with a lie. "Sorry, my hunger seems to be getting the better of me."

"If I had sustenance to offer you, *fraulein,* I would."

I nodded, the pricking of my conscience becoming too much to ignore. My Self wanted me to talk to Manfred but I wasn't sure why. There was just an assurance floating through me that I needed Manfred on my side—that he would prove to be an ally.

"In life, I was a nobody," I said in a soft voice. "I worked at a dead-end job, I was close to my mom and I had a best friend. That's about it." I cleared my throat. "Oh, and I was a member of a medieval re-enactment group."

"*Was ist das?*" Manfred interrupted with a look of bewilderment.

I laughed and felt embarrassment that surprised me. The days before I'd died felt like a lifetime ago. I supposed they were. "I know it must sound really strange to you, but I learned lots of important things from that group like how to make fire and how to sew." Memories of doing DIY alterations to Persephone's porn star wardrobe flashed through my mind like a bad case of heartburn.

His face softened while he shook his head. "You misunderstand, *fraulein.* I am simply amazed that a popular interest in the Middle Ages still persists." He grew quiet for a few seconds before he spoke again. "There is no disgrace in living an ordinary life."

I growled in frustration as I slapped my thighs. "But that's just it! I wasn't living... not really. I was... existing, taking up space, being of service to everyone else and usually being ignored."

He grunted in disbelief. "I find it hard to believe that someone with such striking features could ever be ignored."

91

I felt a stabbing despair at his words. The wretched curse of the supermodel physique strikes again! I gestured toward my body, from my swan-like neck to my perfect legs that went on forever. "I didn't look like this when I was alive."

"I do not understand, *fraulein*."

"It's too long and complicated to explain but let's just say that I got these looks as part of my deal with Afterlife Enterprises." I was quiet for a second as I thought about all the time that had led up to this moment. "Quite frankly, it's a massive upgrade from how I looked before."

"Afterlife Enterprises changed the way you appeared?" Manfred asked, clearly confused.

I sighed and realized I'd have to explain the how of things if he was ever going to understand. "Yeah. I was killed in the most ridiculous accident in modern history. I hit a truck that was carrying a bunch of chickens. And I didn't survive the accident because my guardian angel was nowhere to be found."

A surge of anger towards Bill overcame me when I remembered that lapse in his protection. Yes, we were close now and I loved him but that didn't change the fact that he had seriously fucked up.

"Forgive me, but none of this truly explains why or how you came to the Underground City."

Once again, I hesitated. But what the hell? I'd told him practically everything else. "I mentioned Afterlife Enterprises... do you know about them?"

He nodded. "*Ja*, quite well."

"Well, when I got to the other side, I was stuck in one of their offices with a douchebag weasel named Jason Streethorn. He told me that, through no fault of my own, I'd died and I was slated to spend the next hundred years in Shade..." I held up my pointer finger. "*Unless* I chose to become a Soul Retriever for his joke of a company."

92

"I know of these Soul Retrievers, yes," Manfred said with a clipped nod.

"So then you know we're meant to find and relocate all the souls who were sent down here by mistake?"

"Yes," he answered succinctly.

"Right. And apparently when I satisfy my quota of souls, I'll be free to venture on to the Kingdom where my happily ever after is waiting for me."

At the rate I was going, I doubted my time in the Underground City would ever end. Alaire had some kind of pull with AE and he'd done a spectacular job of throwing me off my game. What good was that apartment in Scotland, an unlimited bank account, or my borrowed good looks if it meant I'd be coming back here forever?

Manfred released the Fury's flank to reach behind him and he covered my hand with his own. "For whatever it is worth, *fraulein*, I am truly sorry to hear about your mistreatment."

That snapped me out of my pity party. What the hell was getting into me? Even at my lowest, I was never a whiner. Why now? Then my stomach and the angry spirit dwelling inside me reminded me why.

Manfred released my hand and gripped the fury's flank again. My next comment was more of a question. "I'm guessing your current bosses are demons, so you've been getting a pretty good education, yourself, on abuse."

The shadow fell on the Red Baron's face again. "*Jawohl...* sadly, that is truer than you know."

He fell silent and I wasn't sure if he wanted me to press. "Do you want to talk about it?" I asked, sounding hesitant.

"You are not the first person who has come to the Malebolge claiming to be a Soul Retriever. Quite a few

93

dead souls of late have been captured by the Malebranche and…"

Even with the acid churning it, a cold knot formed in my stomach. Whatever he was about to say couldn't be good. "Then… they were killed?"

Manfred shuddered. "All such persons who identify themselves as 'Soul Retrievers' are summarily guilty of espionage, according to our orders." The knuckles on his hands started turning white from his tightened grip. "They are not allowed to live, as you can imagine. But the method of execution is solely at the discretion of the commanding officer. So most of your kind are condemned to die a slow, agonizing death by whatever torture currently ranks as the commander's favorite. Most of these executions are too hideous to watch."

My anger started flaring up at his dry recitation of the facts. He'd witnessed such horrible things and all he'd done was *watch*? And remain with the army that inflicted the murders to boot? My outrage was so overwhelming this time that I couldn't keep Donnchadh restrained.

I only had one question for my prisoner, and it needed a damn good answer. "Did you kill any of them yourself?"

He glanced back at me and shame washed across his eyes like an acid bath. "*Ja*… although I tried my best to make their deaths as quick and painless as poss—"

I'd heard enough. Actually, I'd heard way too much. My temper exploded before Manfred could finish his sentence and I grabbed him by the throat from behind. His hands struggled to pry my fingers off his larynx but he couldn't lessen my grip. If anything, his struggles made it more exciting. I didn't want to kill him without a—

No, Lily! A voice screamed from within me.

At that moment, I realized we were about to fall off the Fury's back. I tried releasing Manfred but my fingers refused to cooperate. Neither did the rest of me. My conscious mind was suddenly shoved into the backseat as Donnchadh fought to take control.

Just as I feared, we soon toppled off the Fury and took the express elevator straight down to the ground level. Panic made me rebel against Donnchadh. But I couldn't stop Donnchadh any easier than Manfred could stop me from choking him. The vengeful spirit had chosen this moment to wrest control from me and there was nothing I could do to prevent him.

Still, the warrior spirit wasn't as unaware of our situation as I feared. When a rooftop came too close to us on the right, he suddenly tossed the falling pilot straight towards it. I could hear Manfred crashing into the roof while Donnchadh used my arms to hang onto the nearest windowsill. We were dangling about three floors below the roof but the empowered wraith didn't care. Like a salmon climbing a fish ladder, I scrambled to survive, using my arms to thrust me upward with each clean pull.

My prisoner was conscious but still out of it by the time my interior companion vaulted us onto the roof. Manfred barely got an elbow under him when Donnchadh pounced on his chest, knocking the breath clean out of him. He started pummeling Manfred right in the face, my fists landing as fast and hard as a jackhammer. The punches grew harder and swifter with each passing second while Donnchadh grew angrier and angrier.

After a few more seconds, Donnchadh grabbed Manfred by the collar and snarled through my mouth, "You call yourself a man? Fight back!"

The Red Baron's eyebrows rose up in surprise, his face covered in bruises and cuts. His left eye and lips were swollen. But his voice came out as clearly as if we were still on the Fury's back. "I am a man who is getting exactly what he deserves."

Donnchadh made my eyes blink. He was unable to understand Manfred's words. That momentary confusion finally gave me the toehold I needed. Mentally, I reached out and imagined the runes on my body glowing with the power I required to return my body to myself.

Donnchadh, I banish you! Do not to return until you are directly summoned! I yelled internally.

I felt the anger within me start to abate and my own power began to thrum through my veins, restoring me to myself. The first thing I noticed upon my spiritual reentry was the pain encompassing my entire body. My arms felt like someone had ripped them out of their sockets after Donnchadh's little stunt at window climbing.

I released Manfred's collar to give my sore muscles some relief. For his part, Donnchadh's latest victim sighed as he said, "Welcome back, *fraulein*."

"How did you—"

He coughed up a wad of blood before answering. "I have had the great disadvantage of witnessing many spiritual possessions during my service in the Malebranche. When your eyeballs suddenly turned completely black, it was hardly a leap of faith to conclude that you were in the throes of such an episode."

Crap, at this rate, he would know my whole life story by the time I found Tallis and Bill. *If* I found Tallis and Bill... "Yeah, about that possession thing... it's a long story and not one I like to talk about."

He slowly propped himself up on his elbows to face me. "As you have respected my privacy on personal matters, I shall respect yours. I am, however, relieved to see that you have *some* influence over the beast that inhabits you."

I rubbed my face self-consciously, exacerbating the pain in my shoulder. "I don't suppose you know any handy exorcism rituals to get rid of this guy, or do you?"

"That realm of knowledge is something my superiors have deemed beyond my grasp."

The way he said it made me laugh out loud. I pushed to my feet, wincing in pain, and gave him a hand up. He looked at my still-sheathed blade. "I must admit my amazement when you refrained from using your sword to cut me down."

His comment made me pause as I considered it. I was surprised Donnchadh hadn't gone for my sword. He could have easily carved Manfred up like a Thanksgiving turkey. So why hadn't he? "I can't comment," I said with a shrug. Then I faced him. "How badly hurt are you?"

Manfred palpated his tenderized face with light, careful fingers. "Just a bit battered. Neither the beating nor the fall inflicted much of an injury."

His mention of the fall made me look up at the skies. There was no sign of the Furies anywhere. I whistled, hoping they'd hear me. After a couple of seconds of seeing nothing but clouds, I whistled even louder. I got exactly the same response as before. As in… nothing.

I slapped my thighs in frustration again as I put my hands down. "Dammit! Now we're stuck here." Looking around, I tried to get the lay of the land. "I've got no idea where we should go."

The captain scanned our surroundings with a discerning eye. "If you are willing to trust me, I know where we could go."

I studied his face. Yes, he'd been truthful and honorable ever since he'd become my prisoner. But being back on the ground might give him ideas, the kind that could land me right back in Alaire's clutches. "Where would that be exactly?"

"The laboratory of a married couple whose allegiance to the Malebranche is even more conditional than my own."

His reply evoked my Dr. Frankenstein fears. "But they're still working for the same dukes as you are, right?"

"Technically, but like me, they too have suffered this place's horrors. It has resulted in an immense compassion for all those in need. On more than one occasion, they even defied the Malebranche in order to sustain their ideals."

I didn't need Donnchadh to convince me how convenient this all sounded. Seeing damn little kindness in all of the Underground City... Now the thought of finding it here seemed like a bridge too far. But what else could I do? Wander aimlessly until I got caught? Remain on the rooftop until I got caught?

"How far away are they?" I asked.

"Your doom fix'd deep within me..."
- Dante's Inferno

TEN
TALLIS

I peeked me head inside the building, the stookie angel and the French girl immediately behind me. The cavernous space beyond was about the same size as the cubicle labyrinth we'd been dragged into. The steel walls were replaced by heavy stone but just as sturdy and durable. A collection of nozzles were scattered about the walls, giving the place the look of a public shower. A quick check of the iron door beside me confirmed 'twas solid. Three battering rams would be hard-pressed to make so much as a tiny dent.

The angel started frantically tapping me leg and hissing at me as though to warn me of something lurking. I glanced behind meself to see no one following us and gave the stookie angel a stern look. Aye, I knew remaining out here was dangerous. But there was nae sense in walking straight into a trap, for such could be far worse.

Finally, I was satisfied this old facility was as deserted as it appeared. I walked into the building and waved the angel and the girl inside, sheathing me blade. Our heroine had not said a word since we escaped the mess with Cauchon and the Spites. Of course, I wanted to ask her questions but we needed a place to lie low first, a location we now had.

The stookie angel gave the empty room a suspicious glance as he looked about himself. The bullet hole in his chest had long since closed and the burn on his face was nearly faded completely.

"You sure this place is safe, Tido?"

'Twas a tricky question. "'Tis deserted an' as safe as any place 'tis likely tae be... at least we can catch our breath an' figure out where tae go from here."

The angel's eyes lit up at the sight of the shower nozzles. "Finally! I can address my *Eau de Garbage* aromasol!"

I had to admit he reeked with odor. But I snatched his hand away before he could touch the nearest faucet handle. "Ah wouldnae do that. Them metal monsters shoot out fire, nae water... Ah highly doubt sooch is the sort o' bath ye got in mind, eh?"

The wee fellow took it as well as I expected, yanking his wrist away and punching the nearest wall. "*Fuck*! Can't we ever catch a break?"

The girl's lilting voice cut through his anger like a surgeon's scalpel. "We have managed to escape our captors as well as the torments of those who came for them. Isn't that reason enough to be grateful?"

"Sounds like you gotta be careful of preclapulation, girl," the angel said as he eyed her with the expression of someone who knew something she didnae.

"Preclapulation?" she questioned him and soon faced me with eyebrows arched.

"Ah dinnae oonderstand most things that come from his mouth," I answered with a shrug.

"Preclapulation, girl," the angel repeated. "Clappin' before you know the outcome o' your situation."

"Ah," she said with a quick nod. "Do not count your chickens before they've hatched?"

"Not sure what you're goin' on about but whatevs," the angel replied as I shook me head.

I carefully swung the thick, metal door to the point of nearly being closed, but nae quite. A quick peek through the crack revealed that all was still well. Settling next to the wall sae I could keep an eye on the goings-on beyond the crack in the door, I kept me ear cocked while inspecting our newest traveling companion. "Ah'm afraid Ah never did catch yer name, lass."

She bowed her head and half-curtsied. "Jeanne, *mon seignour.*"

Me French wasnae as fluent at the stookie angel's but I knew enough to understand. "Ah'm nae nobleman, jist a blademaster who calls the Dark Wood me home."

The angel looked at me with genuine confusion. "What? Are ya sayin' the whole 'Lord of Fergus Castle' schtick don't still applicate?"

Before I could rage at him for being so dense, Jeanne stepped between us and took me hands in hers as she looked up at me with genuine admiration in her eyes. Her hands were delicate and soft.

"What may I call you, then?"

"Me name is Tallis. That'll do."

She looked confused. "Tallis? Not Tido?"

Naturally, the stookie angel held back a snicker. I looked over Jeanne's shoulder at him and frowned. "That jist be a nickname the walloper angel calls me... mayhap because he couldnae pronounce me true name. Sooch is whit happens when yer nae able to graduate primary school."

Jeanne held a dubious look upon her bonny face before releasing me hands and turning to face the wee fellow. "So... your name is really William?"

The squat angel looked about the rest of the room as though his mother had caught him fornicating with the milkmaid. "Uhm, yeah... But, I go by Bill or Billy or you can call me Billy-Bob."

101

"I am pleased to meet you both," the girl said with a smile for each of us before she turned to take in her surroundings. "Why would anyone make a room with contraptions such as these?"

The angel shrugged. "Well, sweets, it looks ta me like it's 'sposed ta be a shower room. Now, I dunno how long ya've been dead-ceased but a shower—"

Her interruption was so smooth, it seemed like she replied between his breaths. "These contraptions are meant to clean people?" She glanced between the stookie angel and me, seeing the expressions of surprise on our faces. "And before either of you ask, no, I never saw such a thing while I lived."

"Jist how long ye been dead, lass?"

She shrugged. "I cannot say. I have wandered the Underground City for countless years. But the passage of time here is not the same as in the world above us."

I glanced out the crack in the door before saying, "Well, as Ah said, these showers are nae fer cleanin' oneself. When this place was used proper, it housed those leaders what exploited their people's love an' troost."

The angel stepped in front of me and the stench of him made me wish there *were* a proper shower for his use.

"I gots a better in-quietry fer ya, honey... how'd ya make the Black Death Bee Swarm ignoramus to us?"

She hesitated to answer, giving us both a nervous glance. The daft angel came closer to her and took her hand. "Hey, yo, we've already determinated that I'm an angel, right?"

"Yes."

"Then ya knows ya can trust me, right?"

I couldnae keep me eyes from rolling back. If this lost child had an inkling of the true foolishness of the angel, I doubted she'd invest any trust in him at all.

When she spoke again, her voice trembled. "*Pardonne, mon ami*, but I dared to speak of such matters only once before... with Cardinal Cauchon. I have since vowed never to speak of it again, as it only managed to bring me harm."

I nodded toward the door. "Goin' by the prayer ye muttered back there, Ah'm thinkin' some higher power watches o'er ye?" She attempted meeting me eyes, but couldnae quite do it. I sighed and reassured her, "Ye dinnae hafta answer, lass. Ah think we can agree yer silence makes the answer plain enough. Boot tell me this: whit's the cardinal doin' commandin' demons?"

Fear filled her eyes, mixed with a burning hatred that only the truly faithful can manage to control. "He is a member of the Council of Simon. They broke free from the Fourth Ring of this Circle and started a rebellion against the Malebranche. Some of them command powers great enough to rival the dukes of this Circle, providing the motivation for ambitious demons to flock to the Council's banners."

The dunderheid nodded right along. "Yeah, that makes sense... it weren't just the leaders that got sent here. I seem ta *Total Recall* that this was the spot where the alchemists, prophets, sorcerers an' the occasional mad scientist got punished."

"As according tae Dante anyway," I corrected him. Of course, I knew the truth of those who had and did populate this level of the Underground City but I didnae care to expound. 'Twas better Jeanne nae find out that once my role was master of this dismal place.

I put a gentle hand on her shoulder. "Brave lass... ye saw whit they could do tae ye an' ye still managed tae save the pair o' oos." I gave her small shoulder a gentle squeeze. "Ah'm proud tae have ye by me side, come what may."

She looked up at me with unmasked gratitude. "Were you a father in life, Tallis?"

103

Her question took me back to the days I lived upon the earth and dashed me spirits instantly. "Nae."

Her eyes shone with regret. "That is a shame. I believe you would have been a good one."

"An' what about me?" the angel asked, giving the girl a "woe is me" expression. She immediately turned to approach him, calming his wounded pride with her sweet words.

As I heard the two of them talking, I maintained me post next to the door, unsheathing me blade in the off chance we were overheard. Up until now, no one followed but we couldnae stay here forever. If we'd had Besom with us, our next stop would have been this Circle's shortcut back to the Dark Wood. Me heart ached to think I still had nae idea where she could be in the midst of this war zone. Or if she were even still alive.

Me blade suddenly grew warm in me hands. I felt it vibrating as though I'd struck a solid piece of iron, making me bones rattle. I instinctively shut me eyes whilst tightening me grip...

...and just like that, I was back on the heather moor outside Fergus Castle. It was a bonny scene that stretched before me: clear blue sky, bright, shining sun, peaceful waters of the loch lapping the shore. No one, friend or foe, shared this space with me.

I noticed a faint sound floating on the breeze. It had a harshness about it, like sandpaper mixed with a bird's whistle. As it came from the direction of the castle, I moved toward it. The noise grew a wee bit louder with every step I took, becoming more distinct.

I was halfway across the field when I finally recognized what I was hearing: wireless static. At that moment, I saw the source: 'twas coming from a bluebird. The bird began moving its beak, speaking, "Tangent to Sapphire, come in..."

104

A harsh shake of me arm brought me out of the vision. I opened me eyes and found Jeanne clinging to me forearms, and she had a stricken look on her face. "Are you unwell?"

I shook me head. "Ah'm fine, lass." I took a breath. "Jist went someplace in me mind that's helped me from time tae time."

Her attention shifted over to me blade. One of her delicate hands caressed the side of the metal like a lover's cheek. "I have never seen a *claidheamh mor* like it."

I raised me eyebrows in unbridled surprise and appreciation. "Ye surely know yer arms."

Her expression was caught between embarrassment and shame. "A long time ago, I led many men into battle, carrying nothing more than a banner..."

"A banner?" The angel said with a mocking laugh. "Who'd you hope to kill with that?"

"No one," Jeanne replied as she looked back at him. "I do not believe in killing."

I studied her with rekindled interest, having figured out the nature of her identity though I kept it to myself. "Ah feel the same way, lass, aboot firearms. The simple click o' the trigger an' a life ends. Death should ne'er be sae easy or convenient."

The angel gave her a pat on the arm. "Well, I Dream Of Jeannie, yer not gonna hear any arguments to the contraband from either of us."

She appeared puzzled at hearing the stookie angel's nickname for her and faced me in question. "Dinnae look at me, lass," I said with a shrug. "The walloper's got a moniker fer ev'rybody."

I opened the door a little wider, checking on the landscape outside. We still remained the only people in the vicinity which was just as well.

From behind me, I heard Jeanne say, "I have to admit I envy your skill with the blade, Tallis."

Without looking at her, I asked, "If Ah were willin' tae teach ye, would ye be willin' tae learn?"

"Yes, but there is only so much you can do."

"Knowin' how it's done beats not knowin', Jeannie-gurl," the angel said with a shrug.

I sighed and shook me head. "The stookie angel's got a point. 'twould nae take verra long tae teach ye the basics."

After an extended stretch of silence, Jeanne answered me. "Very well, but in the meantime, I beg you both to stay close to my side."

The angel scoffed. "As if we'd leave ya! I mean, as if *I'd* leave ya. Tido there's a little anti-sociable an' he's moody as fuck."

"Language," Jeanne reprimanded him.

The fool angel shrugged. "Hey, you can take the thug outta..." and then he appeared confused as to what he was trying to say and quieted, thank the gods above.

Jeanne looked at the ground as though all her hopes had just melted there. "If only I knew where Tangent was..."

The name made my eyes widen as surprise echoed through me. "This Tangent... would he happen tae have a wireless, by any chance?"

Jeanne widened her eyes and appeared confused. "A wireless?"

"Sorry, lass, people nowadays refer tae it as a 'radio'."

"But how did you—?"

"An' this Tangent calls ye Sapphire, aye?" I continued, eyeing her with interest. Now I understood the nature of me vision.

"Yo, slow down, Conan," the angel said, holding up his hands in a supplicating gesture. "Where'd ya suddenly manage tae harvest all this insta-knowledge? You some sorta psychic you ain't never told me about?"

Jeanne never took her eyes from mine. "It is as you say. Tangent is among my boon companions in the recent past. We were separated by the Malebranche before Cauchon captured me."

The stookie angel started tapping his chin, appearing to be in deep thought. "You know all our futures or what, Tido?" he continued, eyeing me with a narrowed and suspicious gaze.

I ignored the bloody bampot.

"An' ye were a valued prize sooch that those bastards chased ye straight to Cauchon?" I asked her.

She nodded slowly. "*Oui*, but how did you know that?"

"It's like super obvious," the angel interrupted. Jeanne turned to face him. He tapped his index finger next to his right eye. "As an angel, I got an eye fer auras... an' I ain't never seen one like yers before. So it like just follows that you're somethin' pretty special." He glanced up at me. "Even Tido here figured it out." He grew quiet and studied me again. "But that's 'cause he got some sort of brain power he ain't told no one about yet."

"Whit exactly makes her aura different, stookie angel?" I asked, deciding to ignore the rest of his ridiculous commentary.

He shrugged. "I dunno. It's just different." When he saw my expression, he blew his lips at me. "Look, Tido, if ya want more details, better talk to an archangel. All I can tell ya is this: anybody with her aura gots no busy-ness bein' down here with or without us, yo."

Yet Jeanne, otherwise known as Joan Of Arc, had been here for centuries, long before AE's foul-up involving that damned Y2K virus or bug or whatever they termed it. Hmmm... very interesting.

The angel crossed his arms and gave me an untrusting expression. "Since we're comparifying our psychic muscles, maybe ya can tell us how ta find this Tan-rant an' his merry pals."

"Aye! Radio! That is, if'n we can git one, we might be able tae contact him."

Jeanne stared at me in utter awe. "What higher power guides *you* that would grace you with such insight?"

I frowned at her. "Ah am driven by nae higher power, lass."

"But how..." she began.

The angel impatiently snapped his fingers and I was grateful to him. "Umm, gittin' back ta the radio..."

Jeanne's eyes snapped into clear focus. "The camp from which I fled had such a device. I remember having to turn the dial to 381.4 to speak to Tangent." She winced. "That is to say, someone who knows how to control such a frequency. I have no knowledge or skill, I admit."

The stookie angel threw his head back until he was staring at the ceiling and released a world-weary sigh. "An' since Tido ain't good fer anythin' but skinnin' dead animals an' killin' demons, I guess that leaves only me."

I gave him a dubious look. "Ye know how tae operate one o' them wireless contraptions?"

He nodded. "Yeah, it's totally dead tech but I can wing it."

I opened the door after checking the path was clear and stepped outside. Once I was certain we were still alone, I waved to the others to join me. "Think ye can git us back tae that camp ye mentioned, Jeanne?"

She looked in the direction of the rubble from whence we'd come. "Perhaps... although I cannot guarantee it."

"Remember, people, we're nowheresville without that radio," the angel said.

I grunted at him. "Ah doubt any camp that has sooch a machine will be that hard tae find."

Jeanne started forward and I followed. As I did, I heard the angel muttering, "Yeah, that's exactly what I'm afraid of."

"...and myself who in this torment do partake with
them..."
- Dante's Inferno

ELEVEN
LILY

When I heard shouting, I knew something was
wrong.

Judging by the look on his face, so did Manfred.

The stairs leading off the rooftop were
miraculously intact and we took them two at a time
until we reached the last stairwell that was less intact.
Glancing down, beyond the broken steps, I noticed we
were still a couple of floors up, and way too far to
jump without breaking one or more bones.

I looked around, searching for another way of
reaching the ground, when I spotted a window. Beside
the window was a high pile of rubble. Granted, the
rubble would hardly be solid but it might still be
enough to give us the boost we needed to get into the
window.

"Go," I whispered to Manfred and motioned to the
window. He glanced at it before nodding and then
started for the pile. Following Manfred, I ran towards
the pile of rubble and found myself sinking into it
once or twice before I was able to grab the window sill
and hoist myself inside.

Once we jumped down from the window and
landed on the floor, the Red Baron pointed me forward
and took the lead. That suited me just fine. I still had
his pistol, which I aimed at his back just to make it

known he was still my prisoner. My other hand stayed by my sword, just in case Manfred tried anything. I was more secure with my sword than I was with a gun.

Despite the circumstances of our meeting, I actually wanted to trust the Red Baron. I was starting to appreciate his honor and his dignity. But my suspicions that he could be leading me into a trap kept gnawing at me. I was sure I could take him where my sword was concerned because I didn't imagine he knew much swordsplay and by now, I was pretty much a mavon. And I also had Donnchadh to rely on—no one could triumph against Donnchadh.

However, Manfred was just one person and dealing with him if he decided to make a break for it would be very different to facing off against a whole army.

The only thing stopping me from binding the captain again or ditching him altogether was that neither of us had any other choice in this situation. We were stuck in the middle of hostile territory, with little to nothing to protect ourselves. The odds were pretty good that either side might kill us just because they could. For the time being, all we had was each other, for better or worse.

The shouts coming from around the corner of the half-demolished building in front of us definitely counted as "worse."

I detected some distressed cries beneath the shouts, followed by the sound of gravel being trod upon by clumsy feet. Manfred flattened himself against the corner of the building and looked like he was trying to evade a prison spotlight. I did the same, keeping my gun aimed at his side and well out of his reach. I glanced up, looking for anything in the air that could possibly spot us. The only flying monsters I knew about were the Furies but I seriously doubted they were the only flying abominations in the Underground City.

My prisoner made a sudden break from the corner of the building, bolting across the demolished street. I was about to bemoan trusting him so stupidly when I realized he was simply shifting his position. He glanced back at me and held up his palm, motioning for me to stay where I was.

Then he ducked behind a dilapidated fence that still provided enough cover to hide him. When he reached the building just beyond the fence, he glanced around the corner and jerked his head toward the noises that were coming from inside. He faced me and nodded quickly, encouraging me to join him. I was careful to cling to the shadows as I made my way forward, toward the broken fence and then underneath it.

Shimmying up the side of the building, I finally got my first glimpse of what was going on. No two ways about it, what I saw was ugly. A middle-aged couple were were in the process of being physically dragged out of a very small, squat building that resembled an oversized brick.

I had a feeling this was the couple Manfred had been talking about. Well, it now looked like they needed our help more than we needed theirs. The assholes who were forcing them out of the building were a mix of ragtag humans wearing army fatigues and creatures in three-piece suits. The suits resembled worms if worms were bipeds. The skin on the worm boys was frightfully pale and to say they were ugly would have been an understatement.

Manfred muttered something under his breath in German that didn't sound nice. I kept my voice down as I responded. "That bad?"

He peeked around the corner. "Considering we're looking at a Simoniac detachment, *ja*, I would say it's very bad indeed. It almost makes me long for the more ruthless violence from the Spites."

I watched the couple who were in the process of being yelled at. "Are those worm things going to kill your friends?"

His face became a mask of hopelessness. "Eventually... but first, they will slowly torture them for their secrets."

His description of the troops made me realize something. "So these guys are the ones rising up against your Malebranche bosses?"

He nodded. "Even if *meine lieben freunde* were suspected of disloyalty, the dukes would never dare to treat them so roughly. What they know and can do is far too valuable. The Simoniacs are less... prudent."

My uninvited spiritual lodger began to stir. I steeled myself for more trouble. I wasn't surprised when I discovered Donnchadh's sole intention was to hand the Simoniacs around the corner an epic ass-whooping. On this subject, Donnchadh and I were allied.

I glanced around the corner and did a quick headcount. "There are six of these Simoniacs, right?"

Manfred's voice sounded a little concerned. "*Ja,* that was my count... why?"

I put my hand on the runes around my arm and stood up. "I'm not letting your friends get hauled off to their doom."

Manfred stood up and pushed me against the wall. He grabbed my rune-covered arm like it was a live hand grenade, while pinning me to the wall. My breath caught in my throat and I felt my eyes widen as I stared into his.

"*Fraulein* Harper, I will not allow you to do this! It's sheer madness!"

He was so close to me that we both just stared at each other for a few seconds. I noticed his eyes leaving my own and traveling down to my mouth.

"You have to trust me, Manfred," I said in a soft voice.

He continued to stare at me and I couldn't read the expression on his face. It was like our close proximity had suddenly sucked the words right out of his head.

"Manfred," I said, trying to get his attention.

He found himself again and had the good sense to release my arm and take a couple of steps back. Deep down, my resident raging spirit's bottomless wrath was more than pissed. I gestured for the World War I flying ace to get on the other side of me. He took slow, careful steps but did as instructed.

"Please do not do anything foolish," he whispered from behind me.

"Trust me," I said again.

I felt his hand circle my upper arm and squeeze it momentarily before he dropped it again. I didn't allow myself to think about the familiarity of such an action and instead, mentally began the release chant.

Donnchadh, I free you to take control of my body and destroy the armed men around the corner.

I felt Donnchadh's response which was whether he would be able to kill them all, including Manfred's friends.

They're to be left alone, I thought back to him.

Donnchadh's anger spiked, which was concerning but we had an agreement all the same. After all, I was allowing him to kill. And seeing as how that was his favorite pastime, he didn't have much to complain about.

The release of Donnchadh took place in the space of two seconds. He seized control of me and I felt myself shrinking inside my own body. After a few

114

seconds, I found myself running around the corner. I remotely heard Manfred trying to tell me something but Donnchadh was long past listening. All that mattered now was the enemy in front of us.

Perceiving the gun as a weapon, Donnchadh raised it and started shooting wildly. He emptied the whole pistol clip by the time we reached the Simoniacs. One of the bullets grazed one of the humans in the shoulder but startled the rest of them so much, they remained rooted to the spot. Donnchadh threw the pistol at the nearest demon before we hip-tackled it to the ground. Its arm was stuck inside its coat like it was trying to pull out a weapon.

I laid him out with one rage-powered punch before yanking his arm out. His hand was wrapped around a nasty-looking whip that appeared to be a limp version of a thornbush branch.

Gunshots were coming our way, and Donnchadh rolled us and the worm demon over. The unlucky demon caught every bullet in his back and Donnchadh yanked the whip out of his hand.

One down, I thought to myself.

Apparently, this wasn't the first time Donnchadh had held a whip. With a flick of my wrist, he lashed out at a human behind us, who was firing an automatic rifle. The human squealed as the whip wrapped its thorns around his aiming arm. Donnchadh pulled on the whip. Instead of drawing the human closer, the whip only managed to shred his arm from the wrist to the elbow, leaving thin, bloody strips of flesh in its wake. The man howled out in pain and collapsed to his knees.

Another one down. Five to go.

In a frustrated rage, Donnchadh threw the bullet-riddled body of the first victim at one of the other gunmen, bowling him over with the dead weight. At the same time, he lashed the whip at the other man who was busily shooting at us. The whip embedded its thorns into the man's skull as he gasped and cried out in pain and horror. But Donnchadh gave no fucks and pulled hard on the whip, driving his newest victim to the ground. The spikes of the whip remained stuck in his head.

Four remaining.

Donnchadh threw the whip aside, meanwhile another whip caught my arm. Donnchadh turned my neck to see who the offending party was and one of the worm demons came into view. He was holding the other end of the whip.

The sharp pain in my elbow and the sight of my blood refueled Donnchadh's outrage. He grabbed the thorny whip and pulled hard. I was only midly aware of the searing pain in my hand as the thorns sunk into my flesh. Rearing my leg back in order to kick it out again, two more whips caught me around my legs and held me in their grasp, their thorns sinking into my flesh. Meanwhile, the pasty demon began to approach slowly.

Soon he stood right above me and glared down with pure hatred in his expression. He leaned over and looked like he was about to say something when Donnchadh reacted by smashing his face with a head butt. There was no nose to break, so it was comparable to ramming my head into solid rock. But it apparently did the trick because the worm demon immediately gripped his face at the same time that Donnchadh grabbed him by the neck with my free hand and used my head to ram him again.

Again, I was only faintly aware of the pain. The pasty worm demon fell down in a heap and looked, for all intents and purposes, dead. Or maybe he was just unconscious.

Three left.

116

A third whip entwined my hand that was still tangled in the unconscious demon's whip. Moving solely on instinct, I reached for my blade. The second my fingers touched the hilt of my sword, I felt Donnchadh suddenly thrown back into his cage. As soon as he vacated my body, my nerve endings started protesting all the injuries I'd sustained.

Great timing, I thought, gritting my teeth in defiance against the pain that roared through my entire body. Instead, I focused on the task ahead and pulled the blade free.

I hacked at the whip around my other wrist. My sword cut through the thorny weapon like paper but the other two whips that were wrapped around my legs tugged hard and threw me off-balance. I had no idea who was manning them because I'd thought Donnchadh had taken out everyone who needed it.

The momentum made me land face-first on the ground. Somehow, I managed to keep a death grip on my blade and spare it from the impact. The whips tugged at my legs again, rapidly dragging me toward my attacker. Noticing a faint shadow over my right shoulder, I raised my blade to stab at it and got the satisfaction and relief of a death gasp as the sharp point sank into soft flesh.

Two remaining.

The right whip suddenly went slack, giving me a chance to roll over and confront the other whip-wielder. The worm boy standing over me was clawing at his inside jacket pocket for something, probably another weapon. I sliced the whip off my foot in nanoseconds before plunging my blade straight into his stomach. He nearly fell right on top of me. I barely had time to yank my sword free before doing a quick roll to the right.

Now there's only one left.

117

"...that fear of the dire burning vanquish'd the
desire..."
-Dante's Inferno

TWELVE
LILY

Back on my feet, I noticed the final remaining
adversary was a human who was wielding a sword of
his own. He came at me, holding his sword high above
his head. There was definitely evidence of training in
his swordplay but nothing compared to what Tallis
had taught me. Even as he drove me into retreat, I
managed to block each stroke. The sparks were a little
too close for comfort, however.

The man tried to get behind me but I easily
sidestepped him before landing a hard blow on his
right knee. But he didn't go down. Instead, the pain
seemed to ignite his anger and he came at me with
renewed vigor. The sparks kept flying off our blades as
they clashed repeatedly. I noticed it was getting harder
to pull my blade away from his, almost as if my blade
had a mind of its own and was going in for the kill.
That seemed even more the case when my blade cut
his sword in half.

Even though he was momentarily stunned, he
tried using the broken half but it was no use. All he
could do was hold his ground. And that was a position
that wouldn't last long.

A shot rang out, cutting the man down before I
could land my killing blow. While trying to figure out

where the shot had come from, another shot came a couple of inches from winging me. I dove for cover behind a pile of rubble as I studied the situation.

The guy who'd been fighting me now had a hole in his forehead. The blood leaked down his cheeks while his eyes stared up at the sky blankly. The couple I'd charged in to rescue were now nowhere in sight. For all I knew, they might have fled the scene the second fighting broke out. It would have been the smart thing to do.

A third shot ricocheted off the top of the rubble, putting a quick end to my thoughts. The muzzle flash from the building's roof told me I was dealing with a sniper. Wracking my brains, I tried to figure out what to do. The shooter had the advantage because he was high above me and I had no idea exactly where he was or how I could access him.

The next shot went wild and entered the chest of the guy I'd brained. My attention, however, was fastened on the sounds of a struggle near the sniper's perch. Figuring I should take the opportunity while I could, I ran out from behind the rubble. Staying as low as possible, I darted to the opposite corner from where I'd just come. The welcome sight of a fire escape awaited me once I reached that side of the building. Sheathing my blade, I climbed up the metal staircase as quickly as my rubbery legs would take me.

When I reached the top, I saw Manfred tying up a man with boot laces. The man was wearing what appeared to be a Nazi uniform and a quick glance at the bound man's feet revealed the laceless boots beside him. The rifle that had been firing at me was at Manfred's side, leaning against the slightly raised roof edge.

When I came close, he glanced up at me. "Ah, there you are, *Fraulein* Harper. I trust this assassin did you no harm?"

119

I nodded at him. "Not a scratch, thanks mostly to you."

He waved off my gratitude and finished tying up the unconscious shooter. "*Bitte...* I am merely appreciative that I arrived before one of those dreadful bullets found its way into your vital organs."

I chuckled at that brutal but poetic statement. "Yeah, me too." I took a deep breath as another thought occurred to me. "Did you see your friends while the fighting was going on?"

Manfred let out a frustrated breath through his nose. "*Nein*, unfortunately... but I have every reason to believe they are not far." Manfred snatched up the sniper rifle and aimed it at me. "With sincere apologies, *fraulein*, I am afraid my time as your captive has drawn to a close."

I instinctively raised my hands and backed away as I cursed my bad luck. At this range, there was no way he could miss me. Circling to the left, he began walking between me and the roof's edge. "Now, if you would kindly drop your sword in front of me...?"

I pulled my sword out very carefully and looked in the reflection of the blade. I wondered why my Self had told me I could trust him. My emancipated prisoner cleared his throat and gestured with his rifle at the ground. I tossed the sword his way and he promptly kicked it over the roof edge. I could hear the faint clank of metal hitting rock a few seconds later.

I looked past him to where the sword disappeared. "I'm surprised you didn't take it with you."

"You have treated me very well, *fraulein*. Leaving you defenseless is a poor way to thank you for your courtesy."

"So is pointing a gun at my face."

His lips twitched a little then he shrugged, inching ever closer to the fire escape. "I forbid you to follow me. If you do, I shall be forced to kill you though I do not want to." He paused another moment and then sighed, his eyes never leaving mine. "I really do not want to harm you... Lily Harper."

I took a deep breath.

A voice behind Manfred startled us both. "Do not harm her, Manfred."

The flying ace's combat reflexes kicked in. He swung the rifle around and pulled the trigger once he turned it away from me. I was on the verge of tackling him when I heard the bullet striking glass. An instant later, the whole rifle exploded in Manfred's hands, blasting him backwards and throwing him to the ground.

Standing on the fire escape was the couple I'd just rescued. Directly in front of them were shards of glass, a scorch mark, and some sort of liquid that was collecting in little puddles.

The male half of the couple, an elderly man with a full beard, clucked his tongue. "Well, at least I can say how gratifying it is to know that this particular compound works as it was originally intended."

The woman, younger than the man by about twenty years but still older than me, gave me a concerned look. "Are you unharmed, *mon enfant*?" she asked in a pronounced French accent.

It took a minute for me to get my mouth to work. "Uhm, yeah, I'm-I'm okay. Thanks."

The man chuckled. "Fair exchange! It is only in reciprocation for saving our lives a few moments ago."

He walked over to the fallen Red Baron, who was shaking off the blast that wrecked his weapon. The old man offered him a hand up. "Now, truly, Manfred, is that any way to treat a lady or greet an old friend? I keep saying you are far too fond of your firearms."

The appropriate adage popped out of my lips without me even thinking about it. "When your only tool is a hammer, every problem looks like a nail."

The couple laughed as Manfred accepted the man's outstretched hand, and the woman clapped. She held onto her smile after her laughter died down.

"Just so, *mon enfant*, just so. And thus, by this logic, every problem that our dear Manfred encounters looks like a target that must be shot down."

Manfred looked at me. "*Fraulein* Lily Harper, allow me to present Lord Nicolas Flamel and Lady Perenelle Flamel."

The lady gave him an indulgent smile as I fought to understand why the name Flamel seemed somehow familiar to me. "Shall we agree to ascribe Manfred's lapse in decorum as a side effect of the phlogiston blast your compound inflicted upon him?" Lady Flamel asked.

Nicolas shrugged and made a thoughtful hum. "Perhaps, dear wife, but how would you explain the blind shot Manfred took at me instead of saying hello?"

Manfred turned a little red in the face. "While I appreciate your quick wit as always, it has been a rather trying day," he grumbled. "We should make our way back to the nearest Malebranche encampment."

The second he finished speaking, I started calculating the odds of running past them to reach the fire escape. The last thing I wanted to do was accompany them to the Malebranche because I was more than sure I'd be doing so as Manfred's prisoner. Perenelle drew back her head with a stunned expression. Clearly, she wasn't wild about the idea either.

"And just why on earth would we do that?" she asked.

The flying ace looked at her as though she'd lost her mind. "Protection, of course! The Council of Simon will send more troops momentarily."

"But what about the Malebranche forces?" I asked. "Won't they show up at some point?"

Nicolas pursed his lips and gave me a respectful nod. "Given our positions as premier alchemists affiliated with the Malebranche, you would certainly think so, *mademoiselle*. However, I believe I speak for both myself and my dear wife when I say that assumption fails to play out in practice."

Perenelle smiled at her husband. "For once, your theory is entirely supported by the actual facts, my husband. This marks the third such raid by the Simoniacs within the last month. Every time, we called for aid. Every time, we were ignored."

There was something adorable about the way these two played off each other. It made me wonder why they'd stayed with the Malebranche so long. "So it's a case of three strikes and you're out?" I asked.

Perenelle gave me an indifferent shrug that could only be called French. "A peculiar metaphor, but one that is also factually true. *N'est-ce pas*, Nicolas?"

Nicolas didn't seem as casual about the proposition. "You will recall, Perenelle, my reservations regarding performing such a drastic course of action. One does not walk away from the Dukes of the Eighth Circle without consequence."

Manfred's face lit up. "And that is why it is so vital that we go to the nearest camp now. If we stay here too long, we shall officially be declared deserters in absentia."

Perenelle glowered at this idea. "And what precisely is *Mademoiselle* Harper's fate?"

Manfred looked at her like she'd suggested he take to the air by flapping his arms really hard. "We take her back as our prisoner, of course! To leave her behind would be a violation of the—"

"I won't be your prisoner!" I railed at him.

He turned to look at me and sighed as he shook his head. "I do not see another way, *Fraulein.*" He paused. "And it is not safe for you to remain here... alone."

"It's safer for me to become a prisoner of the Malebranche?" I insisted.

"I would ensure that no harm befell you," Manfred said and by the expression on his face, he meant his words.

"As soon as Alaire realized I was prisoner, he would see to it that I was returned to him," I said as I staunchly shook my head. "And I won't let that happen."

Nicolas's loud sigh cut off whatever Manfred had to say like a chainsaw hewing through a twig. "Oh, Manfred! So very concerned with doing right by those who have never and will never do right by us. Such an extremely noble sentiment, matched only by its utter naiveté."

Manfred bristled and replied, "You have just said yourself that there are serious consequences for breaking ties with the Malebranche."

"So I did. However, I never said that such consequences were compelling enough for me to stay in the Malebranche's employ any longer, *non?*" Nicolas glanced over the side of the roof and continued as he looked over at me, "I am happy to report that your blade is still very much intact and lying exactly where Manfred so gracelessly kicked it, *mademoiselle.*"

I sighed with relief. "That's good to know... thanks."

Perenelle studied my face for a minute before saying anything. "Would you be interested in gainful employment on our behalf?"

I didn't understand and frowned to show as much. "I'm afraid I'm no good with chemicals, neither in the real world nor down here."

Nicolas laughed as he looked at me again. "That area of expertise is quite adequately covered by both of us, so have no fear. But we now find ourselves in need of reliable protection."

Perenelle took up the thread her husband dropped. "And we were quite impressed with your exceptional fighting skills against the six Simoniac soldiers. An expert warrior such as yourself would be most welcome to serve at our side and of course, the cost would be at your discretion."

My one-time prisoner looked at Perenelle again like she'd lost her mind. "Let us not be so hasty as—"

Nicolas waved Manfred off. "There is no haste in good negotiation. After all, the lady has yet to admit if she is interested in the position being offered her."

His wife smirked with a knowing expression. "Well, there is still the aforementioned matter of an acceptable price for such services, husband." She turned back to me. "Perhaps now is the time to speak of money, *non?*"

I already had the price in mind. "I'm searching for two friends of mine whom I was separated from. If you could help me find them, that's my price."

Perenelle looked at me in mock shock. "You would sell your unique services so cheaply?"

"My friends mean more to me than anything else you could offer," I responded.

She placed a motherly hand on my shoulder. "Ah, *pardonne-moi, mon cher.*"

Nicolas raised his finger. "Be that as it may, I must agree that such a price is far too small. May I propose a compromise? In addition to the aid you ask, we shall also allow you one favor of your choosing, something that is within our power to accomplish?"

125

Manfred looked a bit shocked. When he spoke to me, his words came out shaky. "As appalled as I am by this very conversation, *fraulein*, it is no small offer Lord Nicolas is extending. You are one of the rare persons he has ever offered such a favor."

"Just as long as I can leave the Underground City after we find my friends, that's all I care about," I answered.

Perenelle patted my cheeks before kissing both of them. "That is very much our plan as well, I assure you."

Manfred looked at the three of us with alarm. "You can't do that—you... you are risking your safety! If you are caught..."

"We shall be put to death... again," Nicolas finished for him.

"Or worse!" Manfred insisted. "I did not come here to rescue you only to see you place yourself directly in harm's way!"

Nicolas sighed and put a fatherly hand on Manfred's shoulder. "If you must insist on returning to the same superiors who will never repay your undying loyalty to them, I only ask you have the good grace to devise a plausible explanation for events leading up to this point. One that does not involve myself, Perenelle or *Mademoiselle* Harper. Are we agreed?"

Manfred hung his head in defeat. "*Jawohl, Vater.*"

Nicolas smiled and patted Manfred's shoulder. Manfred turned and offered me something I didn't expect, a salute. "*Fraulein* Harper, you have been an outstanding and honorable opponent. I hope that our paths may cross once again someday, but under vastly more pleasant circumstances."

"Thank you," I said and didn't know what to make of it as Manfred closed the distance between us until he was maybe a foot from me. Then he paused and appeared completely uncomfortable before he opened his arms wide and threw them around me, engulfing me in the most rigid of hugs I'd ever experienced. I brought my arms around him and patted his back as he pulled away from me. He didn't drop his arms but looked at me with something akin to longing in his eyes.

"I wish we had met in different circumstances, *fraulein*," he said in a soft voice. Then he cleared his throat and dropped his arms as he took a step back and nodded at me. "*Auf wiedersehen.*"

Words were suddenly unavailable to me but I saluted him in return. He turned to the fire escape and descended it. Nicolas looked over the roof edge again and nodded.

"Your blade," he said as he eyed the object in question. "Not that you require it in light of your excellent unarmed and improvisational fighting skills."

It seemed like a bad time to tell them about Donnchadh. "Just the same, I'd feel better having it by my side again."

Perenelle marched over to her husband and took him by the shoulder. "Yes, allow her to retrieve that exquisite blade while we gather the necessary reagents to meet her reasonable price of employment."

"Reagents?" I asked, frowning.

Perenelle smiled at me in a knowing way. "As alchemists, we have different ways of doing things, my dear."

I wasn't sure what that meant but decided not to question her and reveal my doubt. Instead, I started after my sword and felt an incredible sense of relief suffuse me as soon as I closed my fingers over the pommel. I resheathed it around my waist and started back up the fire escape.

"I believe Manfred was quite taken with you," Perenelle said as she looked up at me slyly.

"Oh?"

"Oui," Nicolas added with a nod. "I've never seen him willingly embrace someone before. It was quite... awkward."

That was a good word for it, actually. I didn't know what to say so I said nothing at all.

"Perhaps you could be a good reason he leaves the Malebranche?" Perenelle continued as she faced me with that sly expression.

"I don't think Manfred is ready to break ties with the Malebranche yet and I doubt anyone will change his mind."

Perenelle shrugged. "Do not underestimate the power of your feminity," she said. "Do you find Manfred... handsome?"

I could see where this was going. "Yes but my heart belongs to someone already."

"He is a lucky man," Perenelle said though I could tell she was disappointed on behalf of her friend.

Nicolas looked over his shoulder at me. "It would be helpful to know the identity of your friends."

I trailed behind them. "Well, there's my guardian angel, Bill and Tallis Black."

Tallis' name brought them both to an abrupt halt. Perenelle looked over her shoulder at me. "You mean to say the very same Tallis Black who was once *Master* of the Underground City?"

By now, we'd all reached the fire escape. "Uh, yeah, that's him."

"Finding them will be a great deal easier than I feared," Nicolas said. "Black is not a man easily hid."

"And an angel!" Perenelle added, from where she stood right behind her husband on the stairs. "They stand out like beacons on a cloudy night." Perenelle grinned up at me. "You are quite fortunate that our supplies come not from the Malebranche but from the current Master of the city, Alaire, himself. He appreciates the value of good quality."

The sudden clenching of my jaw and stomach were clear signs of how *unfortunate* I found that information to be.

"Not scorn, but grief much more..."
-Dante's Inferno

THIRTEEN
BILL

Christ, but I freakin' hate walkin'.

Yeah, yeah, I know... that's how everybody gets around. But c'mon! I'm a freakin' angel. That oughta count for something!

But all my gazillion requestrations to AE for a pair of wings always gets me the same damn answer each time: "disqualified."

Except for the red eye flight on Lils' pet bird bitch and the car rides on the Garbage Truck of Doom and the Little Electric Car That Couldn't, I ain't done nothing but walk since I got down here. And it was seriously getting old.

My in-and-outsoles were screaming with agony while I followed Tido who was too busy trailing our new gal pal, I Dream o' Jeannie. Damned if I knew how long we'd been hoofing it, though. The clock on my phone barely budged since leaving the elevator. We were probabilistically too far away from any cell towers and no way could it have been three minutes, but that was what it said. Still, as extenuational as our travel time was, it gave us a lot of opportunistics to talk. Good a reason as any other for why Tido decided to put the one billion dollar question to Jeannie.

"Ye seen ah certain blind giant recently?"

A bit of surprise cracked open her Lady Madonna mask, one she'd been wearing since she hooked up with us. "Epimetheus?"

Conan actually gave her a smile... at least, that's what I assumed it were under that forested bog he called his beard. "Aye, the verra one, Jeanne... he spoke o' ye as though ye were his personal angel."

She took that complimentary with a shrug. "I could see he was in pain and I wished to do something to alleviate it, if only for a little while."

"Aye, an' yer kindness left a deep impression oopon him. His brother contracted oos with ensurin' yer safety in exchange fer lettin' oos pass by."

I scoffed. "Yeah! And look how *that* worked out, Conan! She winds up savin' *our* asses, yo, 'cause we never seen them ambashers comin'."

The mask dropped back over Jeanne's face. "Everyone needs help eventually, William." She sighed. "At the end of my life, I was denied any assistance. So how could I cruelly deny it to either of you when I could so easily offer it?"

Conan's voice sounded real choked up like when he yapped again. "Ah, had Ah known ye in me life, Ah'd have been proud tae stand by yer side in battle."

I cleared my throat and changed the subjective. "So why didn't you find Epi and Pro before now? I mean, after spendin' centureons walkin' around the Underground City, ya shoulda run into 'em a loooong time ago."

She bowed her head a bit. "In death as in life, I am guided by something I cannot speak of. Wherever it prompts me to go, I must follow."

Sounded a lot like my gig as a guardian angel. Problem was: angels don't stay with their humans after death—they just move on to the next human who gotta need for 'em. So why was I still with Lils? Easy—

131

I'm the exceptionator, not the ruler. "Did ya ever, ya know, *not* listen ta that voice or whatever it is?"

A smile that looked as sad as Tido's shoeless feet took holda her face. "More than once, William, and each time, I regretted it. I now follow this inner guidance without question, wherever it might lead. And it has never guided me here until this very day."

Conan asked a question that made me wonder if he weren't such a dumbass as I thought. "Ye been tae all the Circles aboove oos?"

She didn't hesi-state. "Every one and many times."

"An' yer jist *now* comin' down tae the morgue?" Tido asked, shaking his head like he got a damned tick in his ear. "Yer timin' makes me wonder; why now?"

Jeannie blew a cute, little breath out her nose. "I truly do not know, Tallis. But I shall find out when I need to."

And there it was, the secret sauce of how she kept us mesmer-roused: true faith. Most humans in my experience just go through the motionals. Including most of the folks I watched over. Some of them said they believed, and put on a good enough act to fool everybody else but I always saw right through 'em. Auras are real handy when it comes to sifting out bullshit.

But every once upon a time, you run into the feels real deal. Those people make the human race better. They be so good that you feel bad about yourself for not trying harder to be better. That's probly why most of them don't last. The hippocratical world around them can only take so much gazing in that reflectation before they decide to smash it with the nearest hammer.

All that bullet-training ran through my head when I piped up. "Dunno if I'm speaking fer Tido here but, uh… I hope we can do the same fer you as ya did fer us."

The smirk returned to Conan's lips. "Nae offense, stookie angel, but Ah'm guessin' that somethin' like repellin' them Spites is a wee bit beyond ye."

I blew a raspberry at him. "Yo, ya know what I'm sayin', Conan."

"Ah think that was the first pair o' full sentences Ah didnae need a translator fer."

Watching us speak-spar made Jeannie smile. "You squabble as only *deux freres* can."

Maybe Tido didn't get the French but I sure did. "Him? My bro? If you're right, Jeannie, that's one branch o' the family tree I want chainsawed off."

The big ogre gave me a quick chuckle. "Aye, Ah'd like tae see ye attempt tae work a chainsaw." Then Tido faced Jeannie. "The angel's ah rather useless, girly type."

"Consider yerself lucky to be hanging out with the yeti," I said to Jeannie. "Usually he only comes outta the forest on occasion an' most people don't even believe he exists." Tido frowned at me before turning 'round again. "Dat ass doe."

"Stop lookin' at me arse, man!" he railed.

Jeannie couldn't keep a straight face. She started laughing the way only a free soul can. It made me wonderize, yet again, how in hells she got down here. I've always known AE was an ineffectualized, slug-trail operation with no right to still be in busy-ness. But this went past what Polly'd call "oversight"—guess the word "mistake" ain't in her vocabulary—and straight into what Sally'd call a "travesty." That's her code word for disastrophe.

Any dumbass who could see straight would *know* this was the last place Jeannie should be. An' yet here she was with the rest of us poor saps. Sweet kid deserved a lot better… just like my Lils.

133

***

The big artillerator guns went off and sounded too damn close, even if they weren't nowhere in sight. It was enough to make me tempermentally forget my acherating feet. Guns mean armies. Armies mean base camp. Base camp means radio contact. Guess Jeannie's info weren't as out of date as she thought.

Tido pointed to an open area just beyond us. Once upon a time, a building stood there but now it was no more than a pile of ragged rocks. You could hear and see all the shells firing past it. Tido started running towards the heap an' Jeannie started up behind him before she turned to look at me where I was maintaininating my current walk.

"William, you must hurry!" she whispered.

"Nah ah, not me, sugar lips. I got runner's block."

"You've got what?"

"It's like writer's block but not. I got me a lack o' will or reason to run. It can last up to a few weeks."

"Hurry, ye bleedin' dunderheid!" Tido said as he walked his enormo self back over. Then he was glarin' at me as he started up that junk heap like the bear he resymbolates and Jeannie wasn't too far behind him. Me? I was *way* behind both of them. I was too busy lappin' up the view of Jean-Jeannie's ass-ets and even that couldn't make me climb no faster. Being short's a bigger bitch than Skeletorhorn.

Jeannie, or God movin' through Jeannie, or maybe she was channelin' some other dude like John Cena, but she managed to haul my dumpy ass over the final stretch of the rubble up to the top. That gave me a good look at the situ-aching... which was anything but good. The place was a square gridlock of tents.

"I shaved my balls for this?" I whispered as I took me another once over of the encampment. It looked

134

like the boy scouts had taken over only these ones were way less friendly and I doubted they even knew the first thing 'bout roastin' marshmallows.

Not too far from where we was, I seen those big arse-an-all guns getting reloaded by their crews. Every one of those metal monsters was a Big Bertha, over a hundred years outta date but still pretty deadly. Just past them, I saw the ragged line of humans all loading their rifles. My eyes practically bugfucked out my head when I saw they were also fixing bayonets on the gun barrels. Freakin' bayonets...

I nearly swallowed my own tongue when a guy popped out the nearest tent. There weren't no mistaking those natural blonde curls, matching blonde mustache, deep-socketed blue eyes, and that damn ridicu-louse broad-brimmed hat. He always looked like a kid imposteranating a grown-up. When I heard him talking to his men in that high-bitched, enthusi-asshat voice, I realized things hadn't changed much.

Conan actually *did* utter a groan before he identificated the asshole. "General George Cooster? O' course, he'd be in the thick o' it."

Jeannie looked over at Tido. "You know him?"

I ignored my twisting guts—for once, not because I was hangry—but to fill her in. "We both do, Jeannie. The only reason people rememorate that yellow-haired idiot is 'cause he got hisself an' all his men killed in a battle with Nativity Americans that never should've been fought."

The way Jeannie was frowning, I could tell she didn't understand. "Was it not a worthy cause?"

Tido's whole face, not just his lips, sneered in disgust. "Ah wouldnae say so, Jeanne. An' e'en if it were, none o' the men oonder his command had tae die the inglorious way they did."

135

I wasn't sure if I agreed with the Scottish Sasquatch; if I did, it would be the first time an' I weren't sure I was ready for that yet. "One o' the guys who died that day was one o' mine. I tried tellin' him to GTFO while he could. I damn near screamed it in his ear when Custer got closer. But instead..."

I didn't like how that rememory affectuated me. Right after that, I really started party-hardying just to cope. Sometimes you can lead a human to the trough but you can't get him to shit. Or however the hell that stupid sayin' goes.

The consternation on Jeannie's face clued me in: she finally got on our wave-lap. "Do you both believe this man, Custer, is about to do such a terrible thing again?"

Our perch gave us a clear view of the enema lines. I took out my telenoculars to get a better peek. What I saw in the trenches was anything but encourageous. "I'm seein' a metric ton o' rifles an' the supersized, economy pack o' machine gun nests; I don't believe shithead's about to do a terrible thing, Jeannie. I *knows* it."

When I looked away, Conan grunted like a moose with a bad ear infection. "Cooster probably thought the big cannons would soften 'em oop long enough tae charge the lines."

I gave him something 'tween a laugh and a cough. "Yeah, good luck with that. All those idiots with the merit stars on their shoulders thought that'd work in World War I too."

Jeannie went back to being confrustrated. "One two?"

Conan got me out of that jam by interrupting. "Hol' on now... look down below oos."

"Your doom fix'd deep within me..."
-Dante's Inferno

FOURTEEN
BILL

Since I couldn't see shit, I wiggled up a little closer to the edge. Looking straight down, I saw a tent—hell, it were more like a bumbershoot seeing as it didn't have any sides on it—and it had a lotta comm gear under it. A bunch of perfect-looking kids, vale-dictator-ans of their eugenics class no doubt, were manning the equipment. It was surrounded by four troopers who were probly glad to be spared the Suicide Sprint Custer planned for everybody else.

"Ye think those kids on the machines are Soul Retrievers, stookie angel?"

I gave 'em a quick aura read. "Yeah, pretty safe bet, Conan. They're definitely newlydeads an' the guys 'round 'em got Underground City stamped all over their auras."

Jeannie started tapping both our shoulders. After getting our attention, she pointed at the cannons. The cannon cockers were falling in line with the rest of their battle-buddies, right down to the bayonets on the rifles. I did some quick death math in my head. "You thinkin' what I'm thinkin', Conan?"

"If ye be thinkin' we make our move right after Cooster makes his, then aye."

Jeannie chose that second to hurlicane us a curveball. "No killing."

That threw Tido for a loop. "Nae whit?"

137

She nodded toward the line where General Fuckster was walking to the front. "No killing."

I wanted to say that was impossible an' bullshit but I never got me the chance. 'Cause Conan hurly-burlyed me a second curveball.

"Aye, Ah think we can accommodate ye, lass."

How's we was gonna do that, I had no idear. But whatevs.

"Charge!" Custer's yell was damn near as loud as his cannons. All his boys started hollering just before rushing the other front line. Somebody needed to kick this party off, so I launched myself right on top of the nearest guy's head.

"Light it up!" I yelled before cutting loose with a flashbang aura that blinded everyone but the guy I was riding. He failed ta appreci-ache my feat or regalize that I'd just saved him from a seri-ass blinding while his buddies were aimlessly stumbling around and clawing their eyes.

Dumbass kept swiping at me, trying to pull me off but I was seated pretty good on his shoulders. The good news was: Custer's boys were preoccupated with the whole full-frontal and didn't see us. The bad news: the guy was frantically trying to tear me off his shoulders. I kept squeezing his head the way I would've liked to squeeze a pair of over large breasts.

Tido landed on the back of the one in front of my ride. His big fist smashed the back of the guy's head, knocking the sap out cold. Then Conan laid out the next one with a bomb-punch that sent him flying into the guy ahead of him. They both fell in a heap while sasquatch yanked out his sword. He brained both those guys with the hilt. That left the one guy, who was so busy dealing with me, he had no idea what was happening around him.

Tido reared back his sword, hilt first.

"Off, stookie angel!"

138

No need to tell me twice... I ain't no fool. Soze I jumped off the guy at the same time Tido whacked the dude squarely in the face and he hit the ground in the same exact place where I was! His head slammed into my empty gut so hard, I almost power puked. Too bad I didn't have nothing inside me to vominate.

By then, the 90210 crowd were getting their regularly scheduled insta-vision from their eyeballs again. Every one of 'em backed away from Tido's uniquified blend of bad hygiene and overlarge muscles. One kid in the back looked like Tom Cruise before his plastic-fantastic surgery. He damn near back-walked out the tent saying, "W-W-We don't want any trouble!"

I heard some rocks moving behind us and I assuminated it was more trouble until I saw Jeannie walking out from behind the yeti. The girl next to her was such a looker, I found myself suddenly nursing a semi. The hottie-patotty took a couple steps toward the last member of our not-very-merry band.

"Who are you? And how did you get stuck with these two?" she asked.

Jeannie's dazzling smile could've lit up Vegas for a whole year. "I am Jeanne, *mon ami*. Please do not be alarmed by these two. They rescued me from Cardinal Cauchon."

Tido unexpectedly turned his full at-tension on them and they all looked scared. I wondered if they thought he was gonna eat them? "Unless Ah'm mistaken, ye all moost be Soul Retrievers?"

A super pale kid with a mop of orange hair scoffed and stared at the ground. "Yeah... not that the title means much."

Tido looked at Hottie like he wanted an explantion. She shrugged. "It's the same story for all of us. We get our first job, run into trouble and next thing we know, we're here."

139

"Not like we're prepared," the orange-haired dude added.

The other girl, a blonde, wore the body of a super fit, muscular gym bunny. She grabbed flame-crotch's shoulder and squeezed. "I keep telling you, Harry. We were set up purposely to fail. None of this is our fault."

Harry gave her a look. "I hear you, Kay. I just can't stop thinking we could have done better."

Tido's head turned towards the raging battle. "Water oonder the bridge, lad, an' that's somethin' we got nae time tae discoose. How long ye figure, stookie angel, 'afore Cooster's troops be fallin' back?"

Harry's eyes bugged out a little before landing on yours truly. "Did he just call you an angel?"

Ms. Hottie next to him lightly slapped his arm. "Quiet!"

While the girl hissed, I answered Conan's question. "We got maybe five, six minutes max, yo. Chargin' the front lines that way, one side's gonna be massacrated PDQ. An' I'm pretty sure it's not gonna be the side Curly expects."

Ms. Hottie gave me a shrewd look. "So... what do you need from us?"

Ms. Junior She-Hulk aka Kay looked over her man-shoulder. "Uhm, I don't know if you missed it, Addie, but these two don't look like they need much of anything."

Jeannie stepped up and put her finger on the equipment they were standing in front of. "We need your radio. There is someone I must call before it is too late."

Harry's eyes got harder. "Can we proceed on our way after that?"

Tido did a quick nod. "As ye like, lad, boot Ah'd recommend stayin' with oos jist sae ye got a fightin' chance tae make it out o' the Oonderground City."

Harry frowned but he looked like he wanted to believe Tido. "What do you think, Addie?" All eyes were fastened on her. That pegged her as the alpha bitch of this woof pack. Her answer cementaried it.

"I think we're wasting time these people could use. Yeah, we're in."

Jeannie gave her a relieved smile. "You know how to operate this equipment?"

Harry barked or quacked when she said that. "Sheeit, only reason we're here. That bunch of headcrackers would probably find a pair of cups and a string too complicated to use."

Queen Addie was ready with the radio dial. "What do you need?"

Three steps later, Jeannie was right by her side. "Dial the radio to 381.4. Then hand me the headset... please."

The voice she used to issue that order sounded a lot differentiated from the one she used to talk to me an' Tido. Banner people weren't usually considered command material but here she was, barking out commandments like she did at Army General Boot Camp. What the hell wasn't she telling us?

Tido turned his thousand-yard stare to the thousand yards of battlefield ahead of us. The chit-chatter of the machine guns and popcorn pops of the rifles kept mixing with horrible screams and cries.

"That damn fool's keepin' 'em there tae long."

I stood next to him and felt so... little. "Yeah, anybody else woulda blown the retreat smoke signal by now." I could've telenoculared my way to the fightin', sure. But I'd seen that show too many times. Seeing it again was about as appealing as passaging a kidney rock and about as much fun as chemotherapractice. The radio crackled to life, making both of us turn around.

141

"Tangent calling Sapphire. This is Tangent. Do you read, Sapphire?" A voice sounded over the radio.

Another sunbeam smile later, Jeannie mashed the talk button with her thumb. "Sapphire here, Tangent. Are you safe?"

The relieviated sigh that came over the channel threatenated to blow out the speaker. "For right now, we are. What's your twenty?"

My new favorite gal glanced at the fighting before answering. "The camp... we shall need to move ourselves soon."

"Come back, Sapphire, did you say 'we'?"

Jeannie seemed on the verge of laughter. "*Oui*, I said 'we'! I can vouch for each of *mes nouveaux amis* but we cannot hold our position."

A chorus of whistles an' horns rang up and down the line. I knew what that meant. So I ran over to Harry. "This dump got any food?"

He scrunched up his face while Tangent kept yapping to Jeannie. "Copy that, Sapphire. Rendezvous at the wizard's place and we'll meet your new friends, over."

Queen Addie glow-wormed at me. "This place isn't exactly a Taco Bell, Shorty."

Jeannie didn't seem to notice us while she answered her mystery man buddy. "*Tres bien, mon ami*. We shall see you soon."

Ms. She-Hulk pointed over at a spot behind the equipment. "You'll find food there."

Thankfully, Conan backed my play with a nod. "'Twill have tae do. Best grab as mooch as ye can afore we go. Nae tellin' when ye'll git another chance tae fill yer belly."

Jeannie put the radio mike down and gave the troops a once-over, then a twice-over. "We have a little longer than two minutes before their return, *mes amis*. It would be best to do as they say, *rapidement!*"

Thankfully, the Calvin Klein Clones knew a good idea when they heard one. They started grabbing the boxes of food fast. When Tido walked outside the tent, I saw something behind him that made me feel downright celestialistic. It was a sat phone case right there, just waiting to be opened up and used. I was about to take it when I felt the unmistakable, hairy arm of Tido yanking me back.

"Wha'dya think yer doin', man?"

The tree trunk that he called his arm held me like a vise. "Just need ta make one quick call before we vamoosh, Tido."

He looked angry. "Nae time left fer it! Soon as the lads an' lasses get what they can—"

"We're set!" Harry yelled at us.

I ducked under Tido's hand and ran back to the phone.

"Stookie angel, what'd Ah jist—"

I yanked the sat phone case off the bench. Damn thing weighed as much as me but I did my best to ignoramus that. By then, everybody was lining up behind Jeannie. Since Tido was too busy staring at me, I barked at him, "Well, we goin' or what?!"

That got the hairballs out of Conan's brains. He gestured to all of us to play "Follow the Leader" around the left side of the tent. I could faintly hear the stamping of Custer's boys' feet when we evacuumated the place.

"As to the centre first I downward tend."
-Dante's Inferno

FIFTEEN
LILY

For the hundredth time, I looked through the crack in the door for any sign of trouble. Nicolas glanced up from the tile floor where he was making markings and grunted.

"While I truly admire your caution, *Mademoiselle* Harper, I can assure you that neither side of this wasteful conflict will bother us here."

I tore my eyes away from the outside to answer him. "Look, no offense, but every time I assume I'm safe down here, I turn out to be anything but."

Perenelle's face exploded with joy although she stayed focused on the chalk marks she was making. "And your words have made you *mon nouveau meilleur ami.*"

Nicolas grunted at her. "You only call her your new best friend because the women have now officially outnumbered the men in our immediate vicinity."

She shook her head at him and laughed. Meanwhile, I busily tapped my fingers against the wall. "No *further* offense intended, but this place doesn't exactly inspire good vibes."

That was putting it mildly! The inside of the place looked like a shower room from hell with thick concrete walls, no windows and metal showerheads everywhere. That was *before* I discovered that every one of the nozzles spat out fire instead of water.

144

When the Flamels mentioned a safe place where they'd formerly conducted certain experiments that weren't safe to test in their lab, this wasn't what I had in mind.

Nicolas tapped his chin and nodded. "Vibes? As in 'vibration', *oui*?"

I couldn't mask my surprise. "Yes, but how did you figure that out?" I didn't mean to offend him but clearly he was from another time and place and I doubted contemporary phrases like "good vibes" would be easily interpreted.

Nicolas shrugged as he continued to work on the floor. "In life, I was a humble scribe at a time when literacy was considered a rare and specialized skill. I am also very fortunate to have an affinity for languages in general."

Perenelle chuckled with a little hint of derision. "And how many 'humble scribes' have two shops for writing manuscripts in Paris, not to mention a number of sculptures along with several other pieces of property, dear husband?"

Nicolas took her comments with good humor himself. "Oh, I never actually considered anything my property except for my humble shops, dear wife. We both know that, the prejudice of our neighbors notwithstanding, you actually owned the rest."

"And you owned them when I died... so I am still correct in my assessment, Nicolas."

In spite of my fears, I could relax while listening to their banter. Perenelle noticed and cast a smile my way. "Nicolas, you have succeeded at putting *mon nouveau ami* at ease."

"Well, I figure if you two can be so casual with each other, it must mean this place really is safe," I said.

145

Nicolas hummed thoughtfully. "You would not be the first young lady I have set at ease. The one who works by my side at present was one such lady."

While his wife waved her hand at him dismissively, I asked her, "What did Nicolas mean when he said you actually owned almost all the property you both had?"

She glanced up at me before answering. "Before this charming scribbler worked up the courage to ask for my hand in marriage—"

He interrupted her with, "She lies... I was ready to do so from the moment of our introduction."

She shook her head. "*Oui, oui*, you and countless other would-be *chevaliers* with notions of nobility running through their empty heads."

I remembered Manfred's introduction back at their place. "So you were a noble lady?"

Perenelle chuckled. "No, no, no, no, *Mademoiselle* Harper! Much more than that, I assure you. I was a widow whose two previous husbands allowed me the wealth and means to *choose* the man who would take me to the altar the third time."

Nicolas scooted himself over to draw out the next part of the design they were working on. "And no more than two days after the wedding, you tried to convince me to close my shops and live in luxury for the rest of my born days."

"And now who is lying, husband?" she asked with another laugh. "I saw how you put your heart and soul into your work. I would have no more separated you from it than marry the other *hommes muets* who thought you unworthy."

I was a little confused about something. "So why did Manfred call you 'Lord' and 'Lady'?"

Their eyes showed mutual understanding. Nicolas spoke first. "Do you wish to tell her or shall I?"

146

Perenelle glanced over at his section of the design and pointed to part of it. "Given that the line there needs thickening, perhaps it is best if you focus on your work instead."

Nicolas glanced at the direction she'd pointed and made a frustrated noise in his throat. While he furiously set to fixing it, his wife looked up at me.

"For you to ask that question, it can only mean you are largely ignorant of our reputation."

I heard something under her voice that made me wonder. "Doesn't sound like a reputation either of you wanted?"

Perenelle grunted in disgust before answering. "Given that this reputation conspired to condemn us to the Underground City, who would want it?"

I frowned at her. "What do you mean?"

Nicolas's wife went back to the drawing. "While we both lived, we dabbled in the noble art of alchemy as many educated people of our time did. But we were hardly what you would call ardent seekers of the great magic. We were merely competent enough to make certain effects manifest."

Nicolas couldn't keep the disgust out of his voice when he added: "and yet that apparently was enough to convince Afterlife Enterprises to send us to the Eighth Circle for such marginal, innocuous activities. Since we were freed, I have learned that we acquired an overblown reputation as master alchemists."

His wife looked at him with some sympathy. "Had I known the books on the Philosopher's Stone which you transcribed for that wandering scoundrel would be credited to you, dear husband—"

He looked back at her with unmasked sympathy. "Ah, but do we all not make mistakes we regret? Wishing we could take them back and yet, we never can? I do not blame him for our predicament. Scoundrel though he was, he only acted according to

147

his nature, nothing more. Our fault was our failure to realize the consequences."

Nicholas sounded like he was using some of the principles in my self-help books to cope with his situation. "So who was this scoundrel?" I asked.

Perenelle shook her head as she moved down to the next part of her circle. "We do not repeat his name," she explained. "We are not what I would consider superstitious people but on this one point, we have agreed."

"Why?" I asked.

"To repeat his name would be to welcome bad luck," Perenelle explained. "At the time, he seemed to me a typical example of a self-proclaimed alchemist. He imparted great wisdom but I sensed the treachery under his words. I shall always regret my utter failure to see the trap he laid for us until it was far too late."

I could relate. "Sounds a lot like Alaire whenever I had to deal with him."

My casual observation made both of them stop what they were doing and look up at me. Then Perenelle broke the awkward silence with a hum. "Of course, if you are on familiar terms with Alaire's predecessor, why would you not also be familiar with the current ruler of this place?"

I rubbed the side of my face, keeping my eyes trained outside. "It wasn't by choice. For some reason, Alaire wants me for his latest captive and he's gone to some pretty extreme lengths to make that happen."

"Such as...?"

I wanted to answer but my mind and mouth clammed up tight. Right now, Alaire was the *last* subject I wanted to discuss. "Let's talk about this scoundrel you mentioned. What was his story?"

Nicolas sucked in a breath through his teeth. "My distaste for him and my wife's hatred aside, he had a clear grasp of the transient nature of all things. So toward people and material things, he tended to be... I believe the phrase is 'love them and leave them'?"

Perenelle sneered. "*Mais oui*, love them while they are useful and then leave them to the Underground City, a place that he shall never set foot in himself."

I wasn't sure if pushing the subject was a good idea but I couldn't help my curiosity. "Why? Is he immortal or something?"

Nicolas firmly shook his head. "Even if he were, immortality is merely the delay of death, not a reprieve. As such, he would eventually die. However, even though he was an arch magician, he never once saw the Eighth Circle."

"And why not? Doesn't he deserve it?" I asked.

Perenelle gave me a tight smile that made me think of my mom whenever she was proud of me. "Indeed he does. But the only such sorcerers, alchemists and scientists who are sent to the Underground City are the lesser lights. You shall never find the likes of, for instance, Merlin, Morgan Le Fay, Mag the Ancient, or Prospero of Milan amongst us."

"While we cannot say where precisely they go," Nicolas added, "I have it on good authority of the Malebranche themselves that they are sent to a place far more comfortable than this Circle."

I didn't want to believe it. "Well, the Malebranche are the big, bad, boss demons down here, right? Couldn't they have been lying?"

Perenelle took a deep, steadying breath before answering me. "I accused them of doing that very thing when we were told of this alleged arrangement. I still remember the precise answer from the duke I berated: 'Had we such great men at our disposal, why would we bother with the likes of you?'"

That tore it. Bad enough that AE let a freaking computer bug send the wrong souls down here. Bad enough that they were so crooked as to condemn plenty of people like me to a hazardous and basically impossible job. But for them to actually cut a sweetheart deal with a bunch of wizards in exchange for making good people like the Flamels suffer indefinitely? If one of those smug bastard Malebranche were standing in front of me, I'd have grabbed him by the neck and twisted it hard until his head—

It took me a second to realize Donnchadh was manipulating my anger to bust himself out again. Thankfully, I still had a surefire method to thwart him. Grabbing the hilt of my blade, I shoved him all the way back to where he belonged. It was funny how he didn't howl about it like he did practically everything else. Maybe he knew he was up against a force way more powerful than he was?

I kept my hand on the hilt for a minute just to make sure Donnchadh was good and restrained. When I looked at the Flamels again, I realized they'd been staring at me. Perenelle spoke first.

"Are you aware that both of your eyes turned into solid black orbs, *mon enfant*?"

While I wasn't sure what to say, the close call needed some kind of explanation. "Yeah, there's this pesky, angry spirit who keeps trying to come out whenever I get mad or hungry or tired or whatever. So I—"

Nicolas shuddered as he cut me off. "That is not any spirit, *enfant*. In fact, it displayed a remarkable resemblance to a Spite."

A Spite? Donnchadh? "Huh?" I asked quaintly before shaking my head. "That can't be right. The Spites are part of this big, killer, flesh-eating cloud that..."

Perenelle was the one to cut me off this time. "Almost all of them, *oui*, but there has long been one exception."

Obviously, I needed more information to understand what they were talking about. "An exception? What do you mean? And what exactly *are* the Spites anyway?"

Nicolas warmed up to my question like I'd asked him to tell me his favorite bedtime story. "You are aware of the legend of Pandora and her infamous box, *non*?"

While I was nodding, Perenelle held up her index finger to her husband. "In actuality, husband, it was an urn."

He waved off the distinction like it was a bad smell. "Regardless of the receptacle's true form, it was nonetheless a wedding present given to Pandora upon her marriage to Epimetheus the Titan."

That sounded as appropriate as giving someone a ticking time bomb for their birthday. "Why would anyone give something that horrible as a wedding present? I mean, outside of a jealous ex."

"Well, for one, the happy couple was never informed of the true contents of the box—or urn, if you prefer. For another, Epimetheus was the brother of Prometheus, who stole the Divine Fire to give to humankind."

I searched my brain for what little I could remember about Prometheus. "I seem to vaguely recall that Prometheus was cruelly punished for pulling that stunt."

Nicolas smiled and pointed at me as though I'd just given him the correct answer on a test. "Indeed he was and Epimetheus was also found guilty by association. However, the latter was considerably more slow-witted than his clever brother, and thus, a

151

much easier target to inflict additional penalties upon."

Perenelle tapped her pointer finger on the floor. "Pandora was given one simple instruction when she received the urn: never open it."

Okay, that part of the story, I *definitely* knew. "But, of course, she did anyway."

Nicolas nodded. "And that unhappy action loosed the Spites upon the world, inflicting all their evils onto the whole species of mankind."

I felt for Pandora. None of what happened was really her fault. Like me when I first sat in Streethorn's office, she, too, was set up to fail from the very start. Perenelle must have read my expression because she added to the story.

"Of course, not all the spirits that were trapped inside the urn fled upon its opening."

"Not all of them fled?"

"Oh, no, *Mademoiselle* Harper, there was one spirit who was of a far more benevolent nature, symbolized by its taking the form of a diamond."

Nicolas's eyes got a bit more watery in the dim light of the shower room. "It was the spirit of Hope, the one force in this universe equal to love. Without Hope, a man is condemned to a fate far worse than here."

Perenelle raised her finger at Nicolas again. "As are women, *n'est-ce pas*?"

Nicolas replied, "A mere figure of speech, dear wife. You are correct, of course."

I started tapping my fingers on my blade's hilt. "So whatever happened to this Hope spirit?"

Nicolas shrugged as he began to stand up. "That is something no one knows. However, if Cardinal Cauchon is any indicator, there are many who would pay very dearly to find out."

Perenelle also stood up and stretched out her back. "I am unconvinced the ploy you used to make Cauchon leave us alone was still a wise course of action, Nicolas."

Nicolas twisted his torso back and forth, presumably getting all the kinks out of his back. "I could either deliver what Cauchon believed was the true Hope Diamond or become his unwilling prisoner. At the time, I saw no better option."

I gave the hilt a hard tap with my finger. "That was why the Simoniacs were raiding your place when Manfred and I came by."

Perenelle nodded unhappily while pulling out vials from inside her leather apron. "I believe so. It is probable that the cardinal decided to use our most convincing fake in an attempt to protect his people from the Spites; and it failed utterly." She glared at her husband. "It is even more probable that I am married to a man who lacks basic good sense. A clever man, I imagine, would have moved our laboratory to a safer location after Cauchon's visit."

By then, Nicolas was pulling out his own vials. "Had we followed through on such a course of action, we would have incurred the wrath not only of the Malebranche but of Alaire himself. Both were very explicit in their instructions to stay where we were."

I held up my hand like I was still in school. "Wait... Why would Alaire care where you were? I thought he just gave you your ingredients so that the Malebranche—"

Perenelle cut me off with the pop of a vial stopper. "The Malebranche has no knowledge of our arrangement with Alaire. And if you are as acquainted with him as I believe you must be, you would surely know that Alaire is anything but a generous man."

I felt a knot lodging in my gut. "What was his price?"

Nicolas made a point of keeping his eyes fastened on the floor while he spread his powders. "In exchange for supplying us with the necessary reagents for our work, we must find both the lost Spite *and* the true Hope Diamond. Why he seeks such things, I cannot say."

Me neither but I could make an educated guess. As long as both of those things were floating around, Alaire couldn't control the Spites. But if he had them in his custody...

Once again, Perenelle interrupted my thought process. "I believe we are ready to put you in contact with your friends. Do you possess any material things that connect you to either of them?"

I pulled out my blade and looked into its mirror quality reflection. "Tallis forged this for me. And it's got some odd properties unique only to it."

Nicolas clapped his hands in delight. "*Magnifique*! It sounds like the perfect instrument to reach out to him. When would you like to perform the ritual?"

I gave the door one last glance. "There's no time like the present."

Following their instructions, I lay down in the middle of the elaborate circle they'd been drawing while we were talking. They positioned themselves opposite each other in the circle and said a number of phrases that sounded like Latin. Then Nicolas rounded the circle three times, holding up my blade while he chanted. He passed the blade over to Perenelle, who walked around the circle three more times in the opposite direction. She used the tip of my blade to touch my forehead.

A split second later, I lost consciousness.

"So that now in tears thou mourn'st!"
-Dante's Inferno

SIXTEEN
TALLIS

While it was hard to tell, with the buildings in such ruins, I think we were mayhap three blocks from Custer's camp when we finally came to a halt. Everyone was too fatigued to do more than pant breathlessly. Me gutsack also chose that moment to remind me how little I'd stuffed into it. Much as I longed to tear into the provisions we'd secured, we had to get to a safer place.

Being just as short of breath as the rest of us, the handsome woman called Addie didnae seem too happy about it. "C'mon, we gotta keep moving!"

The stookie angel, panting like a dog, pointed down the wrecked street. "Hey, go for it, Ms. Hottie-Patotty. But the rest of us gotta actually get some air into our lungs first."

The way Addie's eyes narrowed at the angel, I knew it wouldnae end well for him. "You know, the longer I'm around you, the harder it is for me to believe you're actually an angel."

"Must be like how hard it is fer me ta believe that in life, you looked anywhere close ta how good you look now, huh toots?"

Next thing I knew, Addie charged him with some type of Karate-Ninja kick and the angel was flung across the street into the nearest wall. The breath he was sae keen on enjoying, was knocked out of him in

a rush. Addie marched over—probably to kick him—
when I got in the way. That made her turn her glare
upon me.

"Oh, you want some too, hairball?"

As impressed as I was that me bigger size didnae
intimidate her, I was nae in the mood to play games
with a slip of a lass. "Yer point's been made, lass.
Leave it be."

The other lass who was quite muscled—Kay—
gently tugged at Addie's arm. "If you're serious about
not wasting time, we're doing exactly that."

Meanwhile, the stookie angel slowly picked
himself up off the ground with help from the lad,
whose name was Harry. The angel nodded his thanks
and looked over at Addie.

"That's some mule kick ya got there, Xena."

Addie's eyes darted 'tween him and me. I shook
me head ruefully. "Dinnae look a' me, lass. Tha's the
closest tae nice he ever gits."

The wee fellow walked past me in a huff. "Thank
you very little, Conan!"

Harry, meanwhile, was riveted on every nook and
cranny for the first sign of trouble, while clutching two
boxes piled high with food close to his chest.
Watchfulness was a virtue in a situation such as ours.
But the kind of distress I witnessed from him was just
as bad as if he were oblivious to his surroundings.
Jeanne must have agreed for she put a hand on his
shoulder that made him jump.

"It will be some time before General Custer's
troops catch up with us, *mon ami*. They have just
suffered a severe rout, and we have deprived them of
much-needed supplies, not to mention they have
many wounded to attend to."

Harry relaxed a wee bit but he wasnae completely
convinced by Jeanne's wisdom. "B-B-But won't they
come after us eventually?"

156

I nodded at him. "That they will, lad. So if everyone's got their breath back, Ah'd say we best be movin' oan."

Kay gave me a sour look as she scrunched up her face. "Where? Nobody said jackshit about where this 'wizard's place' is located."

Jeanne gave the horizon ahead of us a careful sweep with her eyes. "We still have some distance to cross yet. And, as Addie noted, we will get no closer to it by staying here and arguing."

Addie threw open her arms as if she wanted to embrace Jeanne. "Thank you!"

The stookie angel opened his mouth to make a remark he'd regret. I shook me head at him and pointed to our guide. He gave me a disgusted look and mouthed, "Fine!" before doing what I had hoped he would: shutting his geggie.

Harry remained close to Addie and Kay, his posture revealing he had no business in a place like this. All three were carrying the foodstuff boxes. The stookie angel walked behind them, studying the rear ends of the lasses. Harry fell behind until he walked alongside me. I glanced down at his burden. "Want me tae take that load off yer hands, lad?"

Harry looked up at me. "Nah, I'm good."

"As ye like."

He smiled. "Besides, for all I know, you'd just run off with whatever's packed in here." Then a wee smirk took over his lips. "With all that extra hair, you'd probably trip if you tried to run. I mean, Jesus, man, haven't you ever heard of scissors or a razor?"

I smiled at him, hoping the shape of me lips emerged from the overgrown beard. "That's the sort o' thing ye can expect when ye been locked oop in a dungeon fer months on end."

His face went from smirky to sympathetic in an eye blink. "Ah, shit, man, I'm sorry. I didn't—"

I cut him off with a shake of me head. "Ye meant nae harm, Ah know. Anyway, ye an' yer friends wound oop in mooch the same state as the blatherin' angel an' Ah did, aye?"

His face tightened. "I still think there was more I could have done, more all of us could have done to at least try to fight them."

I nodded at the back of Kay. "The strong lass ahead seems tae disagree with ye."

The lad looked at the ground. "And she's probably right. I just don't wanna believe it." He looked up at me then. "See, back when I was alive, deals were my thing. There wasn't anybody I couldn't talk into or out of something. I just had this natural instinct to be persuasive, you know?"

"Aye."

When he saw my nod, he continued talking. "So when I wound up in that home office nightmare they called Afterlife Enterprises? I figured 'Cool... beats a burning lake of fire by a mile. So maybe I can talk my way outta this." He dropped his hands back to his side as he looked up. "And the funny thing is I was thinking that I nailed it. I laid down my conditions and the guy I'm talking to says it's no problem, making me think I'm getting the better end of the deal."

'Twas practically Besom's story from point to point. I could see where this conversation was headed. "Then it came time tae do the job an' ye found out why AE was so generous, aye, lad?"

The lad's eyes returned to the ground. "I didn't even get close to the soul I'm here to Fed-Ex back up top. I'm not here two minutes before I get caught by these worm dudes with whips."

"The Mephits."

"Yeah, whatever," he said. "Next thing I know, I've got new friends in the same situation and a job I absolutely hate." He looked at me with guarded suspicion. "So... are you and the homeless angel gonna make us pay for bailing our asses out?"

I shrugged. "Ah dinnae know... how good are ye at coottin' hair?" The panic in his eyes gave way to a smile.

He pointed at Jeanne. "So what's her story?"

I decided not to tell him Jeanne was Joan Of Arc. I figured if she wanted that information known, she'd have told him herself. "The most Ah can say is that she's been down here a long time an' she's guided by somethin' she dinnae like tae talk aboot."

Harry put his finger on his chin and started tapping it. "When it comes to this army stuff, she seems to know her shit."

"Nae arguin' that. Ah've had me own share o' battlefields an' she knows as much as Ah do. Still, Ah'd feel better knowin' exactly where we're goin', same as ye."

"You're telling me you don't know where we're going?"

The lad gave me a sharp look and I held up a hand. "Ah'm followin' her jist the same as the rest o' ye."

Harry exhaled a breath out his nose. "Better not tell that to Addie. The last thing she needs to hear is that *nobody's* got a handle on our safari guide."

I was about to answer him when the world suddenly started spinning. I faintly heard a humming in me sword just before I stumbled. I felt meself falling down and Harry was quick to try to stabilize me but I was too large and weighty and caused him to stumble alongside me.

Then all turned to black...

***

I found meself nestled in a meadow of soft, green grass. I looked up and saw the clear blue sky above me. I used me arm to brush the rest of the dirt away. I couldnae ignore a nagging feeling that this felt familiar. I wondered why until I caught a glimpse of me lost and beloved Fergus Castle in the distance.

I only came to this living memory of me home in times of true need. It never failed to remind me of the man I once was.

I pulled meself from the ground and began looking about. No crackle of radio static … everything around me was just as I remembered it. Usually this dreamscape meant I would be visited by Besom but now I was alone.

And as I sat upon the damp earth, I found meself sorely wishing me Besom was nearby.

At the thought, I spotted a person far away and down by the loch. 'Twas mere seconds before this person began racing towards me and when she came into view, I recognized me Besom. She smiled and waved while shouting something but I was too far away to hear her words.

At the sight of her, me legs started moving on their own, quickly going from a walk to a full gallop charge. She crossed half the distance between us before I finally swept her up in me arms. The thrill of feeling her lithe body was divine, and I almost uttered a prayer of thanks to whomever made it possible.

"Lily," I whispered and the happiness within me heart was impossible to keep within.

After I twirled me wee lass 'round a few times, she seized the back of me neck and forced me neck down. I gazed upon her, never wanting to break the path of me eyes for she was so beautiful. I had missed her. Oh, how I had missed her.

Before I could comment, her lips were on mine. And then her tongue was in me mouth. But even if me mouth weren't full of hers, I wouldnae complain. Just to behold her, to feel her within me arms—it was enough. The memories of our last time together surged forth in a rush.

"Lily," I repeated her name and held her to me, never wanting to let go of her again.

"Tallis," she said and pulled away from me, smiling up at me as I held her head in between me hands. I wanted naethin' more than to just look upon her, to fill me eyes with her so I could convince myself she was real and she was safe.

Her first words were a bit of a puzzle. "I can't believe that worked!" In true Besom fashion, she shook her head and contradicted herself in the next breath. "Well, I mean, there was no reason to believe it wouldn't *work. The Flamels looked like they knew what—"*

The mention of the surname made me interrupt her. "Ye dinnae mean Nicolas an Perenelle Flamel, do ye, Besom?"

Lily's face took on an expression I'd come to know well. She was worried she'd made a mistake. "Yeah, uhm... they're not secretly bad people, are they?"

I laughed, a deep and full feeling releasing through me. "Nae... they're good folk, when all's said an' done. If it weren't for that treatise Nicolas pooblished in—"

"He said the work he did on the Philosopher's Stone wasn't really his. Nicolas just transcribed it for... someone else."

I gave her shoulders a gentle squeeze. "I never said it were, lass. Just that pooblishin' it was the reason why he an' his wife wound up in the morgue. Speakin' o' the Eighth Circle, I'm guessin' that's where ye are right now?"

She let out a shaky breath. "Yes." She looked about herself for danger we both knew wasnae there.

"After the way I left, I'm pretty sure Alaire wants me back worse than ever. I took off with his prize spirit."

I felt me teeth clenching at the reference to me passenger. *"Has Donnchadh—"*

She put up her hands. *"I've got him under control, now anyway. Now... what happened after Alaire threw you out of the castle?"*

We spent the next few minutes relating our adventures. Besom was proud beyond words that the wee angel saved me hide back in the Asylum. She even muttered, *"Maybe there's hope for the little lecher yet."*

For me own part, I was properly impressed with me Besom. She had nae only managed to keep Donnchadh in check but she had also survived a plane crash, captured the Red Baron, and applied all me lessons of bladecraft to a fight against six demons and humans.

When we finished swapping anecdotes, Besom's face took another look I'd come to know well: deep thought. *"If I'm reading between the lines correctly, it sounds like Alaire is supplying both sides of this civil war. He helped the Flamels by providing ingredients for their alchemy, which only aids the Malebranche. But if Bill's right, it sounds like Alaire's also funneling arms down to the Council of Simon through those dummy shipments."*

There was still one other part of this puzzle that Besom had no way of knowing. *"Maybe nae jist arms, lass. There's nae many demons that will follow mortal souls, especially ones that were their prisoners nae so long ago. Fer such an arrangement, the orders moost come from someone far greater than them."*

To her credit, she understood fairly quickly. *"Like, say, the current Master of the Underground City giving them an ultimatum?"*

I smiled. *"The very same, Lily, me love. Weapons are a good start fer any fight. But even without 'em, the*

162

likes o' those worm beasties would overwhelm any human troops in nae more than a fortnight."

Besom took her right hand away from me and rubbed her temples as though she were overwhelmed. "But why do any of this at all? The weapons, troops, and infrastructure... everything is getting wrecked the longer this war goes on. Why doesn't Alaire just back one side or the other and be done with it?"

I shook me head. "Nae, Alaire learned tae fight from the bastard Romans. Divide and conquer was how they prevailed... Git the enemies fightin' against each other, weakenin' the other through a long battle an' then sweep in tae take the territory o' the winnin' side afore they can regroup."

'Twas the very same tactic the Romans had used on me and me kin to claim our lands.

"Okay, when you put it like that, it makes sense. But why would Alaire do this in territory that's already technically his? Doesn't the Malebranche answer to him the same way everyone else in the Underground City does?"

Me smile turned rueful. "That's so, lass, but it dinnae mean them dukes aren't always plottin' a way tae git out from oonderneath Alaire's thumb. Mayhap Alaire got wind o' a plot o' theirs. Mayhap he jist decided tae make sure nae such plot comes tae pass. Either way, the fightin' continues apace."

"And then there's Jeanne." Besom looked upon me with a suspicious sort of cast to her eyes. I winced. I had a nasty suspicion this part of the conversation might make me long for a rematch with the Wendigo in the Asylum.

"I swear tae ye, Besom, there's naethin' goin' on—
"

She flashed me a smile and stroked me bare chest in reassurance. "And I believe you, you big, silly Scotsman. From what you've told me, Jeanne sounds like the kind of woman I would have called a friend back when I was..." Her voice trailed off and she looked down at herself. "...Not like I am now."

I could sense something else behind the words. "Is there somethin' I can help ye with, lass?"

She bit her lip as she looked up. "I don't know." Her face relaxed again. "Getting back to Jeanne... you think she might have been another Soul Retriever who got stuck down here after AE screwed her over?"

I shrugged. Even as Joan of Arc, it stood to reason that maybe Jeanne had more recently been offered the position of Soul Retriever? Certainly, she didnae belong down here an' she wasnae an escaped spirit who belonged in the Kingdom. "'Tis possible but that still dinnae explain how she were able tae repel the Spites? An' it wouldnae explain whose voice she hears."

"Or how, if she's a first-timer in this Circle like me, she knows all about this place."

This comment, I could address. "Well, she spent a good many days attendin' tae Epimetheus. An' she made some friends who may well have been down here even longer."

That earned a nod from Besom. "Okay, that leads me to my next question. This level is supposed to be made up of those who practiced magic, right?"

"Aye."

"As far as I've seen, there haven't been a whole lot of magically inclined people here." She shrugged. "How many people in this circle can really be called 'wizards'? Even if they aren't Merlin or Gandalf or Dumbledore, you'd think they'd stand out from the other prisoners stuck here."

"Ah'd only be guessin' if I ventured tae answer ye."

There was something I wanted to tell her since laying eyes on her again. As I grabbed her shoulders in me hands, I decided now was the time. "Lass, there's a

164

shortcoot tae the Dark Wood in this Circle. If'n I tell ye where it lies, will ye go there an' wait fer me?"

Her eyes grew as steely as the blade I had made for her. "I know you didn't just suggest what I think you did."

I sighed and tightened me grip upon her shoulders. "Every second ye stay down here is another that Alaire could use tae git ye back in his clootches."

If anything, her eyes grew harder. "The same goes double for you... and probably Bill too, at this point. And now that you're without Donnchadh, you're susceptible to whatever atrocities Alaire has in mind for you."

"Ah still possess me own Druid magic, Besom," I insisted.

"It's not enough," she said as she closed the distance between us and looped her arms 'round me neck. "I want to make sure you escape this horrible place just as much as I want to escape it, Tallis."

Why did Besom pick now, of all times, to live up to her nickname? "Now that Ah'm a free man, I can take care o' meself long enough tae—"

Lily pummeled me chest with a pair of meaty slaps before bracing her face against me. "Either all three of us leave together or none of us do."

As ever, I sighed at her ingrained stubbornness. "An' there's nae a thing Ah can say tae change yer mind, is there?"

She looked up at me and smiled in that girlish way of hers. "What do you think?"

Right after she released her hold 'round me body, she continued. "Have you considered that maybe Jeanne is leading you and everyone else into a trap?"

I shook me head. "An' here I thought ye said ye wasnae jealous."

"Not jealous, just aware, Tallis," she corrected me. *"If Jeanne weren't a young and pretty girl, would you be so trusting of her?"*

Great Morrigan, when did she become so suspicious? "Ah've long troosted me own senses when it comes tae knowin' what sort o' person someone is. Ah believe Jeanne tae be genuine enough. She isnae traitor. But Ah cannae say the same fer her friends."

"Yeah, that was my thought too. We both know Retrievers have a track record of going bad down here. Hell, for all we know, they may be inside agents for Alaire, playing games to keep the conflict going."

Her face settled into a thoughtful expression again. "You know, between what you've told me about Jeanne and what the Flamels told me about themselves, I'm really wondering how many undeserving people are actually down here in the Underground City."

Me guilt hit me chest at those simple words. "'Tis me disgrace that only now, long after Ah coulda done somethin' aboot it, that Ah'm wonderin' the same."

"That was long ago and you're a different person now, Tallis," Besom said with a curt nod. Then she changed the subject. "And what's the deal with the Spites? Are they the reason Alaire launched this master plan that..."

The light of the overhead sun began to fade. And 'twas far from the only thing that was waning. The rest of the landscape around us became less and less solid. It was also beginning to glow as it faded. I released me Besom and looked upon her one last time.

"We've talked as much as we are allowed, Besom."

She seized me hands and yanked me down to her level, giving me a quick, warm kiss upon the lips before pulling away. "I'll find you, Tallis Black... no matter what it takes."

Before I could reply, all the scenery turned white...

"Thus cried I with my face uprais'd..."
-Dante's Inferno

SEVENTEEN
TALLIS

I awoke to something hitting me cheek. 'Twas soft
enough to be a hand. The voice that accompanied it
told me at once to whom it belonged.

"Don't you freakin' die on me, sasquatch!"

When the hand hit me left cheek, I grabbed it and
opened me eyes. As expected, 'twas the angel. What
surprised me was the panic on the stookie angel's
face. I'd only seen him so worried over Besom.

I grunted as I propped meself up on me elbows.
"Good Lleu, man, how's beatin' me down soopposed
tae wake me oop?"

"Fuckin' fuck," he grumbled as the wee fellow let
out a relieved breath and turned to the rest of our
traveling group. "Now that we know the yeti ain't dead,
where's that grub?" He punctuated his demand with a
few fast claps with his hands.

The well-built Kay approached with a piece of
dried meat. The aroma made me think 'twas from the
Dark Wood. With the look of an angry nursemaid, she
handed me the food.

"Why didn't you say you were starving?" she
demanded. "It's not like we're short on food supplies."

I caught the look in the angel's eyes. Wee fellow
knew it wasnae the lack of food that dropped me. But
he wanted to preserve me dignity, me secrets or both
by telling them such.

167

In between bites, I answered her. "Wanted tae at least git somewhere closer to a safe place before Ah dug in, lass. The rest o' ye could well have been hoongrier than me or the stookie angel here."

She gave the angel the stink-eye. "After watching him stress-eat? He gobbled one of our boxes empty!"

I glared at the bloody angel for being his usual indulgent self. He just threw up his hands. "What? The grub was there, so I chow-bow-wowed down. So sue me!"

I looked up at Kay who was still standing over both of us. "Please tell me he left somethin' fer the rest o' ye."

Her smile reminded me of an executioner with whom I was once face to face. "Let's just say he knows to leave well enough alone from now on." As soon as I finished me meal, she stretched out her sinewy hand. "Need a hand up?"

I clasped me hand in hers. "Ah'll nae say no, lass."

It took a bit of effort on her part but she pulled me back to me feet. That's when I noticed some of our crew were missing. "Where's Jeanne and Addie?"

Harry, who'd been standing in front of the food boxes, angled his head back towards the next block. "They went on ahead of us. Jeanne said to come find her whenever you woke up."

Kay gave an exasperated sigh before looking back at me. "So, you steady enough on your feet now, Mr. T?"

Harry gave her a look. "Oh, you did not just call him Mr. T!"

It took me a moment afore I realized they were both talking about me. The angel began laughing heartily. "Gotta say, yo, I'm likin' Harry-man's new nickname fer the big galoot."

I held up me hands. If I hadnae, they'd be gabbing about this well into next week. "Names aside, aye, Ah'm more than able tae keep goin'."

Harry pointed at me. "Yeah? Then let's get this show on the road!"

Kay nodded before taking point. I had nae idea how she planned to handle anything coming at us without any weapon of her own. Mayhap she was trained in martial arts or the such. After me little collapse, she probably had doubts as to whether I were in any shape to fight, blade or nae blade.

The stookie angel fell in line with me as we trudged onward. "Well... all that went better than I extrapolated."

I noted the plastic case he carried by the handle. "Still looggin' that piece o' machinery 'round, Ah see."

He nodded, his face growing serious. "Soon as we're in a genu-wine safe spot, I'm gonna make that call I tried to make on the way up from the Asylum, yo."

I hummed at a high pitch. "Assumin' that machine's in decent enough shape, nae reason why ye shouldnae try agin."

The angel got a shrewd look and quieter voice. "Now that we're out o' ear-shock o' the kids, wanna tell me what all that fallin' down was about?"

I answered him in a murmur of me own. "Aye... 'twas Besom. She reached out tae me. She is close."

The angel damn near choked upon his own tongue. "Wait, what? How'd she do *that*?"

"Dinnae rightly know, man," I answered. Even though Besom and I shared a certain connection that had allowed us to communicate in the past, I wasnae certain this most recent incident was a case in point or mayhap it should have been attributed to the sorcery of the Flamels. "Besom mentioned roonnin' intae some magical folk. They're the reason we could talk fer... how long was Ah out agin?"

That annoyed the wee fellow. "How the hell should I know, yo? I was too busy lookin' at you to make sure you wasn't dead! I wasn't keepin' track of the time."

It took all me strength to ignore me own frustration but I was still hungry and exhausted to boot. "Christ, man! Did it seem a few minutes, seconds, an hour, what?!"

After giving me a growl, he almost looked ashamed of himself. "Well, definitely wasn't no hour but... a little longer than a few minutes." Then he changed the subject. "Anyways, back ta Lils... where's she at?"

"Ah've nae idea regardin' the particulars. All Ah know is she's somewhere in the morgue."

The angel pulled his head back in surprise. "What, Blondie finally got tired of her?"

"Nae, she escaped him. Only reason she's down here is tae come git oos."

The wee angel's face fell again. "Dammit, it's supposed ta be the other way around. We're supposed to be gettin' her!"

"Och aye," I said with a nod. "Dinnae forget that Ah swore tae protect her..."

"Well, we both did a bang up job on that."

"At least she be close by to oos now," I said with a weary sigh.

"Does that mean you're happy she's in the morgue? Frickin' place was the worst, yo! I ain't happy poor nips is stuck there at all! Damn, yo, you're a weirdo! Know what makes me happy? Beer, grill porn, strippers, Netflix..."

"Grill whit?"

170

"Them catalogs that come out 'round July 4th all about barbecues an' smokers." He took a breath. "The things that make you happy are f'd up, Tido."

Sweet Bran, but he could be tiresome! "Happy? Ah amnae happy aboot Besom bein' in the morgue, ye addled dunderheid! Boot there's nothin' fer it. She's there an' we're here an' the sooner we git ourselves tae her, the better."

The angel looked over at the kids we'd pulled from the camp. If they heard the two of us jabbering, they gave no sign. "Didja tell Lils where we were?"

"Aye, Ah mentioned it."

His face held an expression I didnae think he ever could be: thoughtful. "Before Jeannie and Queen Addie took off, Jeannie said we weren't too far from our final destination, maybe ten blocks or so."

"'Tis good news indeed." It didnae seem like a good idea to add my doubts. I simply hoped 'twould work out as we planned.

***

LILY

My head felt like it was stuffed with steel wool when I came to. Every part of my body felt as hard and stiff as the tiles I was lying on. Even opening my eyes was enough to make me groan.

Back when I was alive, I'd tried some astral projection experiments for hours and didn't get anywhere. Now that I'd succeeded—with a little help from the Flamels, of course—I was wondering if my early failures were such a bad thing after all.

My vision was a little blurry before it cleared enough to see Perenelle kneeling next to me. She popped open a vial and put it to my lips. "Drink this, *Mademoiselle* Harper... slowly."

171

I opened my mouth wide enough for her to pour the contents down my throat. It burned like cheap rum. But a few minutes later, the rest of my body felt a bit more fluid, enough that I could move.

Nicolas's wife nodded with approval. "*Mieux?*"

I squinted at her. "I'm not a cat."

She grinned and shook her head. "*Pardonne-moi.* What I meant to say is... do you feel better?"

I rolled my shoulders forward. "Yeah, good enough to stand, anyway."

Despite my declaration, Perenelle made a point of supporting my right arm and elbow to make sure I didn't fall again. I saw my blade leaning against one of the freestanding shower walls. When I started for it, I spotted Nicolas beside the barely open door. He held a stoppered vial in his hand like it was a grenade.

He relaxed a little when I stepped in front of him and offered my sword. "I'm surprised you're not using my sword in your attempts to locate my friends?"

Nicolas shrugged. "In any struggle, one is always better off using one's preferred tools. And I have never been much of a swordsman."

I pointed at the vial. "Does that one explode too?" I asked, recalling my introduction to Nicolas when Manfred shot the vial and it exploded into a downpour of glass.

Nicolas shook his head while turning his attention toward the cracked door. "*Non.* The Devouring Lion is a rather strong acid which can eat metal and flesh with equal ferocity. But it does not explode."

I instinctively took a few steps back. And here I thought demons were fierce.

Perenelle lightly touched my shoulder. "Were you successful in making contact with Tallis Black, *mon enfant?*" The smile I gave her made my nod redundant but I nodded anyway.

172

I spent the next few minutes telling them about my conversation with Tallis... well, most of the conversation. I left out the easy exit from this Circle to the Dark Wood. For one, I didn't have any idea where the shortcut was. For another, telling them now might give them the perfect excuse to ditch me later.

When I was finished recounting the details, Nicolas and Perenelle looked at each other and exchanged a mutual sigh. I couldn't really blame them. "Yeah, that's about how I felt. Even though we made contact, it's not like we can just GPS each other's location," I started and then realized they probably had no idea what GPS even was. I smiled and explained: "It's not like there's a directory down here."

Perenelle nodded but the frown on her face suggested there was more to it.

Nicolas stepped between us and frowned a bit. "It is certainly in all our best interests to rendezvous with your friends as soon as is feasible."

Perenelle frowned. "But it still does not answer the open question of *how* we are to rendezvous with Tallis Black and the angel, dear husband. Had we the time to experiment, I would propose we modify the ritual we just performed as a way to locate them."

"We do not have the time, my dear," Nicolas said. "Every second that lapses, our safety becomes more in question."

I felt my jaw clenching. "I thought you said this place was safe."

Nicolas didn't miss a beat. "*Oui*, for now it is. But there is always later, *n'est-ce pas*? As talented as you are in the arts of war, we both know you are no match for an army of sufficient strength and size."

Perenelle held up her finger. "The same cannot be said of Tallis Black, however. His prowess at bringing

173

whole armies to heel is legendary in the Underground City. Such a man would prove an asset to us."

"That reminds me..." I started as Nicolas gave me his direct attention. "You said something about escaping the lab being a strict no-no with the Malebranche and Alaire. Does the fact that you're hiding out here mean you're in trouble with both of them?"

Nicolas shook his head. "Not necessarily. Should Perenelle and I return within... let us say a day's time, there would be no 'hard feelings.' Is that how you say it?"

His wife harrumphed at his statement. "I am far less confident than Nicolas in both parties' understanding nature. For the 'crime' of abandoning our post a third time, we could well be taken prisoner or even outright killed as punishment for our continued disobedience."

"It sounds like your best bet is to throw in with the rebels, the Council of Simon?"

Perenelle didn't take that suggestion well. "Need I remind you that these self-same barbarians were quite eager to execute us before your timely intervention? Why should we think that an attempted defection to their cause would secure us your desired result?"

Nicolas hummed with equal parts of disapproval and deep thought. "Do be less harsh on our protector's suggestions, dear wife. She merely wishes that we—"

"*Oui, oui*, husband. But it makes her suggestions no less unworkable." Taking a breath, she looked at me and smiled. "I confess that I am put off by the sheer arrogance of the Council of Simon. They hold the erroneous belief that their many years of imprisonment qualify them to be the new masters of this Circle."

I tapped my chin. "And you think because it's such a self-defeating circle jerk, the damned have no business leading the damned?"

Perenelle sighed and gave me a look I couldn't decipher. "I have to admit that your colloquialisms seem to come in only two categories: those beyond the scope of my knowledge or those that are crude to the point of pornography."

I grinned at her. "Compared to my guardian angel, Bill, I'm a complete amateur where crude is concerned, but I apologize if I offended you. Seems Bill is rubbing off on me."

That's what she said, I said to myself and then groaned.

Nicolas grinned. "Even so, dear Perenelle, you must admit that our little warrior perfectly captured the essence of your counter argument. And perhaps you will recall that I suggested the same regarding joining the rebels after the first raid."

"I feel outnumbered," Perenelle said with a frown.

I raised both my hands. "Guys, look, I'm not taking anyone's side with this conversation. I'm just like you... trying to figure out the best way forward."

Nicolas's face turned grave. "Indeed... Which is why I am increasingly inclined to think Perenelle and I should join your exodus from the morgue altogether."

I was debating whether now might be a good time to mention Tallis's emergency exit through the Dark Wood when Perenelle responded to her husband. "And where would we go upon making such an exit, hmm? It has been centuries since we trod the world above. We have no friends nor allies waiting for us there."

"And we have even less friends and allies down here," Nicolas argued. "It is difficult to escape the feeling that the list of our enemies continues to grow with each new raid on the laboratory. The situation is becoming untenable."

I replied with a bit of verse that suddenly popped up in my head. "*Turning and turning in the widening gyre, the falcon cannot hear the falconer; Things fall apart; the center cannot hold; Mere anarchy is loosed upon the world, The blood-dimmed tide is loosed, and everywhere, The ceremony of innocence is drowned.*"

"Returning to behold the radiant stars..."
-Dante's Inferno

EIGHTEEN
LILY

Perenelle and Nicolas looked at me in awe.

"That is lovely," Perenelle said on a sigh.

I shrugged as I glanced between them. "It's by a poet: William Butler Yeats. He was a little after your time."

Nicolas nodded in appreciation. "To hear such verse, one would think *Monsieur* Yeats had endured our own trials and tribulations in this place. Regardless of who triumphs in this conflict, the winning side will likely dispose of us once our usefulness comes to an end."

Perenelle's face paled. "Perhaps such a fate need not be so terrible. So long as we go together, the pain will be lessened."

Nicolas sagged against the wall like a deflated balloon. "I do admit that I am growing weary of this constant struggle. And the obstacles in escaping from the Underground City are as formidable as you have implied."

That fatalistic talk made my temper kick into overdrive. Donnchadh was behind a lot of it but I was pretty irritated on my own. *Donnchadh, I summon you to manifest your presence in my eyes until I've scared them out of this shitty plan they're hatching.*

When my vision started developing a crimson haze around it, I realized I was in the process of

177

getting what I asked for. The trick now was making sure I kept Donnchadh in check.

Once they caught sight of my eyes, Perenelle took a few steps back in fear while Nicolas prepared to toss his vial my way. I could hear the roughness of Donnchadh's voice overlaying my own while I talked. "Surrender is the dumbest idea either of you could choose. These bastards will never offer you anything other than an eternity of torture. You'll be brutalized and made to watch each other suffer forever." I felt my vocal cords tightening as I struggled to spit out the next words. "While we are together, there will be no surrender... no pity... no mercy... no—"

Dammit, Donnchadh was fighting me for control and this time, I could feel him pulling out all the stops. My hand only got halfway to my blade before he stopped it cold. I forced my hand to keep going while he kept pushing back against it. It was like arm wrestling a ghost.

Even when I forced my hand up nearly to the hilt of my sword, I suddenly weakened. Donnchadh turned out to be much stronger and more prepared than I'd assumed. If I didn't grab my sword in the next few seconds, he would do a full takeover and then we'd all be screwed.

Fight him, Lily! I yelled at myself.

I clenched my eyes as I collected all the memories of people I ever cared about—my mom, Bill, Tallis. The thought of Tallis made Donnchadh recoil a bit before he started pushing against me even harder.

Noting Donnchadh's reaction to my thoughts of Tallis encouraged me keep my mind fixed on my bladesmith... my guide... my lover. Tallis had endured this monster for centuries and Tallis had ultimately prevailed over Donnchadh. Tallis had found the inner strength to keep this angry spirit at bay, and had done so for centuries.

178

I pictured a flash of the tree tattoo on Tallis's back before Donnchadh's hold on my hand weakened. He was still fighting me but he wasn't quite as strong now. I continued imagining the black ink outline of the tree's branches as I felt my hand rising up to the blade of my sword.

I felt the unmistakeable burn of Donnchadh's anger deep within me as he was forced back to the deep recesses of my psyche.

Exhaustion suddenly claimed me and I leaned back against the freestanding wall as I fought to catch my breath. Goddamn, that was too close.

Both the Flamels looked too stunned to do more than stare at me. I took a deep breath before saying, "Remind me never to use Donnchadh as a motivational speaker."

Perenelle still looked astonished. She faced her husband. "Is there any remaining doubt as to this spirit's true nature?"

Nicolas's head shake was slow and deliberate. "None whatsoever... only a Spite would manifest itself in such a fashion."

That accusation got enough adrenaline pumping in me to make me stand up straighter. "That can't be. Yeah, Donnchadh's the spiritual equivalent of the devil but he—"

Nicolas slid his words into my statement like he was sticking a scalpel into my skin. "...has far more power than any mere spirit should possess, regardless of its age. I should know... much of my time in the Malebranche's service was spent writing treatises on these awful spirits."

Perenelle's face grew sad. "And an equal portion of my own has been spent hunting down their true history. Hard though it may be to accept, *mon enfant*, you are indeed host to a Spite."

179

I didn't doubt their sincerity, but I was sure they weren't correct in their assumptions. If Donnchadh were truly a Spite, Tallis would have known about it. And more so, he would have told me... right?

"Oh, c'mon!" I said as I waved away their wide-eyed surprise. "Since Donnchadh got rammed into my subconscious, I've been reliving his mortal memories. Last time I checked, no Spite could ever walk across a battlefield as a man, which Donnchadh was."

To his credit, Nicolas didn't dismiss my comment. "You are fully certain these memories are of this Donnchadh and not some mortal that he—"

Inspiration lit up Perenelle's eyes and she swung her head to her husband. At the same time, they said the same word. "Rebis."

Having no idea what they were talking about managed to cool my temper down. "Should that word mean something to me?"

Perenelle looked over at me again and put a gentle hand on my shoulder. "Rebis is the final aspirational goal of the alchemical Magnum Opus, the complete merging of opposites into one whole being."

"Um... what?"

Nicolas looked a little sad. "In the usual sense, the rebis is the result of great spiritual, emotional and physical trials that improve the person undergoing it. But in this instance, something far more terrible has occurred, I fear."

I let the new information sink in before responding. "So... what you're saying is that somehow, Donnchadh merged with a Spite on the spiritual level and that's why he's such a flaming asshole now?"

Perenelle gave me a chuckle that sounded anything but amused. "Would that it were so simple, *Mademoiselle* Harper. For such a union to be possible, there have to be similarities between the two beings that are gradually brought to the surface."

"Indeed, dear wife," Nicolas concurred. "It is more likely that your Donnchadh was already quite horrible when he was a mere man. I shudder to think what processes of putrefaction were employed to make the being within you possible."

But there was one missing piece to the puzzle. "But Spites strip their victims down to the bone. How would Donnchadh have lasted long enough to be—?"

Nicolas cut me off with a raised finger. "This current incarnation of the Spites is also the end result of a long process of purification, albeit of a vastly different bent. In the earliest days, the Spites could possess a mortal if the host contained a sufficient amount of hatred within him or her."

Perenelle looked up at the ceiling and sighed. "Not that such mortals lasted long. The relentless fury of the Spite within them drove them into murderous frenzies which would always end with the host being destroyed by his comrades."

I covered my discomfort by clearing my throat. "So, uh, for Donnchadh to have bonded with this Spite, he had to have beat those odds, right? Lasting longer than all other possessed people?"

Perenelle met my eyes cautiously. "As improbable as such a hypothesis may seem, I can think of no better explanation based on what we have observed thus far."

Nicolas nodded. "So far as I can tell, there is now no real difference between this Donnchadh and a Spite. They have become one and the same."

Perenelle's eyes took on a distant look as she repeated under her breath. "One and the same..."

Nicolas held up his vial and shook its liquid contents slightly. "What you carry inside you makes this compound safe as purified water."

181

Perenelle startled both of us by slapping the wall. "I have it!"

As she delved into her apron, I asked her, "Just so we're on the same page, what exactly do you have?"

She dug up a couple of vials and looked at me with a grin. "A way to find your friends, of course! And it all goes back to your blade."

Nicolas gave her the look I'd seen from numerous husbands toward their wives. It usually happened when the former didn't understand what the latter was getting at. "As both of us would like to assist you, Perenelle, would you care to elaborate?"

His wife put both of the vials in one hand and snapped her fingers with the other. "Bring forth some powdered mandrake root, my husband, and I shall explain."

Since Perenelle's new plan centered on my blade, I pulled it out and held it to her. She uncapped both the vials with her thumb and poured their liquid contents on the length of the blade. To my concerned stare, she shook her head.

"No harm is being done to this fine weapon, I assure you. However, it is being repurposed to serve as the solution to your dilemma."

By this point, Nicolas had crossed over to his wife, handing her what I guessed was the requested vial of powder. His eyes never left the door, however, and he was quickly back at his post before Perenelle finished adding the powder to the liquids. Once that happened, the whole blade began to give off a faint glow and I felt a sudden tug to the right. The glow intensified even more when I let the sword swing in the direction it wanted to go.

Perenelle put the vials away and clapped her hands. "*Merveilleux! Impressionnant! Prodigieux!*"

I raised an eyebrow at her. "I take it this is a good thing?"

182

"Oh, the best, *Mademoiselle* Harper, the best! Because the sword was forged by Tallis Black, himself, and you share a deep connection to both it and him, the sword can now lead us directly to his location."

Nicolas cautiously opened the door a bit wider. "Then may I suggest we be on our way? Just because danger has yet to show itself does not mean it will never arrive."

I noticed that I had some trouble pulling the blade away from the direction it was pointing. "Is this enchantment going to alter my ability to use my sword if I need to?"

Perenelle let out an aggravated growl before slapping her head with both hands. "Idiot! I should have remembered that part of the formula."

Nicolas pursed his lips before swinging the door the rest of the way open. "Perhaps a tincture of argent salt will mitigate any ill effects?"

Perenelle clapped her hands together. "*Parfait*! You do, of course, have some?"

I decided they needed a push. "Uh, guys, not to be rude but could we sort this out on the road? I'm with Nicolas; I don't want to stay here any longer than we need to."

Nicolas looked between me and the now-enchanted blade. "Will you be able to move the blade sufficiently to exit?"

It took a little more effort to make that happen but I did all the same. By the time Nicolas retrieved the argent salt, we were already heading in the direction the sword was pointing.

"When thou with pleasure shalt retrace the past..."
-Dante's Inferno

NINETEEN
TALLIS

Me heart sank as soon as I saw the pennant hanging over the pile of rubble that at one time had been a building.

The banner was a simple design, a white horse prancing across a black background. 'Twas nae just the flag that caused me reserve. Even more concerning was what existed above the banner and the rubble pile: trees. Nae just any trees, either, but the sort of healthy, living trees that have nae business existing in the Underground City, never mind the morgue. It bore the signature of only one wizard. I cursed me bad luck.

What I heard next made me guts clench: laughter. It wasnae just the wizard's laughter. I recognized Jeanne's voice in the chorus of three.

"Bloody hell," I grumbled.

The stookie angel, doing his best to carry one of the foodstuff boxes, gave me a nervous look. "That bad, Conan?"

I looked down at the wee fool as though I was about to charge a battlement. "When it comes tae the Welshman, it always turns out worse than ye can imagine."

He nodded slowly, looking back at the trees. "Well, he ain't gonna pull no Costcop shit on me..."

Kay looked at me. "What's he talking about?"

184

The angel faced her with a stern expression. "Costcop, yo! The Po-Po at Costco who won't let you leave the damn place without checkin' your receipt!"

Kay faced me. "What's wrong with him?"

"Ah dinnae know, lass, boot tae often have Ah asked meself the same question."

Kay shook her head and then brought her hands to her hips. "Who is this Welshman? And why is he such bad news?"

I nodded towards the pennant. "'Tis a wizard an' a powerful one at that. His proper name's Gwydion fab Don, nephew tae Mag the Ancient, starter o' wars, breaker o' oaths an' ruiner o' far tae many lives. An' that's on his good days."

Harry blanched at me description of the Welshman, clutching his own box closer as though 'twas a loved one. "Oh shit! And Jeanne's just up there acting like nothing's—"

"O' course she is, lad," I nearly spat back at the boy. "Gwydion is charmin' when ye dinnae know his tricks." Then me brow darkened as I added, "'Tis a damned good thing Ah do."

I started to step forward but Kay gripped me arm. "Tallis..."

I looked down at her and saw her concern as I shook me head in exasperation. "Fer the last time, lass, Ah'm fine. Ye dinnae have tae—"

The muscular woman would have none of my explanations, pushing me back a step. "If that wizard's as bad as you're saying, I want first crack at him."

"Nae, lass," I began but Harry interrupted me.

Tucking his box under his arm, he grabbed Kay's arm and tried to tug her back. He'd have had better luck moving a boulder. "You don't know what you're saying, Kay!"

She eluded his grip and turned her grim eyes towards me and then the broken path ahead. "If the wizard does anything to me, Bigfoot, cut him down."

That would be the moment when the angel decided to be stupid. He set his box down and pushed ahead of all of us. "The problem with all o' youze is that you're mortal an' can still get killed."

"So?" Kay insisted, hands on her hips.

The angel glared at her. "So ain't nobody playin' mar-turd today. Ima do it myself."

I reached down to grab the stookie angel. "Dammit, ye dunderheid!"

The wee fellow barely dodged the swipe of me hand but 'twas enough to escape me. A second later, he was off towards Gwydion's camp, marching as though he were leading a battalion into battle.

The stookie angel moved faster than I imagined him capable. But all those months of starving had taken off enough blubber to increase his speed.

Harry dropped his box and ran past me other shoulder, trying to catch up to him. "Hold up, Shorty!"

But the angel had already disappeared 'round the corner. The lad was nae slouch a runner himself and he stayed on the stookie angel's heels before disappearing after him.

I shook me own head in frustration as I hoisted the dropped boxes from the ground, placing them upon either of me shoulders. "Guess we're all goin' oop then!"

Kay didnae try to stop me this time. As I rounded the corner meself, I could make out her steps right behind me. In between strides, I took the time to mutter a few choice words in Gaelic that would hopefully serve me at some point in time.

***

186

The pennant and trees surrounded a canvas tent. This tent had the same look as those from Custer's camp, causing me to wonder if the Welshman came alone. The four trees—which I realized were oaks now that I was closer—formed four corners and a perimeter 'round the tent. Inside the perimeter grew verdant green grass that was better suited to Fergus Castle than this horrid place.

Me attention shifted to the angel as he began yelling incoherently at a young man with a hawkish, handsome face. The man laughed as though the stookie angel had told him a funny joke.

The man wore a simple yet finely tailored jerkin and trousers. He was thin—but nae scrawny—and his auburn hair fell to his shoulders. He casually sat upon the grass, leaning his back against one of the oak trees as though he hadnae a care in the world. And he wore his usual grin, which was as clear as his deep green eyes were bright. He appeared to be in a jolly mood. And why nae? Gwydion delighted at making people angry with him, deliberately or otherwise.

I dropped the two boxes of food rations as soon as I stepped foot inside the perimeter of the wizard's encampment. Then I unsheathed me sword and prepared meself for whatever lay ahead.

When the Welshman continued to laugh at the now outraged angel, the walloper did something I didnae see coming. He walked up to Gwydion, pulled back his flabby arm and punched him right in his face!

Gwydion, still laughing, allowed his head to roll back with the punch and standing to his impressive height, shoved the wee angel towards the tent. The angel fell over his own feet and landed upon his arse in the dirt which sent Gwydion into peals of laughter.

187

Harry thought such a time a good one to involve himself and went for Gwydion, but the Welshman caught him 'round the throat with his bare hand and threw him. The poor lad was launched into the air as though he had been fired from a cannon before gravity embraced him again.

"Harry!" Kay called out after him, shock and horror plaguing her face.

As Harry fell, I focused what remaining energy I possessed into the grass knoll that appeared just below him. Channeling me Druid magic, I imagined the knoll recessing into the earth as though it were a huge, padded net and below it, naethin' but air.

When Harry touched down, the grass appeared to gobble him up which startled Kay but seconds later, the ground spat him out again. He appeared whole and unscathed. And surprised. As was Kay, who turned to me with wide eyes as though to ask if such was my doing. But my attention was nae longer upon the lad. Instead, I watched the tent where Jeanne was just emerging. The angel began stumbling across the uneven ground, nearly falling over himself. But Jeanne caught him before he lost his balance.

Addie walked out of the tent right behind Jeanne, looking as though she just stepped out of a bath as her hair was wet. When I glanced back at Jeanne, I noticed her clothing was much cleaner and in better repair. Addie, too, wore an improved version of her former wardrobe.

Addie's eyes widened when she watched Harry slowly picking himself up from the ground.

Jeanne glared at her host. "Why did you treat them so roughly, Gwydion?"

The Welshman's laughter died down as he shrugged as though to say 'twas nae his fault. "Well, I couldn't very well allow either of them to attack me, now could I?" His eyes were now firmly fixed on the trio standing before his tent. "And since I didn't want to cause them any undue harm—"

Me shadow fell over him like a dark cloud, thanks to the fact that I was a good two feet taller. I held me broadsword at the ready. "That'd be a first, Welshman."

Gwydion turned 'round slowly, which was smart. If he moved tae quickly, I'd have felled him where he stood. His shining eyes didnae lose one whit of amusement as he smiled up at me as though we were long lost comrades. I didnae return it.

"Ah, Tallis Black." He paused to smile even more broadly. I felt me stomach drop. "Even though the circumstances are less than ideal, it's good to see you again."

I leaned over him far enough that me beard fell into his face. "Forgit yer pleasantries, nephew o' Mag. Ye know as well as Ah that we are nae friends."

I looked past him to see Addie, Jeanne and the angel tensing. Harry, who stood closer to the wizard, seemed ready to strike another blow at his head but looked at me for the order.

Gwydion pretended not to notice his surroundings, instead centering his full attention on the rapidly approaching Kay who looked as though she were ready and able to commit murder.

Gwydion gave her a careful look before shifting his gaze to the others. Then he glanced up at me again. "I was under the impression you were in need of help. Was I mistaken?"

Harry's voice sounded behind me. "Wait, he wants to help us?"

I threw up me hands without taking me eyes off the Welshman. "Nae, lad, dinnae be fooled sae easily," I grumbled as I narrowed me eyes upon the wizard.

"The lad hasn't been fooled," Gwydion announced, shaking his head. "I do wish you help you."

189

Me glare grew more pronounced. "An' whit exactly dae ye git outta helpin' oos?"

He shrugged as he turned his back to me. "Oh, goodwill, a future favor, the knowledge that some poor, deserving souls are getting the aid they so desperately need…"

Harry stepped closer to the wizard. Gwydion snapped his head 'round, his eyes and smile taking a hard edge. "Careful, young one. I admire your fighting spirit, but tread carefully."

Harry didn't flinch. "Not to question your motives, but Tallis here talks like you're one slippery SOB. Is he wrong?"

The Welshman chuckled the way he always did when confronted with the truth. He even patted the lad's shoulder a few times. "You would do well to listen to your guide, son," he said as Harry frowned, clearly confused.

Gywdion continued. "Given that I arranged the rape of my sister, restarted the war between North and South Wales, and executed enough misdeeds to incur a year of humiliating transformations, I have more than earned my place in this Circle." He eyed the rest of us, his smirk broadening. "I do believe I am rather… unique among this Circle's residents."

The stookie angel walked up behind him. "Ya do realize that yer not exactly argumenting the case fer trustin' you, right?" he asked whilst he rubbed his bum which was obviously sore from his scrap with the wizard earlier.

Gwydion shrugged as he regarded the much smaller man. "Lying is no way to do business, little angel." Then he looked up at me. "And neither are threats."

Addie approached the angel. "Look, guys, I'd be the first to tell you if I thought this was a trap. But Gwydion has been nothing but kind to us and generous. And Jeanne trusts him." She took a breath then motioned behind her shoulder. "There's a bath waiting in that tent for anyone who wants it as well as changes of clothing."

The Welshman nodded towards the stacked foodstuff boxes beneath one of the trees. "I'm also able to provide you with sustenance." His eyes fell to the boxes I'd dropped once we stepped into the perimeter of his encampment. "But you've already managed that necessity or so it appears."

"Aye," I said.

It grew quiet and Gwydion eyed me as narrowly as I did him. I felt everyone's eyes on me, each pair asking the same question: what to do next?

"Well, Tallis Black, will you accept my offer?" Gwydion asked.

I took a deep breath but then nodded. Whatever I could accuse Mag's nephew, he'd never violate the laws of hospitality when it came to providing for his guests. Even within the most evil of people, there exists a code that must nae be broken. And providing meals, a wash, and a bed to wary travelers was one such code that had existed for centuries and would continue. Even in this—the most wretched of places.

Addie placed a concerned hand on the angel's shoulder. "Why don't you bathe next? You and our Scottish throw rug over there have been in need of cleaning up longer than any of us."

The angel nodded. "Guess it's time I took care of my fauxgiene."

"What?" Addie asked.

The angel shrugged. "Combo of faux and hygiene, babycakes."

Addie frowned at him. "I got that much."

"It's like half-heartedly cleaning yoself but not 'cause you like wanna be clean. More due to the social pressure to appear like you actually give a shit."

191

"If you weren't an angel and incapable of dying, there's no way you ever would have lasted this long," Addie said.

"True dat, true dat," the angel responded as he began whistling and started for the tent.

Once he was inside, Kay called out after him, "And don't take too long!"

Jeanne reassured her with a smile. "Time moves quite differently within the bounds of the tent. Indeed, you may be quite shocked at how little time it takes to clean yourself and dress."

Given his slovenly habits, I had me own suspicion the angel would require even less time than Jeanne expected. Nae two seconds later, the angel emerged. He was still dressed in his dirty clothes but his face was shaven and there was considerably less dirt upon his person. Kay rolled her eyes before stepping into the tent herself.

In the meantime, I moved the box of foodstuffs to join Gwydion's beneath one of the oak trees. When I turned back around, the Welshman was approaching, with a pair of blade shears. He clicked them together suggestively, which made me eye the obviously sharp blades of the implement warily. That, in turn, made Gwydion scoff.

"Oh, come now. You cannot argue that you could use a trim after all those months of captivity."

Me wary gaze moved from the shears to his eyes. "Sae ye heard aboot that, then?"

The Welshman dipped his head to the side. "I was told of your time as Alaire's captive, yes."

"An' who told ye?"

"The lovely Jeanne."

Gwydion's mention of Joan Of Arc caused me to look at her. While the others busied themselves with bathing and dressing within the tent, Jeanne was vigilant, carefully searching for any signs of trouble.

192

I wondered if Gwydion knew Jeanne's true identity but decided nae to ask. He most probably had figured it out and if not, 'twas better nae to alert him.

Gwydion drew me attention back to him by tugging upon me beard. "You must have been a prisoner for a long time," he said, eyeing the length of me beard. Then he glanced up at me head. "All that hair must be terribly uncomfortable, not to mention the bugs and lice."

"Ah've managed. And Ah can manage a while longer if need be."

Gwydion held up his hand. "I offer my services."

"An' Ah deny them."

He shook his head. "Come now, Tallis Black, let this be the moment when we put our pasts behind us and look toward the future."

"An' why should we dae that?"

"Because we are both powerful men, are we not?"

"Aye."

"Then could we not find it within both our best interests to become allies of some kind?"

"Allies fer whit?"

He shrugged. "For whatever may come our way."

"Ah dinnae troost ye. Never have."

"Well, you are a smart man as surely as you are powerful." He glanced down at the shears in his hand before looking up at me again. "I swear on the soul of my beloved nephew, Lleu Llaw Gyffes, that I shall do you no harm in the course of cutting your hair and beard."

I wanted to call his bluff, but he swore on the name of the only person he loved. There was nae way he would harm me. And 'twas true that I sorely needed a shave and trim. Thus, I sat down upon the nearest rock with me back to him, but only after I put me blade in me lap. "Aye, well, git on with it, then."

193

"Thus downward from a craggy steep we found..."
-Dante's Inferno

TWENTY
TALLIS

The sound of snipping shears began at the back of me neck.

"Come, come, Tallis. We both know your lady love will be quite relieved to see you cleaned up."

"Me lady love?" I felt me eyes narrowing of their own accord. I didnae like the fact that Gwydion knew of Lily. I tried looking over me shoulder at him. He gave me a quick "uh-uh" and pushed me head back to the front. "An' was that somethin' else Jeanne told ye?"

"No, no, whispers of your more recent exploits seem to be all the buzz lately. Rumors even managed to penetrate all the way down here, if you can believe it," he continued, sounding as though he was discussing the weather. The metallic clicking of the shears continued. "When I heard a woman from the world above was traveling with you, well, I was truly warmed. I suppose you can call me a romantic at heart."

I grunted. "Nae so certain yer sister, Arianhrod, would agree."

The weight of me hair diminished with each snip of the shears, landing in me lap in clumps of black. "Be that as it may, if there is any truth to the rumors, I'm quite happy for you. You've been alone far, far too long, bladesmith."

Clumps of me hair were being thrown about willy nilly and me suspicions rose again. "Now, would ye be collectin' me hair tae use in a spell?"

Gwydion hummed in the negative. "Oh, every last strand will be burned when I'm finished. You are, after all, my guest. And such deceit would be terribly rude of me, not to mention against the code."

"Aye, ye have always lived accordin' tae the code."

"Of course!" Gwydion said upon a laugh. "And so shall I continue."

Seeing as the bastard was in such a chatty, chummy mood—as always—I figured I'd try to get something useful out of him. "Would Ah be rude meself if Ah asked aboot the goings-on at the morgue?"

The tent flap rustled from behind me and I heard the sound of footsteps and laughter—a sound which was sae foreign in the Underground City. Meanwhile, Gwydion's shears reached the middle of me head.

"Hardly, not when knowing such things might help keep yourself and your companions alive," he answered me question. "What do you wish to know?"

Me eyes swept through the wreckage in front of me as I asked me first question. "Whose side dae ye favor in this fracas?"

"The same one I always do... my own."

"And have ye told either side aboot yer allegiance tae yerself?"

"Goodness no!" he laughed. "Why ruin the surprise? We both know how repetitive everything eventually becomes down here. I've found these silly wars quite entertaining, actually."

"Sae how did these wars come aboot? Ah'm nae surprised by the fightin' now that the prisoners are free, boot—"

"But you wonder how they became freed in the first place?"

195

I would have nodded but me head was playing captive to Gywdion's hands and shears. The proximity of the shears to me scalp made me answer "Aye" instead.

"If you'll kindly turn towards me...?"

I did as he asked, careful to balance me blade in me lap. Once I was resettled, he grabbed the bottom of me beard and applied the shears. "I hate to disappoint you but I have no true knowledge of this conflict's origins. The first time I heard about it, I was in the process of being released from that rack you strapped me to."

He handed me a mirror I hadnae realized he'd brought with him. Of course, he could have simply magicked it from the very ether that surrounded us. Something that was more probably the case. I glanced at me reflection, noting me hair which was cropped tightly to my head. And me face was beginning to show skin again as he cut the beard away.

"Mayhap ye should retire yer wizardry skills in pursuit o' a barberin' career? Ye are quite good."

Gwydion laughed but there was nae real humor in the sound. "Very funny, bladesmith."

Once his laughter died down, I moved back to the subject. "So ye've nae idea why the fightin' originated, then?"

"Oh, I've always got plenty of ideas. Some of them are just more appropriate than others."

"Any o' them involve the Spites?"

He chuckled softly as if I'd stated the most ridiculous idea possible. "Oh, no, I doubt they were part of *anyone's* plan. Even Alaire would never be so rash as to think he could control the Spites. No one can."

"But Alaire *is* involved in this, aye?"

He snipped off another piece of me beard that landed in me lap. "Aye," he answered, having a go at

196

me accent. "Along with practically every other resident of the Underground City. Were things any different when you were in charge?"

I felt me mouth tighten. "Ye nae be sayin' that Alaire an' Ah are one an' the same, are ye?"

"Of course not!"

"Then whit are ye sayin'?"

"Given what the Spites became, what's the point of releasing them? They're incapable of being controlled and all they've done is wreak havoc upon both sides. All those centuries of extracting the worst instincts of men made those vicious spirits a ravenous, mindless hive."

"Speakin' from experience, are we?"

He clipped away the last of me beard and gave it a closer look. "Why do you always refuse to give me the benefit of the doubt?"

"Why do ye always act like ye know more than yer lettin' on?"

The shears found me bushy upper lip. "Touche, as the French say."

I waited until he finished me mustache before asking me next question. "With all that concentrated strength ye mentioned, could the Spites have broken through Pandora's Box on their own?"

"You mean Pandora's Urn."

"Aye," I answered with impatience.

Gwydion nodded. "All anyone knows for certain is this: some months ago, the Spites broke loose and have been roaming the morgue ever since." Going to the other side of me face, he added, "There was one other bit of information you might be interested in."

"Go oan."

"When I last saw Alaire, he took a rather inordinate interest in the Spites when he met with the Malebranche."

"And?"

197

He frowned and tapped his cheek with the shears as though he were deep in thought. "Or was it the Council of Simon?" He shrugged. "Well, either way, it doesn't matter now."

I shook me head. "Nae, I dinnae sooppose it does."

Gwydion's smile indicated his smugness and I knew I'd been had. "No, I mean, it *really* doesn't matter now." He stepped aside to reveal Jedidiah and Jebediah's rifle which was pointed straight at me head. I exhaled heavily as I turned right round and found the pack of Fenrir surrounding me. Further apace, the angel and our group emerged from within the tent, a pack of human soldiers at their backs. All of them were armed with weapons, from pistols to rifles.

"Ye broke yer word," I said to Gwydion.

He shook his head. "I promised never to harm you whilst I cut your beard and hair. And as I have finished with both, my allegiance to you is thus ended." He shrugged. "Though I still could make a case for the fact that I haven't broken my word at all."

"How sae?" I demanded.

He shrugged again. "Any harm that comes to you, Tallis Black, will not be from my hand."

Jedidian kicked me blade out me lap, hard enough to knock it against the tree. I faced Jedidiah with disinterest. "Surprised yer still alive."

A smirk oozed onto his lips. "I suppose I have you to thank. Braining me with your sword knocked me out of the Spites' path. Most of the others weren't so lucky."

"And was the cardinal so unfortunate?"

"His holy flames protected him. And he asked me to tell you hello."

While we were speaking, Harry raised his hands with obvious resignation as he eyed the soldiers surrounding him. Suddenly, his eyes went wide with recognition as he focused on one of the few girls among the human forces. She held one of those ridiculous machine pistols and appeared with a large frown upon her otherwise pretty face. Her skin was the color of coffee and her large, dark eyes gave her an innocent look. Quite ironic given the circumstances.

"Dahlia, what the hell?" Harry asked.

Her face was as unemotional as Jedidiah's when she aimed her gun at Harry. "Don't make this worse. Just get over there with the rest of them."

Harry did as he was told and I started to rise to me own feet. Jedidiah ground his rifle barrel right into me forehead. "Not you."

I gave him a tight grimace. "Now is that any way tae treat a man what jist saved yer life?"

Gwydion grinned at me as he leaned against the tree behind us, the shears still hanging from his fingers. "He does have a point!"

The slave hunter swung his rifle around at the Welshman. I started to move when the growls of the Fenrir made me stop at once. Oblivious to this, Jedidiah took careful aim at our betrayer.

"Unless you want to eat my first bullet, trickster, stay out of this."

Mag's nephew gestured around him. "If you insist I leave…"

Jedidiah tensed, and he appeared seconds away from pulling the trigger. "We both know why that would be a fatal mistake on your part."

The Welshman crossed his arms and smirked at Cauchon's flunky. "So we do. But have no fear, I wouldn't miss what's going to happen for anything."

But there was something wrong. It took me a moment or two to put me finger upon it. But there was something off in the way Gwydion was baiting Jebediah. Gwydion only baited those he considered

199

marks. Aye, he gave his allies plenty of grief, to be certain, but this baiting was different.

Jebediah pointed at the Welshman while looking at Dahlia. "He does anything questionable, shoot him."

Dahlia nodded and trained her gun on Gwydion. His smile only widened as he nodded at her. He acted as though he had no fear of being shot. Actually, he acted as though he had nae fear of anyone or anything. Meanwhile, Jedidiah swung his rifle back towards me brow.

"Now, as to your question, I'm about to give you the best gift I can offer you: a quick death."

Out the corner of me eye, I noticed a wee figure peeking from behind a tree. With all eyes drawn on us, nobody noticed the angel creeping his way up to the tree directly ahead of him.

I turned me full attention back to the man holding the gun on me. "'Tis a mighty peculiar way o' sayin' 'thank ye', Jedidiah."

I could see his trigger finger tightening. "Compared to the alternatives? You should consider yourself lucky, Tallis Black."

The click of his rifle was nae louder than the dry snap of a branch. And just as impotent. Jedidiah popped out the intact bullet and fired again. All he got for his trouble was another dry click. As he furrowed his brows and adjusted the lever of the gun yet again, I seized the rifle by the barrel, yanking me captor closer before headbutting the bridge of his nose. Instantly, a deluge of blood poured from his face as I pushed him away and he dropped his weapon, his hands moving to his face as he wailed in pain.

A dozen or so clicks came from the other weapons as Harry and the rest of our crew fell into a general brawl with the others. Jeanne slipped out of the fracas and ran towards me discarded blade. While I was swinging the useless rifle like a club to keep the Fenrir at bay, the Welshman laughed long and hard.

"Did I forget to mention the bladesmith put a gunpowder dousing charm on this area?"

I wasnae surprised the clever bastard had overheard me lick of Gaelic I'd muttered upon entering his encampment. What *did* surprise me was that he'd managed to keep that information to himself. What did he have to gain by pulling a triple cross like this?

I had nae time to ponder such things. The demon wolves kept coming at me. By the time I had beaten them back apace, I was bleeding from a dozen or more bites and the rifle butt was cracked clean in half. I was in dire need of a new plan.

A pair of strong hands seized me round the middle from behind. The smell of fresh blood told me 'twas Jedidiah, ready to take his revenge.

"Get him!" The slave hunter's shout deafened me left ear when the nearest Fenrir made a dive for me nethers. Something small leapt in front of the wolf's mouth, yelling loudly as the latter clamped down. Despite his pain, the stookie angel reached out and thrust his stubby index fingers into both eyes of his tormentor, making the Fenrir instantly release him.

Meanwhile, I struggled to break loose from Jebediah's manacle grip at the same time that I kicked back the other Fenrir, which wasnae an easy task.

Jedediah continued sidestepping me footstomps and dodging me backwards headbutts. And with both me arms pinned, I wasnae able to elbow him good and proper. A whistling in the air could be heard behind us, ending in a thud that made Jedidiah cry out. The moment his grip loosened, I slammed his ribs with both me elbows, feeling them shatter. He fell backwards just as one of his pet wolves launched itself at me face.

I punched me way into its mouth, knocking several of the sharp teeth down its throat. But its jaws were sae tight, I couldnae yank me hand out. Someone stepped out from behind me and I felt the cold steel of me blade being placed in me right hand. I wielded me blade as a flash of grey passed me eyes and cleaved right through the wolf's neck. The wolf dropped, revealing Jeanne standing before me. She appeared stunned that me blade could cut down me attacker sae easily.

Even in death, the damned wolf wouldnae release me hand. I yelled at Jeanne as I threw me blade to the right of her and it buried itself into the green grass, "Keep them fiends off me!"

Jeanne nodded as she pulled me sword from the earth and held it alight, swiping at the pack with me blade. The angel soon joined in, taking up the rifle and using it like I had, as a club.

Fighting to free the dead wolf head off me arm, me nose caught the scent of blood again. I turned to face Jedidiah, who pulled a hunting knife out from under his coat. 'Twas bigger than a stiletto but half the size of a butcher knife. He made a feint for me stomach before shifting the jab towards me face. I stuck the wolf's head between me and the knife point. The blade sunk into the demon wolf and severed something which, in turn, loosened the jaw, freeing me hand enough to slide it out. I threw a blind punch with me other hand. The blow landed right on the side of Jedidiah's head.

As he fell, I caught a glimpse of the fight happening in front of the tent. Our side was losing against Jedidiah's. All the while, the Welshman leaned against his tree while smiling in amusement as though he were watching a film. A glance over me shoulder revealed Jeanne and the stookie angel losing ground to the Fenrir. I yelled at them, "Git intae the tent!"

Jeanne obeyed first, running past me to help the others. Jedidiah attempted snagging her ankle but she slipped out of reach and kept going. The angel made a point of whacking the slave hunter on the back of the skull before running past himself. The rifle butt was completely cracked off now, leaving naught but a jagged stub with a bit of a sharp edge.

Jeanne began wailing on the attackers with the flat of me sword, which must have been the same way she'd used it against Jedidiah. Though 'twas nae the way the sword was meant to be wielded, 'twas effective enough. The angel attempted something similar by clubbing our enemies but the damn rifle was sae heavy, he could barely keep his balance.

Hearing the growl of the Fenrir behind me, I raced towards the fighting meself. A pair of hands grabbed both me ankles before yanking me straight down again. I lacked any time to protect me head before I struck the hard, broken ground with me jaw.

Dazed momentarily, I felt me legs being pulled forward and when I looked down, I saw Jedidiah. Alas, the man was exhaustedly strong. How I wished for Donnchadh's power at that exact moment! But 'twas nae to be.

Jedidiah released me and I thrust me right leg back. It caught Jedidiah's shoulder right before he grabbed me left leg again. 'Twas enough. I rolled meself over with me right hand before aiming me second kick right at the slave hunter's face. It landed true on his broken nose which made him pause but didnae stop his bloody wolf pack from running straight at me. Just over Jedidiah's left shoulder, Gwydion suddenly appeared. As he grinned broadly, he made a circling gesture with his hand.

"Now how is this fair?"

Jedidiah instantly transformed into a hog, squealing in disbelief at the sudden unexpected change of circumstances. The fresh pork on four legs made the wolves instantly forget about me and, instead, turn their hungry gazes to their former master. With another horrified squeal, the Jedidiah hog turned and ran into the ruins. He barely managed to stay ahead of the Fenrir pack, which was right behind him. I heard a new chorus of hog squeals and a quick glance over me shoulder revealed me group standing over a pack of hogs and staring at them in wonder.

As I struggled to stand up to me feet, I looked at the Welshman. "Ah dinnae oonderstand," I managed.

He shrugged and smirked. "I just didn't want you to miss the good part." Before I could ask him which part that was, he vanished from sight.

At that moment, a whip wrapped 'round me right wrist. I yanked the other end with a tug to the left but wasnae able to do much as a second whip struck me back before a third wrapped 'round me other wrist.

As the lash slammed into me back a second, third and fourth time, a figure stepped out from behind the tree Gwydion had just vacated. This figure had curled ram horns as pale as porcelain, the horns the same lack of color as his skin. He was easily me same height and build. The muscles encasing his bare chest looked like white marble. He wore leather breeches and his white feet were bare. His most prominent feature was his tail: a long and great, scaly snake that thrashed back and forth like the whip that beat me.

"Malecoda," I said to the Malebranche Duke who stood before me.

He smiled with straight, even teeth that didnae match his other monstrous features. "Tallis Black, I believe you have something I want."

204

"That this dark wave resounded, roaring loud..."
-Dante's Inferno

TWENTY-ONE
LILY

As convenient as it was to have a physical object that acted like a tactile GPS, being yanked around by my blade was more than annoying. The compound Perenelle had put on it made it less annoying, but it still felt like I was being tugged by a big dog on a short leash. I looked back over my shoulder at the Flamels. "Are you sure you two can keep up?"

Despite catching her breath, Perenelle managed to smile. "If such were not the case, *Mademoiselle* Harper, I assure you we would say as much."

Nicolas was huffing and puffing a little more than his wife. "Just the same, Perenelle, I have to admit one regret: that I never followed your sensible advice regarding the importance of exercise."

She grinned and playfully poked his chest. "Your wife does know best, you see?"

The sword pulled me around the next corner and the landscape changed drastically. To the point that I couldn't actually believe my eyes.

The first thing I noticed was the trees: big, green, beautiful trees.

Life.

And life that didn't belong down here, in the Underground City. The trees were like a Greenpeace sign in a toxic waste dump. Below the trees was a flag with an image of a pale horse dancing against a dark background. Before I could further question what the flag was and why it was here and, furthermore, how it was possible that trees were growing all around it, I heard the unmistakable sounds of a brawl: shouts, punches, and growling.

My heart skipped a beat as I tried to prepare myself for whatever we were about to encounter. My blade continued to yank itself forward, nearly pulling my arms out of their sockets. It was all I could do to stand in place.

The blade seems to think Tallis is down there which means he could be in the middle of that battle, I told myself as a wave of fear and worry overtook me.

And then I heard his voice.

"Get them fiends off me!"

My heart sped up as tears started in my eyes and my blade about pulled itself right out of my hands.

"He's here!" I yelled back to Nicolas and Perenelle.

As I started running in the direction the sword was pulling me, I heard Nicolas cry out "*Mademoiselle* Harper, wait!"

Yeah, no thanks.

I'd done all the waiting I could stomach just to get to this point. I didn't care if I was walking straight into another fight. I had to see Tallis and make sure he was safe and if not, make sure I helped him through whatever it was he was facing, no matter what the consequences.

The trees were about two blocks from my location. Despite the demolished buildings in front of me, none of the debris piles were low enough to allow me to see what was going on. I heard Tallis shout a second time, something about getting to "the tent," and I hastened my pace. For all I knew, that could mean he was losing the fight.

All of a sudden, a swarm of pigs rounded the corner in front of me. Stunned and wondering where in the hell they'd come from, they damn near ran right into me. I had to leap onto a nearby pile of rubble just to avoid their stampede. That indignity caused Donnchadh to turn up my anger a couple of notches.

Just before the hog horde disappeared down the road, the Flamels finally caught up with me. This time, even Perenelle was panting heavily. I pointed at the departing drove of pigs. "What the hell was that?"

Nicolas looked at me with unmasked surprise. "You no longer have pigs in your world?"

I ignored my tugging blade for a moment so I could reply to the scribe-turned-alchemist. "I know they're pigs, Nicolas," I said with a "duh" tone. "My question is: why are they here and where did they come from? Last I checked, there wasn't such a thing as livestock in the Underground City."

Perenelle pursed her lips before answering. "My guess is they are transmogrified beings; they were something else a few moments before they became pigs."

The next sound I heard caused my stomach to drop yet again: Tallis's agonized grunts. I also detected the signature crack of a whip. Before I could start in the direction of Tallis' cries, Perenelle gently grabbed my wrist.

"You will benefit no one by carelessly rushing in."

I frowned, knowing she was right. But if I waited too long, Tallis might be dead by the time I got to him. Nicolas fished out the Devouring Lion mixture from his apron. Perenelle released my hand to reach into her own apron pocket. She pulled out a vial and faced me with interest. That was when I understood. They weren't telling me to go slow so much as they were asking me to let them back me up. I nodded and we all made fast tracks towards the trees.

***

When we arrived, I was glad I'd waited for the Flamels. At least a dozen of those worm demons were all over the green glade of trees. Half of them surrounded a group of clearly frightened people, possibly Soul Retrievers, near a tent. I could only imagine it was the same tent I'd just heard Tallis mention.

It was then that my eyes narrowed on my guardian angel.

"Bill," I said in a whisper as I took a deep breath and tried to keep the joy from overcoming my entire body. I still had work to do and from the looks of it, my angel was in trouble.

He was currently being guarded by two of the worm things. Each of Bill's arms were being restrained by the ends of a whip on either side of him. Meanwhile a strange plastic case lay in front of him.

Beside Bill was a girl who was wearing a muddied, medieval-looking peasant style of clothing that seemed outdated even down here. She was getting the same treatment as Bill, where she kneeled beside him. Her eyes remained fixed on the ground like it had the solution to their dilemma. Tallis's blade stood next to the tree behind them—unattended.

And that was when I rested my gaze on my bladesmith. And any joy I'd just felt at seeing Bill, immediately fled.

Tallis was in terrible shape. He looked battle-worn and was covered in lashes and open wounds. Like Bill and the girl, Tallis was being held by two whips attached to either of his hands. Meanwhile, one of the grotesque worm demons were ruthlessly lashing him with a third whip. I immediately recalled my own fight with them in front of the Flamels' lab.

208

I was just about to charge in when someone stepped out from behind the nearest tree. He had a snow-white complexion, curly horns on his head, and a big lizard tail that looked like it could hit just as hard as the whip that was lashing Tallis's back. He waved at the worm doing the whipping, and made the torture come to an abrupt stop. Then he leaned down and sneered at Tallis.

"I already told you what I wanted, Black. Why are you so insistent on denying me my prize?"

Tallis spat at the ground before glaring up at his captor. "Ah dunno, mayhap Donnchadh dinnae like bein' told whit tae do anymore than Ah do. An' mayhap he's jist seein' how mooch he can piss ye off!"

I felt the air being sucked out of my lungs. This bastard obviously thought Tallis still harbored Donnchadh! And Tallis, being Tallis, was perfectly content to allow the torture to continue just to ruin the other guy's day.

Just then, the girl beside Bill suddenly turned her head and looked right at me! I was shocked because we were still far enough away that no one else had noticed us and we were hidden beneath the foliage of the trees.

Regardless though, the girl had definitely spotted me and she continued to stare at me now. There was something about her gaze: it was forceful yet soothing but demanding all the same.

A name floated into my head as we stared at each other: "Beatrice."

I was shocked momentarily as, of course, I wondered if this was the same Beatrice from Dante's *Inferno*? The Beatrice who had aided Dante in his journey and was an allegorical representation of spiritual love. But could this girl actually be *the* Beatrice?

209

She held my eyes for a second longer before returning her gaze to the tailed demon boss who was still waiting for Tallis to give him something that wasn't there.

The girl's, Beatrice's, eyes returned to me and her eyebrows inclined slightly. I nodded.

She looked at Nicolas and at the worm man who stood to the left of Tallis. She did the same to Perenelle and the whip on Tallis's right. Despite being bound, she was calling the plays for our attack.

I tightened the grip on my sword while Beatrice slowly drew in a deep breath. When she finished, she glanced at all three of us one last time. Then she blew out her breath in one long burst. And I recognized my cue.

I ran into the grove just as I heard the tinkling of glass shattering on the nearest worm man. His screams filled the otherwise silent air. Meanwhile, a vial flew past my shoulder and struck the other demon who was whipping Tallis. He lit up in flames of blue, his screams adding to those of the other worm demon.

The pasty white demon with the horns and tail looked dumbfounded as another of his worm demons caught the magical blue fire that engulfed his brother and both burned amid a chorus of screams. I faced the pasty white demon and charged him, my blade leading the way.

Two inches before my blade would have penetrated his skull, he blocked my attack with a sword he pulled out of thin air. The sword was as black as the shadows that surrounded it, appearing as a mist.

The horned demon turned all the way around, trying to use his tail to sweep me off my feet. I jumped over it and brought my blade down on the shoulder of his sword arm when I landed, causing a huge gash in

210

his arm but not severing it all the way off. He yelled out in pain as he tossed the sword over to his other hand.

"Bitch!" he screamed at me, his eyes going wide as they turned from black to glowy white, matching the rest of him. He opened his mouth to reveal rows of pointed and large teeth and a long, red tongue that ended in a fork continued to pass in and out of his mouth as though it were tasting the air.

We crossed blades a few more times before an odd rumbling began to shake the ground. The tree behind Bill, Beatrice, and the worm captors suddenly fanned its branched arms out wide before leaning over them. It slammed its branches into the worm demons who were restraining Beatrice, then onto the ones holding Bill. Judging by his astonished expression, pasty white demon dude was just as surprised as I was.

Because he was momentarily sidetracked, I took my opportunity and wielded my blade high, thinking maybe I could get him in the neck and sever his head. I brought the blade down but he deflected the blow and struck a few of his own, driving me back. I caught the whistle of an incoming whip to my right and sidestepped to the left. The whip caught Pasty in the eye, and he screeched more in anger than pain as he threw the smoking black sword at the worm demon on the other end of the whip. The sword impaled the worm demon onto a tree and the black mist that surrounded the sword suddenly misted around the demon. The creature screamed as the black mist ate his flesh from his bones, leaving nothing but his skeleton when it was finished.

Meanwhile, I aimed my blade at a closer, more accessible target: Pasty's tail. I held the blade aloft then brought it down as hard as I could. The demon shrieked when my blade sunk into the lizard-skin of his tail, even though my sword got stuck halfway through. Before I knew it, he slammed his fist into my jaw, knocking me to the ground. I released my sword which was still buried in the demon's tail.

Donnchadh went apeshit the second I hit the ground, manifesting in the red heat that claimed my skin and the sudden ire that boiled up from my stomach. As tempting as it was to release him, I was beginning to realize the drawbacks outweighed the benefits. I channeled Donnchadh's anger into picking myself up while Pasty gripped my sword and yanked it from his tail. A whole lot of gross green stuff started oozing out of the wound and sizzled when it hit the ground. Then Pasty turned his murderous gaze on me as I started to crab crawl backwards. But he was much faster and leapt through the air, only to land on top of me.

He opened his palm and his black sword flew from where it had just killed one of his demons, landing in his hand. Pasty pulled the sword up above his head and was about to bring it down on top of me when something slammed into him from behind, throwing him away from me.

I rolled away, to my right and caught my breath as I got onto all fours and then looked up. Standing there in his burly, beautiful glory was Tallis, his blade held firmly in both his hands.

"Ye dinnae touch her!" he screamed at the demon.

Tallis wasted no time hammering on my opponent but it did no good. The demon was still blocking his blows just as easily as he'd blocked mine.

"*Capture!*"

No sooner did I hear a female voice yell the word before I watched my blade suddenly come flying towards me. I caught it by the pommel and glanced forward, in complete shock as I tried to understand what had just happened.

Beatrice stood there, maybe twenty feet from me, smiling before she turned around and went running off to the tent. The Flamels had apparently concocted more of their homebrewed chemical weapons because the worms in suits were reeling—some caught by the blue flames, others apparently choking on something invisible to the naked eye while still others rolled on the ground, screaming and crying in pain.

The rest of the humans who appeared to be part of Bill and Tallis' crew used the distraction to push past their captors, but the odds weren't necessarily in our favor. Bill launched himself in the middle of the chaos, grabbing a dropped whip and handing it off to a human man with bright orange hair who stood just beside him.

My eyes returned to the fight between the main demon and Tallis. The bladesmith was definitely giving him plenty of grief but he couldn't punch through the guy's defenses any better than I could. That was when I thought to myself that two swords were better than one.

Before I could finish the thought, I was already back in the fight, adding my own sword to the equation. Tallis seemed a little stunned by my sudden entry but didn't pause from his offense. Pretty soon, we were both driving Pasty into retreat. Meanwhile, I glanced down at his tail and noticed it was no longer leaking nasty green stuff. In fact, it looked completely intact and healed. When I glanced up at his shoulder, where I'd cut him earlier, that wound too was healed.

Great.

More of our strikes hit their target, cutting into his flesh and impeding his efforts to defend himself. I could see the desperation spreading across his pale face. He knew he was about to lose this fight and I was looking forward to exactly that. Too much so because I dropped my defenses just enough for his next move to be successful.

I sank my blade into the demon's right forearm and pulled it out again at the exact same time that he pulled his left arm, that was holding his blade, all the way back before driving it forward. It felt like slow motion as I glanced down at the blade and watched it run me straight through my middle, the black mist moving around the blade and then traveling up, towards me.

The demon pulled his blade out of me in one motion as I felt myself suddenly totter backwards. I glanced up at Tallis to find his eyes wide with shock and something more—pain. It was an expression I'd never seen on him before.

I heard my sword fall just beside me and with what remaining life force I had, I reached out to it and wrapped my fingers around the pommel. My vision blurred as the world took on a red haze, Donnchadh's trademark. And that was when I remembered I couldn't die.

I growled at the white demon, who stared at me dumbfounded. He didn't see Tallis striking his hand until the blade had already severed his wrist. He screamed but then immediately thrust the green-hemorrhaging stump right into Tallis's face. The green goo got onto Tallis' skin and began oozing in double time, burning him as Tallis staggered backwards and dropped his sword.

My would-be killer then placed his dangling hand back onto his severed wrist and I watched it seal itself together. Then, he turned the blade around and faced me, making Donnchadh rage even harder.

"The bladesmith doesn't possess the spirit anymore. You do," the demon hissed. He twisted his weapon again. "Free the spirit to me and I end this."

I spat in his face, causing him to plunge his sword into me again. I cried out and my raging spirit cried with me, eager to rend and tear. I kept willing my hand to hold onto my blade while hoping I could put the weapon to good use. But my strength was draining away with each passing second.

No, I couldn't die but I could become weakened with every thrust of the demon's blade inside me. As I glanced at him, he pulled his arm back and thrust the black blade into me once again. Though the black mist tried to spread from the blade to my body, it couldn't. It was as though I was buffered against it with some magical shield.

I glanced down at my own blade when I thought I saw it beginning to glow. At first I thought I was hallucinating. But no, after another second, I realized the glow was legitimate. And it spread from the blade, onto the hilt, up my arm, until the glow covered my entire body. A humming started from presumably beneath me and began to encompass my entire body. Little by little, I felt my strength building.

Pasty tried to push his sword through me again, only to get thrown backwards when my body expelled the metal with the force of a gunshot. Tallis was standing right behind the demon as if prepared, his eyes clear and blade raised. The burn marks from the demon's ooze had left a raw wound on his cheek but he didn't seem to notice it now. Instead, he swung his blade right through the bastard's torso in mid-air, cutting the demon in half. Both halves tumbled beyond the grove and landed next to the nearest pile of rubble.

As for me, I was still glowing and humming. My vision went from a bloody crimson to a cool blue. I was possessed by something but even though I didn't have that much experience with Donnchadh, I didn't think this was him. It felt different—there was no anger, no ire, no nothing. Just a coolness that washed over me and bathed me in a feeling of calm.

I felt like I was watching a movie as my gaze settled on the two halves that were once the white demon. As I watched, both halves of the body began to move toward one another like magnets. Then they began undergoing the messy process of joining together the way his hand and wrist had.

I gripped my sword even harder. I approached the mending demon and once he was back in one piece, I extended my foot and pinned him to the rubble. I put my Day-Glo blade under his chin. "Tell your brethren, leader of the Malebranche, that Donnchadh is beyond their reach."

I was both me and not me at the same time. Though the voice was my own, it felt like the words were coming from somewhere else. And wherever that place was, it wasn't Donnchadh.

The demon lifted his sword as if to strike me but once it encountered the glow of my body, his sword completely evaporated into nothing, taking the black mist with it and leaving the demon defenseless. He looked up at me with utter horror.

"What are you?"

I wasn't interested in answering his question. "Tell them."

The same inky blackness that comprised his sword suddenly formed behind him, creating what appeared to be a portal. Before I could stop him, he was sucked into it as if it were a vacuum. The portal closed too fast for me to follow.

Its job apparently done, the glow faded from my body, but the cool feeling remained on my skin. The first thing I did was glance down to check the stomach wound Pasty had inflicted. It was completely gone without leaving so much as a scratch.

216

A nasty laugh made me turn back towards the grove... or what had been the grove. Everything—tent, trees, grass—completely vanished by the time I faced it. Everyone else appeared just as confused as I was. I thought I heard Tallis muttering under his breath "Damned Welshman" while he started towards me.

Sheathing his blade, he planted both his big hands on my shoulders. "Besom, are ye—"

I lifted up my leather tunic. "See for yourself."

He didn't seem to believe what he was seeing anymore than I did. "How's it possible?"

"I... I don't know."

Tallis and I just looked at each other for another few seconds before he gripped me tighter and then pulled me into the warmth of his chest. I wrapped my arms around him and closed my eyes as I breathed in the scent that was the bladesmith.

"Tallis..." I whispered, just because I wanted to hear the sound of his name.

He held me even tighter and leaned down to kiss the top of my head. And we would have stayed that way for a long time if Bill hadn't interrupted.

"Lils!" he screamed out. "It's good to see you're back, nips! But we gotta save us the welcome backs 'cause we gotta get us the hells outta here!"

I glanced up but didn't budge from Tallis's side. Instead, I focused on Beatrice who appeared distraught.

"But this was supposed to be our safe haven!" Then she cast a wistful glance at the place where we'd entered. "And the departed were supposed to be my friends." Since I couldn't see her clubbing around with demons, I figured she was talking about the drove of trans-pigs we'd encountered on the way here.

I didn't know when Perenelle and Nicolas had joined us but I heard Perenelle's voice coming from beyond Tallis.

"Then perhaps it is fortunate that my husband and I have a location that suits our needs perfectly."

Beatrice seemed stunned by Perenelle's accent. "*Etes-vous Francais?*"

Nicolas held up his hands. "*Mais oui, mademoiselle. Je suis Nicolas Flamel et voici ma femme, Perenelle.*"

She nodded and replied, "Jeanne."

I looked at Tallis in confusion. "I thought her name was Beatrice?"

"Beatrice? Nae," Tallis said as he shook his head and smiled down at me as he tightened his hold around my shoulders.

"Then her name is Jeanne?" I continued as I started to really notice her clothing. "As in..."

"Aye," Tallis interrupted. "Aye."

A pale man with red hair who was also sporting a prominent bruise on his chin and numerous cuts up and down his body, stepped out from the crowd. "Look, this is all fascinating but we gotta go. It's not safe here."

Nicolas nodded in understanding. "*Bien sur, jeune homme.* If you will be so kind as to follow us...?"

Everyone looked to Tallis and me for the go-ahead. When I nodded, Perenelle began to lead the group in the opposite direction from where we'd come.

"Into the deep abyss..."
-Dante's Inferno

TWENTY-TWO
TALLIS

Seeing as we'd just come out of battle, 'twas nae easy for our group to keep up the pace between their injuries and exhaustion. I wasnae exactly in the greatest shape meself after the whipping.

Mayhap such was the reason why the angel stuck so close to the kids, although he didnae engage any of them in his usual yattering. Truth be told, none of us talked on our way to the Flamels' stronghold. On the other hand, 'tis rarely a good idea to talk more than necessary on any battlefield. By keeping quiet, we could preserve enough energy to make the long trek ahead of us... or so I hoped.

Speaking of hope, Besom stuck close to me at the back of our ragged troop. Her arm wrapped 'round me while carefully avoiding me open wounds. I couldnae stop looking at her and nae entirely because I was delighted to be near her again. Aye, there was a part of me that wanted to be sure she was really here in the flesh and still another part that merely wanted to look upon her.

But there was another reason I couldnae tear my gaze away from her. I couldnae help remembering her fantastic lightshow at the grove and the way her entire body had lit up with a glow I had never seen before. But 'twas nae just the glow that caused my stupefaction.

When she had taken upon the glow and defeated Malecoda, her entire person had changed. The Lily I had come to recognize was nae the same person. Her body had been nae so long and thin but more curvaceous and her face had taken upon it a softer roundness of the cheeks and chin. While I found her beautiful nae matter what her form, the fair woman she became while amid the glow was truly magnificent. It was the kind of beauty I'd nae seen in centuries and obviously created by a force to be reckoned with.

Ever since I'd witnessed this spectacular vision, I wanted to ask her what had been the reason. But with so many folk about us, I had nae choice but to wait until we were alone.

Jeanne walked a few steps behind the Flamels as the alchemist couple led the rest of us. Jeanne kept stealing glances back at our ragtag crew to make certain we were keeping up. Like meself and Besom, it may well have been a matter of comfort and familiarity rather than leadership that kept her so close to Nicolas and Perenelle. A mutual connection from a shared origin goes a long way in a strange and unfriendly land.

I almost wondered if Jeanne was also staying close just in case the Flamels proved to be traitors? After the truth of Gwydion was revealed, I doubted Jeanne would ever trust easily again. As to me, I wasnae the sort to trust easily as well but Ah knew the Flamels an' believed them tae be a good sort.

I think it was Harry who gasped as we rounded the corner of the leveled block. At first, all I saw was a few heavily battered skyscrapers. Jeanne said something in French to the Flamels that sounded like a question. Old Nicolas just pointed to a spot between the two towers. I had to squint meself but I eventually glimpsed a modest, two-story house.

The house had a mottled coloring scheme—
probably owing to the war—but it looked like it
belonged in an American suburb rather than this
Circle, even on the latter's best days. As I came closer,
I realized me eyes were fooled regarding the mottled
colors on the outside. The house was constructed
from various mason and concrete fragments of fair
sizes. Given the mixes of browns, greys and blacks, all
the pieces had obviously come from different
buildings. Some parts of the roof looked like they
formerly belonged to the nearby skyscrapers. The
hodge-podge made me recall old Nan's patchwork
quilt, if such were turned into a dwelling.

Nicolas walked up to the brown brick door and
knocked upon it nine times in a complicated pattern.
A series of glyphs appeared, prompting him to say
something in a bastardized version of the Roman
tongue. The door soundlessly swung open and he
gestured us to enter.

The interior of the house was vastly larger than
the exterior would suggest. At the right of the door
was a single flight of stairs leading up to the next
floor. Ahead of us was an open space with a set of
curtains covering the windows on the back wall. The
solid right wall had a row of seven hospital-style beds
with decent mattresses upon them.

The left side of the room was a massive, solid
collection of shelves that occupied the whole wall.
Each of them was filled to capacity with a number of
flasks, vials, pots and urns. Containers of glass were
filled with powders or liquids, some that bubbled and
others that glowed unnaturally.

Besom asked the obvious question. "How did you
manage to create a setup like this?"

Nicolas's wife approached the shelves and replied,
"Oh, it was truly no great matter. This makeshift

221

storage unit and clinic came as repayment for services rendered on behalf of the Cyclopes."

Young Harry looked about himself with heavy doubt upon his pale face. "How could a bunch of one-eyed guys build something this good from a collection of Jenga blocks?"

That question I could answer. "They're more than jist the one eye, Harry. The Cyclopes actually earned a well-deserved reputation as master forgers an' artisans. A few o' 'em are even engineers, fer whom a house sooch as this'd be naethin' special."

Perenelle pulled a vial off the shelf and nodded with a smile on her lips. Then she gestured for me to come closer and I obeyed. Meanwhile, Nicolas nodded his approval at me answer while looking over more shelves.

"Indeed, *Monsieur* Black, I can think of no other race that could so well accomplish a task using such disparate resources as their base material."

His wife raised an eyebrow at him. "Not even the alchemists in our esteemed circle, dear husband?"

Nicolas snatched up an urn and gestured for Harry to join him. "Had we been given the advice of a Cyclops, *ma cherie*, I expect we would have discovered all the secrets of this universe in a single afternoon."

A shock of pain ran up and down me back when Perenelle touched a piece of cotton dipped into some liquid to me open wounds. I clenched me jaw when more of the painful jolts followed. The dabs from the cotton swab dipping into me whip wounds hurt nearly as much as the whip itself. I distracted meself by looking at Nicolas. He was carefully treating Harry for his bruised jaw with a dark paste he'd pulled from one of the urns.

Perenelle smiled at me. "It is good to see you are no longer the master of this domain." She paused.

"Though I must admit you were a much fairer master than is Alaire."

"'Tis good tae see ye both again, Lady Flamel," I said.

Though I could still see the marks of the whip around her wrists, Jeanne worked as a proper nurse for Nicolas. The old scribe looked past Harry to see the others falling into line, nae doubt to have their wounds treated as well.

Nicolas said something in French to our battlefield angel. She, in turn, grabbed more vials and flasks from the shelves. Meanwhile, Besom and her stookie angel went off to the corner of the room, near the stairs. They were engaged in a deep conversation, punctuated with a few hugs and sniffles. 'Twas good to see them reunited again.

I felt a few reassuring pats on the unwounded portions of me back in place of the swab. Perenelle looked over the rest of me body as she walked in front of me.

"All done, *Monsieur* Black. Unfortunately, I lack a proper set of bandages to protect the wounds while they heal but—"

I held up me hands and shook me head. "Ah've ways o' speedin' the healin' along, nae worries, lass, boot thank ye all the same."

She hummed and frowned a little. "Even so, I highly recommend you keep your back, as much as possible, undisturbed until those wounds have closed. There is, I fear, a significant danger of re-infection otherwise. Do you understand?"

"Aye, and Ah'll be as careful as I can, *Madame* Flamel." She nodded but the frown stayed upon her face. I raised an eyebrow at her. "Ye nae believe me?"

"That would depend, *Monsieur*. I noticed a number of scars across the length of your back that have long since healed but are nonetheless quite… striking."

I glowered at her. Me scars were me own business. "With all respect, me scars are nae anyone's business boot me own."

She seemed unoffended by me curt tongue as she nodded. "As you like." She looked around me side at Besom, who was staring at us. "Now, if you would be so kind as to ask *Mademoiselle* Harper to join me, please…?"

After the stabbing Besom endured, I was about to suggest it meself. I walked over to me beloved and said, "Yer new friend would like a word an' a close look a' yer stomach as well."

"Yeah, that's probably a good idea." As she walked past, she reached up and stroked me chin. "See you upstairs, bladesmith."

I was startled by her comment and the barely hidden overture included therein. True to her nature, me Besom didnae repeat herself but offered me a smile that told me everything I needed to know. Her failed guardian angel was attempting to restrain his own amusement at me confusion.

"As long as we ain't all subject to the lip banging, that's all I ask," the angel grumbled.

"The whit bangin'?" I insisted.

"When a couple starts making out more furiously than's called for an' right in front o' everyone else," he responded with a shrug. I felt me cheeks color which caused me to clear me throat. Besom looked upon me and laughed. 'Twas a sound I had direly missed.

After Perenelle checked me Besom's stomach and announced she was as healthy as healthy could be, Perenelle showed us to our room upstairs. We ascended the top floor where three separate rooms on the left had closed doors. Perenelle opened the nearest door, the one on the right, as soon as we came closer.

Inside was a simple bed and a nightstand with a wash basin full of water sitting upon it.

"I am quite certain you two would like some privacy to get reacquainted," Perenelle said with a devilish glint to her eyes.

I said naething but Besom smiled as she dropped her face and I noticed a reddish hue staining her lovely cheeks. The grin stayed upon her face as she escorted Perenelle out and locked the door behind her. I placed me blade next to the nightstand and couldnae understand the butterflies that suddenly plagued me stomach. I turned to face me Besom as she placed her own blade beside the doorframe. Then, her eyes moved to me chest.

"How's your back?" she asked.

I nodded. "*Madame* Flamel—"

I couldnae finish me sentence because Besom began pulling up her leather tunic and bared her breasts as casually as I might wipe me brow.

"Actually, they call her Lady Flamel down here," she corrected me but I couldnae say I was actually paying attention. Instead, me eyes fastened themselves to her perfect breasts as the butterflies in me stomach began in double time.

"Thine eye discover quickly, that whereof thy thought
is dreaming..."
-Dante's Inferno

TWENTY-THREE
TALLIS

Besom's areolas pointed at me like fingertips. The heat rising from her body gave me a good idear what was to come next and the rising of me todger was me body's answer.

"Ah moost admit, Besom, Ah'm a mere man an' cannae, fer the life o' me, remember whit in blazes we were talkin' aboot."

Besom laughed and approached me, running her fingertips down me chest. She pushed her breasts against me skin and was careful to wrap her arms about me without disrupting the wounded flesh of me back. She inhaled deeply as she closed her eyes and I ran me fingers through her hair.

"I missed you so much, Tallis," she whispered.

"Nae as mooch as Ah missed ye," I said in a soft and low voice. I pulled her away from me so I could look down upon her lovely face. I brought me rough thumb down the line of her cheek as I just stared at her. "Ah dinnae know how Ah ever managed tae win yer love boot Ah'm the loockiest man fer doin' sae."

"Nae more talkin'," Besom said, in a terrible rendition of me accent. She smiled up at me as I chuckled an' watched her pull her breeches down the length of her legs. She stood before me then as naked

226

as the day she'd been born and I felt myself swallow
hard.

She reached forward and took me left hand,
bringing it to the junction of her thighs. "You seem
shy, Tallis," she said as I mentally berated meself for
nae taking control of the situation.

"Ah dinnae know whit's come over me, lass," I
managed. "Ah feel nae like meself."

She laughed and stood upon her toes as she
stared into me eyes. "I can be in charge for once," she
laughed as she gripped the back of me head and
pulled me lips to hers. I wrapped the hand that
wasnae between her thighs 'round her head and
forced her mouth even closer as I thrust me tongue
into her mouth and tasted her. Meanwhile, me index
finger parted her lips and I felt the sticky wetness of
her sex covering me finger.

I broke the union of our mouths as me todger
damn near forced itself through me trousers. But
there was a desire I had to sate before I gave me cock
what it wanted. I said naething as I backed Besom
against the wall and then placing me hands beneath
her armpits, easily lifted her above me head, propping
her against the wall.

"Tall...Tallis," she started in surprise.

"Ah moost taste yer honey pot."

"My what?" she laughed. I looked up at her and
found her smile broad. "Don't ever call it that again."
The giggle died upon her lips once I brought me
mouth to her folds and separated them with me
tongue. The taste of her was exquisite and I eagerly
sucked upon her nub before bringing me tongue down
to her entrance and forcing it inside. She gripped me
head and moaned as I buried me face into her sex.

"Tallis, I want to see you naked," she muttered
between groans as she squeezed me head as though
she were trying to pop it off me neck.

I brought her back down to the floor again and licked me lips, wanting to fill me mouth with every last drop of her. I pushed me fingers between the lips of her now drenched sex but she pushed me away and began to fumble with me breeches. I heard a growl start in me throat as I forced her back against the wall.

"Dinnae deny me whit Ah want."

She closed her eyes as I forced me thumb against her clit and began rubbing her. She bucked when I pushed two fingers inside her as a loud moan tore from her mouth.

"Ye are sae tight, Besom," I whispered as she rocked against me, grinding her hips into me hand as I fucked her with me fingers.

She opened her eyes then and looked right into mine, her moans quieting. Then she reached forward and pulled me closer to her, beginning to fumble with me trousers once again. A second later, she damn near tore them off.

"I'm ready for you," she whispered as she looked down upon me engorged cock.

"Aye, ye've been ready for me," I answered on a laugh, pulling me fingers from her dripping sex.

She sidestepped me then backed up to the bed before laying down upon it and spreading her legs wide. I couldnae remove me gaze from the pink folds of flesh between her legs and me todger stood out straight, leading the way. I settled meself between her legs and she was careful to wrap them 'round me, below the whip abrasions upon me upper back. She lifted her pelvis, rubbing her wetness upon me throbbing cock.

"Lily," I started but she shook her head.

"No more talking, Tallis, please," she whined and pushed herself against me harder, trying to force me rigid cock inside her. But I pulled back.

228

"Ah want ye to know somethin', ye wee hellcat," I said upon a laugh.

"Tell me when you're inside me," she answered but I held her heads atween me hands sae she would see I was serious.

"Ah love ye, Lily Harper," I said as her eyes widened slightly but before she could respond, I pushed the full length of me dick into her and she arched her back below me as she clenched her eyes shut. I pulled all the way out and then shoved meself back in again, reveling in the feel of her tight and wet passage.

After that, our bodies began moving on their own, settling into a rhythm that we both accelerated. 'Aye, this was nae the first time I had experienced me Besom but 'twas the first time we had ever been able to enjoy one another without the threat of danger looming in the background.

Back in the dungeon, I was too drained and weak to fully appreciate our coupling. But here, I could feel me Besom in all her unbridled glory. Ah didnae ever remember a joining that felt this incredible.

As I reached me climax, Besom wasnae too far behind. And rather than screaming, she latched her mouth onto me shoulder and howled into it. I felt me eyes shut tight as I forced meself into her as far as I could and me seed released from me cock, filling her womb.

As I collapsed upon her, utterly exhausted from our lovemaking, I nearly rolled onto me back. Besom grabbed me by the shoulder. "Tallis, your back!"

We shared another brief kiss and Lily glanced around me side to where she'd left her sword leaning upon the wall. She studied it for a few seconds before she returned her attention to me face again.

"Wha's on yer mind, Besom?"

She looked back at me with concern still etched on her fair features. "When you made my blade, did you do anything special to it? Like enchanting it or something?"

I remembered the peculiar glow and form she'd encompassed at Gwydion's tent. "Aye, Ah created a bonding enchantment that allowed yer blade tae be one with ye."

She nodded but then frowned a bit. "Would that explain why the sword was able tell me where it was in Alaire's castle?"

"Aye, mayhap," I answered with a wee shrug. "When ye an' yer sword are bonded, 'tis as though yer sword is another of yer appendages—as mooch a part o' ye as is yer hand or yer foot."

She nodded but still appeared perplexed. "But how was my sword able to turn me into a warrior princess back there and I think... I was glowing?"

I knew she wouldnae like me answer for it was nae much of an answer at all. "Ah wish Ah knew, Besom."

The smile returned to her face and she stroked me cheek. She kissed me nose and then me mouth while her hand continued caressing me. "I guess all that matters is that you and Bill are alive."

"An' that ye are alive, me love."

She smiled down at me. "I don't know if I'll ever get used to this side of you."

"Whit side?"

"The loving, caring side," she giggled. "I'm used to the brooding, rude and private bladesmith I fell in love with."

I chuckled. "Are ye complainin', lass?"

"No!" she said as she tickled me which failed as I amnae ticklish. "I love this side of you," she finished as she kissed me nose again.

230

Now 'twas time for me to ask some questions of me own. "Did ye have any notion that ye was fightin' the Head Duke o' the Malebranche?"

Her eyes went wide with shock. "*That's* who I was up against? That white demon with the tail?"

"Aye."

"Wow. He just disappeared into that portal."

"Aye," I nodded again. "Bloody bastard."

"Where did it go?"

"Ah dinnae know fer certain. Somewhere within the Underground City, Ah reckon." I was quiet for a moment. "When ye were battlin' Malecoda, the duke, yer body changed as though ye werenae the same Besom as ye are now."

She was quiet for a few moments. "I could see myself glowing but I didn't realize I actually looked different."

"Aye, ye changed shape. Ye werenae say tall nor thin. An' yer face was also different."

She looked at me nervously. "Was I as... attractive as I am now?"

I ran me fingers down the side of her face. "Ye are always beautiful tae me, Besom, nae matter whit ye look like oan the outside." I touched her heart. "'Tis whit's inside here that made me love ye nae yer bonny face."

She smiled and then inhaled deeply. "I've seen this reflection of myself before—where I'm different than I am now and different than I was in life but somehow I know whoever this person is, it's still me. The real me."

"'Tis a spirit?"

She shrugged. "I don't know. I call it my Self."

"Ah moost admit, Ah quite like this Self o' yours," I said as I took her nipple into me mouth and sucked upon it as though I were a babe.

"It seems somehow attached to my sword," she continued. "That's why I asked if you'd magicked my sword somehow to make this Self of mine appear."

"Nae, Ah didnae," I said as I shook my head and separated myself from her breast. "Truth be told, the way ye changed yer shape an' glowed back there reminded me o' what Jeanne did tae stave off the Spites."

Besom's face grew serious. "She's a lot more than what she claims to be, Tallis. That whole unspoken plan of attack on the grove? That was all done by her; she was pointing me and the Flamels at the targets we needed to hit."

Another thought occurred to me and I sighed.

"What?" Besom asked as she placed her fingers beneath me chin and propped me head up.

"Malecoda's been loostin' after Donnchadh fer more centuries than Ah can count. An' now that he knows ye have Donnchadh within ye, he'll nae stop tryin' tae take the spirit from ye."

She closed her eyes and arched her back. "Great... more problems we don't need."

"Aye an' then there's the master wizard, Gwydion fab Don. Ye didnae see the Welshman afore he took off. Boot those trees belonged tae him. 'Twas on account of Gwydion that the trees knocked down the demons holdin' Jeanne an' the angel captive."

"So is Gwydion on our side?"

I didnae think so and I shook me head. "If so, it wouldnae explain why the shifty Welshman decided tae invite the likes o' Jedidiah an' Malecoda tae the party he were throwin'. Ah'm thinkin' he's playin' a deeper game."

"And what exactly is the goal of this *deeper game*?"

That question triggered a headache that always arose whenever talk turned to the wizard. "Ach, Ah gave oop on figurin' out the ways o' Gwydion when Ah placed him down here fer the last time. He does what he does an' the rhyme an' reason make sense tae naught boot him."

She gave me a light kiss on the lips and I began to move away from her when she grabbed me shoulders. "And where do you think you're going?"

"Jist a little tae the right so Ah dinnae lie so heavily oopon ye."

She reached up and hugged me closer. "Just lie right here, okay? Don't get up… not just yet."

I shushed her and gently kissed her ear. "Aye, Besom, as long as ye like."

Just then, a frantic set of knocks sounded upon the door.

"Nips! Tido! We gots trouble, yo!"

"Ever to that truth, which but the semblance of a
falsehood wears..."
-Dante's Inferno

TWENTY-FOUR
BILL

When I went downstairs, I kept a close ear out for
Lils and Conan. Earlier I'd been trying not to listen
but the thunderin' that was coming from their room
made that lil request impossibles. All them sex sounds
did nothin' but remind me how all I seemed to be was
acquaintance-zoned which is like the uglier cousin of
friend-zoned.

The scene on the ground floor was a little different
from when I left it. All the kids from Custer's Camp
were sacked out on the beds, fast and furiously
asleep. Never woulda pegged Kay as the loudest
snorer. Jeannie and the Fabulous Flames were
yakking away in French. My hearin' is good but even it
has its limits. Probalistically, I'd say they were
comparing notes on what lay outside the Great
Warland.

Greybeard Flame spotted me outta the corner of
his eye and they all shut up in a hurry. That's always
a tattle-tale sign... Whatever's under discussion, it's
for their ears exclusivarily. Him making a big show of
wavin' me over just clenched that diag-notion.

"Ah, there you are, *Monsieur* William! We were
just discussing what kind of treatment your injuries
might require."

I'm pretty sure Jeannie gave him the skinny—or in my case, the used-to-be-fat—on what I required. And he looked smart enough to know that the insultjuries those damn wolves did on me weren't nothing serious. I just needed a slick line to get outta this. "Look, no offenstration, Big Grey, but anything that happened to me is inconsequational. I'm a self-healer, ya know. It's one o' the few percolators I git fer bein' an angel."

Lady Flame arched an eyebrow at me like she had X-rated vision and saw through my bullshit. "And how, pray tell, did you ever become so malnourished during your involuntary stay at the castle of Alaire, hmm? Was that also something you could heal from naturally?"

I felt gawkyward. How do other people talk their way outta jams like this? "Hey, that was a whole 'nother ball game, Lady Frenchie. I had ta lose a few pounds anyway... Maybe not *that* many pounds but still..."

Jeannie sighed with a smile that, under any other circumcisionstances, would've given me a semi. "Oh, do come over and let us evaluate you, William. As far as any of us know, the Fenrir may have transmitted a special poison that could prove quite harmful to you."

And here I thought she couldn't do decepticon. Anyone starts talking like that, they wanna pump ya for what ya know. Well, I wasn't born yesterday—as a matter of fact, I was born at the beginning of time—so no way was I gonna go along with it. I had to do one last, little thing first.

I grabbed what I came for, the plastic-fantastic case with the sat phone in it. It was sitting next to the stairs and I shook my head at them. "No, folks, really, I'm feelin' fine. If that changes, I'll let ya know, yo. But there's something else I really need ta do right now."

Jeannie's expressionation reminded me of Lils. "I shall hold you to your promise, William. And I shall be quite upset if you break that promise."

I spread my arms as wide as the wings I wished I had. "Hey, I'm an angel, yo. We angels hafta keep our word, right?" No point admitting that I'd been partying on the job for the last hundred years or so.

None of them Frenchies looked convinced but at least they didn't stop me from going back upstairs. When I reached the top, I let out my breath. Not the most graceful exit...

It didn't take me long to Manhattan Transfer the number from my cell into the sat phone. The line was ringing. On the third ring, a cheery voice answered. "Vice President of Afterlife Enterprises Requisitions Department, Thalia speaking."

I sighed with relief and let the wall hold me up for a second. "Goddamn if it ain't great ta hear yer voice, Sally."

Her reply practically blew out my eardrum. "Billy! We've been wondering what happened to you. Well, at least I have and we both know that Polly—"

I glanced at the door and stairs to see if anyone heard Sally's verbal equivo-quation of fireworks when I heard a click on the line with Polly's stern voice right after it. "Where in the name of Hades have you been? We've been trying to ring you since they found that missing car outside the Asylum."

The door was still closed and nobody was coming up the stairs, so I guessed that nobody but me heard Sally. "Yeah, um, I was kinda beyond cell tower range fer a while."

Sally gasped in horror. "You mean you're *still* down in the Ninth Circle? With all those demons?"

I made my lips fart... softly. "Hell, Sally, you'da found my chub ass frozen into a snowball if that happinionated. Nah, me an' Tido blew out o' there a little while ago."

"Who's Tido?"

I sometimes forget not everyone knows my nicknames. "Tallis Black... ya know, ex-head honcho o' the Underground City an' recently turned antisocialized he-man hermit o' the Dark Wood?"

Polly did one of her little hums, the sound she makes when she's trying to choose between asking for more info or giving me the roots-rock-riot act. "You say you're beyond cell tower range. Then you're not in Dis?"

"Uh-uh, nowhere near Dis."

"You're not in one of the upper circles?"

God, I hated when she did that. "Look, Polly, lemme save ya some time on yer little Socreatic method an' tell ya where I am, okay? I'm somewhere in the morgue."

"If you're in the Eighth Circle, getting a cell call out should be impossible. I personally requisitioned the fiber optics that—"

"Well, actuality, this place ain't in such great shape right now, yo. In actual-factual, ya could call it a literarial war zone."

Polly's tone got sharp enough to cut Tido's hair. "What do you mean by 'war zone', Bill?"

Yeah, she didn't want to believe me but I knew she couldn't be *that* dense. "Geez, Polly, what d'ya think?! I've been in enough o' those bone-grinders ta recognitize a war front when I see one. If I didn't know no better, I'd swear I was back in Ypres fer the fourth time."

Sally's moan was even more unnerving than Polly's sternness. "Oh, no... I remember Ypres. A hundred years ago, it was a horrible place to die... full of rifles, machine guns, mustard gas—"

Polly cut her off like a driver who used GTA to learn the rules of the road. "Yes, yes, I was there too, Thalia." She paused and started in on me again. "And now that you've upset my sister, you slovenly angel, tell me what this is really about."

That right there tore it for me. I understood why Polly didn't like me too much. But being a hardass ain't the same as being a dumbass. "Yo, ya remember all those shipments you misplaculated? I'm pretty sure we just found 'em down here."

A long moment of dead air told me I finally got through the reinforcefield around Polly's brain. "What were they actually?"

"Weapons, Polly... big guns, little guns, planes, comm equipment, maybe a few nasty things we ain't worked out yet. Leavin' asideways the comm equipment, all the rest of it is stuff I ain't seen since the war that Ypres was part of. An' the Malebranche seem ta have truckloads of it."

Sally's next comment was what separated her from a bimbot. "But that's kind of stupid. I mean, the Malebranche rule that Circle with an iron fist. If they were having trouble, you'd think they'd get better weapons than the antiques you're talking about."

I scolded myself for not thinking of that first. "Yeah, well, let's just say there's some serious rust in that iron yer talkin' about, kiddo."

That's when I took the timeout to explanate the little uncivil war that was going on 'round here, including what we knew about the big players. When I got to the part about the Spites, Polly stopped me again with a shout that nearly outdid Sally's.

"What do you mean the Spites are on the loose?!"

She made the proposition sound like an even worse idea than it already was. "I've seen it with my own eyes, Polly. They're out an' about, on some regular migraine flight plan, one that prick Cauchon knew all about. Everybody but him is scared shitless of 'em."

Polly's voice went from am-bitchous to out-courageous in a blink. "As they should be... No one benefits from those foul spirits roaming free."

"So why did someone set them free, then?" Sally asked.

I couldn't believe what I just heard. "Say what?"

Neither could Polly. "Really, Thalia, of all the random nonsense you could bandy about—"

But Sally had enough pluck to push back. "Think about it. None of those bastards could have ever broken out of *that* Urn. It's made out of Primaria Materia, which we all know *never* breaks down. So someone had to release them... again."

Polly made another irritated grunt. "Look, fact-free speculation aside, the current situation is one that upper management would never tolerate if they knew about it."

I had my own raisins for that but I figured Polly wasn't in the mood to hear them. "So I take it yer gonna tell 'em?"

And just like that, Polly got ambitchous all over again. "Without any corroborating evidence to back up the claim of a few mislabeled shipments? Are you *trying* to test my patience, Bill?"

God love her but Sally always knew the right thing to say before Polly and I came to a blow-down. "I think what he's really asking, sis, is what exactly do you need from him that can help make our case?"

No sense in telling either of them what I really meant to say. "Yeah, what she said. Just a little FYI, Polly: me an' everybody else are still a loooooong way from safe down here."

Polly was pissed because Sally once again proved she wasn't a ditz. "All right, all right, you've both made your points. If you could get some of your people on the phone, I could record at least a little of their testimony and take it to my superiors."

I didn't like the sound of that. "Yeah, uh, did you dis-remember that part about how we're all stuck in the morgue right now? You never know who might be listenin'. I'm usin' a sat phone I had ta... ya know, borrow."

"Oh, do have the dignity to at least call your theft by its proper name, Bill."

I pretendulated she didn't say that. "Plus, we're bone-tired, an' some of us are wounded an' I'm sure a few of us are pretty hangry right now."

"And what does hunger have to do with—"

Sally's bubbly voice rescued me a second time. "He's saying it's a bad time to get all that info, even though he knows you need it. And c'mon, Polly, we're talking about people who just escaped some pretty vicious captors. You think they're going to be in any shape to talk after all they've experienced?"

I heard a tapping next to the receiver, probably Polly's fingernails drumming on the desk. "We *still* need something in order to start a meaningful investigation. Otherwise, this conversation has just become a waste of *everyone's* time."

Even though she couldn't see me, I shrugged. "Okay, how 'bout names o' yer future wit-notices? That good enough ta start?"

The tapping stopped, replaced by something heavy that landed next to the phone. "I suppose it will have to do. Whom do you have with you at the moment?"

I looked up at the stone ceiling while I pulled up the list of names from my head. "Well, there's Tido— Tallis Black—"

"Yes, we got that much," Polly snarked. "May I assume the charge you so miserably failed, a Miss Lily Harper, is also among your pack of escapees?"

240

"You know it, Polly. But she ain't the only Soul Retriever down here in Residence Evil."

"There's another one?" Damn if Polly didn't sound as eager for that as a college coed for good sex.

"Try three o' them! They're the kids we yanked outta George Custer's little summer army camp on the way over here. They were there to run the comms. The rest o' Custer's boys couldn't figure out an old school telephone."

Sally suddenly giggled hysterically. "Oh, wow. If Georgie Custer is leading the troops, you know the Malebranche are desperate for good help."

Polly hissed at her before talking to me again. "Who are they?"

"All I got are the first names or maybe they're nicknames... Harry, Kay, and Addie..."

A few scratches later, Polly asked, "Anyone else?"

"Yeah, three more. One o' them's a cute peasant girl who's been stuck down here fer ages. She calls herself Jeanne."

The scratching stopped cold. "Did you say Jeanne?"

Polly was back to business just like that. "Yeah, mean anything ta you?"

A couple of taps later, she gave me my answer. "Aside from 'cute', what does she look like?"

"I dunno, young... nineteen maybe if I had ta guesstimate. Dark hair, doe eyes, likes ta wear super frumpy, out-of-date clothes, seems pretty tacticool when it comes ta movin' an army, guided by something she don't like ta talk about. What's the punchline here, Polly?"

Another few seconds of dead airspace passed. Then Sally chimed in again. "Are you thinking what I'm thinking, sis?"

There were a few more scratches before Polly replied. "If you're thinking Jeanne D'Arc aka Joan of Arc, Thalia, then the answer is yes."

Okay, when ya put it like that, it was Crystal Cathedral clear. Didn't stop me from getting floored, walled and ceilinged by what they'd just said though. "You shittin' me? Joan of the Fuckin' Noah's Ark?"

"We aren't shitting you, Bill," Polly said.

"Holy Fuck me."

Polly sounded smug. "Yes, that enlightened conclusion was something upper management finally concurred with in 1456." Then she sighed and I heard a rubbing sound. "Such a pity it took Jeanne's conviction being overturned in the world above to make them see the truth."

The more I heard of this story, the more pissed I got. "I'm still waitin' ta know what Jeannie's doin' here."

Sally picked up the thread. "Oh, it's just as messed up as the conviction was. The order for her release came down to her holding cell in Dis. We even had a couple of your brothers dispatched to escort her back to Afterlife Enterprises."

Polly let a metritoxic ton of disgust come out in her voice. "But by the time the angels arrived, Jeanne was long gone. They'd already released her and sent her out into the streets."

Okay, even for AE, that was boner-shrinkingly stupid. "Why the hell would they pull that bullshit?"

Sally's usually cheerful voice got a nasty edge to it. "Oh, Billy, you should have heard the excuses we got from Alaire. If you had to boil them all down to one sentence, it would have been 'none of this is my fault.'"

Polly harrumphed like a cat clearing a hairball from her throat. "Regardless of fault, the point remains that Jeanne has been under the radar ever since. There's been the occasional sighting but never any solid information that can be acted upon."

I made sure Polly heard the shit-eating grin on my face. "Until now... How bad do yer bosses at AE want Jeannie out o' here?"

"Bad enough that, if you can get Miz D'Arc back to the office for debriefing, they would wipe the slate completely clean; and that goes for any Soul Retriever that brings her in."

I made a little "oooh" sound when I heard that. Screw the Dark Wood! Jeannie could be Nips's real ticket outta the Underground City once and for all. But then I thought about Skeletorhorn and Blondie and all the other guys with them that we still didn't know jackshit about. What if handing Jeannie off to AE was really handing her off to Blondie himself?

Sally snapped me out of it. "Are you still there, Billy?"

"Huh? Yeah, yeah, still here. I just got lost in my thoughts is all."

Polly snorted. "I never imagined you had enough thoughts to get lost in."

Oh, that burned my ass. Well, time to show Polly she didn't know everything. "Something else Lils told me a while ago, something I wanted ta run past you two."

Sally sounded surprised. "Wait, you mean there's more?"

"Oh, yeah, goes back ta that Spite situational. Lils told me about a couple o' spirits that ain't part o' that flyin' death squadron runnin' around."

Polly gasped this time. "At the risk of repeating myself, that is impossible. The Spites act as a hive mind these days and thus—"

"Yeah? Well, apparenthesisly, one o' the beez didn't make it back ta the hive. An' git this, he's

Heath-Ledgerly been seen out an' about fer a few centuries now."

The tapping on the other end really got fast this time. "That sounds far too much like an unsubstantiated rumor."

"Ya mean like Jeannie's location was?"

Polly gave whatever she hit so hard a whack, I wondered if the thing she used to hit it with survivaled.

Sally hummed thoughtfully herself. "You said there were two missing from the Spites, right?"

"Yeah, the spirit of Hope... or is that a rumor too?"

"Uh-uh, no way, Jose!" Sally squealed. "That one's definitely been off everybody's radar for a long time. It's never been as big a priority as Jeanne is but..."

When Sally trailed off, Polly took over. "The bottom line on both is exactly the same, I'm afraid. We have no more knowledge of either spirit than you do... and shall I assume you don't know where they are at present?"

I felt like a real shitheel for not telling them the other part Lils told me: that Conan's resident psychopath spirit was supposed to be the Big Bad Spite. But like some of my humans found out the hard way, ya never know who might be listening in. "Yeah, the closest I ever got ta Hope was a phony diamond that the Fabulous Flames used ta con Cauchon while he was holdin' onta me an' Tido fer a hot second."

"You and your demented nicknames! Can you for... tell... names of..."

I couldn't make out what she said when static came over the line. "Polly? Polly, can ya hear me? Polly?"

I started banging on the phone like *that* would make things better. But dammit, I couldn't think of anything else to do! That's when I heard a voice.

"I'm sorry but this call has been disconnected. Please try your call again later, preferably on a phone that doesn't belong to *me*."

I swallowed hard at hearing Blondie's voice. He didn't sound any less pissed now than he was back at the Ice Palace one floor down. Still, I had enough sense to turn my cell's recorder on and scrunch it next to the receiver. "Last I checked, Blondie, the righteous-ful owner o' this piece o' hardware was actually Georgie-Porgie Custer."

"And how, pray tell, do you believe he received that particular piece of equipment? In fact, there's not a single weapon or communication device down there which didn't originate from my generosity."

That sounded like evidence of cor-robber-ation on Polly's theory about those shipments. Maybe if I kept him talking, I could get more useful shit outta him. "Gotta say I'm disappointed. I figure a guy like you'd be out-fistin' these boys with something better than iron musketeers from the Great War."

"While I admit that is a fair point, it is also worth considering the troops I must equip. Do you think any of them have the slightest idea how to handle, say, a jet fighter? Or a modern M16 rifle for that matter? No, it was best to give them simple, basic armaments if they are to be of any use to me."

That's right, keep talkin', I thought. "So yer sayin' the Mephits ain't got the brain-cells ta pull a trigger, yo?"

Blondie snorted in disgust. "Please... you may recall they are literally worms. Higher thought is as far beyond them as celibacy is to you. Giving them anything more sophisticated than the Pain Whips they carry under their coats would be a wasted effort." I heard his voice shifting gears like an old Harlequin Davidson. "Of course, it is also in my best interests to keep the conflict balanced. That is why I signed them to exclusive contracts among the commanding officers of both the Malebranche and Simoniacs."

Okay, he'd been free and easy with the info so far. Time to double down or nothing. "Here's what I don't git, Blondie. You already own all this real-deal estate anyway, yo. Why go to all the trouble o' tearin' it up like this?"

There was a pregnant pause on the other end that soon miscarried. "Just between us, there *is* a fascinating story behind this move that I would dearly love recorded for posterity... much like everything else I've just said."

My throat and guts clenched at the same time. I wanted to say something but that was in serious conflictation with my sudden need to puke on the spot. Blondie just kept on talking.

"You really thought I didn't hear you turn on whatever recording device you're holding up to the receiver, you disgrace for an angel? Or did you think I'd be telling all of this to *you,* of all people, without good reason?"

It took a little extra work but I managed to get my vocallout chord-ination working again. "So what's yer game, Blondie?"

"The same one as always: chess. And now that I have a certain piece on the board moving in your direction courtesy of the tracker on this phone, the word 'checkmate' comes to mind. I will send your regards to Polyhymnia and Thalia when I catch up with them." He paused for a moment. "And give my regards to Ms. Harper. Truth be known, I miss her terribly and so do look forward to the moment we reunite."

"You ain't never gonna hurt Lils again, you..."

Blondie laughed. "My goal is not to hurt her, you fool. My goal is to tame her until she wishes to be my queen... of her own inclination." He paused. "And that day will come. Until then, I wish you and yours adieu."

Even if the smug bastard didn't hang up on me, I would've still dropped that sat phone like the hot potato it was. One thought kept running laps through my head in a vicious cycle: *This is bad, this is bad, this is bad.* We needed to get outta here... right now.

In no time flat, I was banging on Lily's door like a jackhammer. "Nips! Tido! We gots trouble, yo!"

"Through the gross and murky air I spied a shape
come swimming up..."
-Dante's Inferno

TWENTY-FIVE
LILY

"Whit's the matter, stookie angel?" Tallis
demanded as he looked at me with an expression of
bewilderment.

Bill's voice on the other side of the door sounded
panicked. "Somethin' big's gonna be the matter if we
don't split like yesterday!"

Before Bill finished talking, I slipped back into my
leather tunic and grabbed my sword. Then I threw
open the door and found him sweating and panicked.
"Get back downstairs and let everyone know we're
shipping out!"

I reached for Tallis' blade and tossed it to him as I
opened the door wide, noticing the panic of everyone
downstairs. Even though neither Tallis nor I had any
idea what was going on, I figured we'd find out later.
For now, I trusted Bill enough to know whatever was
coming, it wasn't good.

The Flamels and Soul Retrievers gathered what
few things they had to their names and watched us
with anticipation as Tallis and I took the stairs two at
a time.

"Let's go," I said and motioned to the front door.

But when Harry tried to open the front door, it
wouldn't budge. Kay rammed her shoulder into it,
followed by Harry doing the same, but the door held

248

fast. Addie came up behind them both and aided in the attempt to strongarm the door into opening which failed yet again. She slapped the door in frustration.

"Why won't the goddamn thing open?!"

Nicolas shot her a stern rebuke. "Do *not* take the Lord's name in vain, *jeune femme.*"

"Well, excuse me for worrying about getting out of this deathtrap!"

Perenelle ran over to the shelves and snatched a couple of vials. "As the house has proven less than cooperative, perhaps this will help us achieve our egress."

While she spoke, I heard something familiar coming from overhead. It was the humming of propellers spinning on a plane.

Perenelle hurriedly uncorked the vials and handed one of them to Nicolas. She poured the contents on the top door hinge while her husband followed suit with the bottom one. The metal hinges hissed and popped, sounding almost as loud as the incoming propellers.

Harry and Kay gave the door one more shoulder ram. This time, it fell off its hinges and hung precariously, blocking our path. Kay jumped over it while Harry lifted one edge and held it open for the rest of us. We all ran outside as fast as our legs could carry us.

I could hear Harry nearly choking behind me as he screamed out in pure fear. "Go! Go! Go!"

Whatever he saw indicated our attacker was way too close for comfort. I heard him drop the door as his pounding footsteps sounded behind me. His breath was coming fast and in raspy gasps. Whatever the hell he'd seen had spooked the crap out of him.

We'd just reached the end of the block when a big boom went off behind me, to my left. I felt scorching air a second before the blast lifted me off the ground.

A few seconds later, I face-planted into the ground. I didn't feel any pain right away but the second I tried to sit up, I was overcome with dizziness. I shook my head until my wits returned and then I took stock of my situation.

Everyone else in my small group had been rocked by the explosion as well. They looked as dazed as I felt and were taking a while to push themselves back to their hands and knees. While some of them were a little woozier than others, everyone appeared to be mostly okay. Or at least, there wasn't any blood to make note of and everyone's appendages appeared to be intact.

You couldn't say the same thing about the house, though. It had been turned into a pillar of flame. The conflagration was so hot, it melted the standing stone of the skyscrapers. I glanced up and caught a glimpse of something that looked like it was trying to be a World War I prop plane. It immediately vanished into the clouds.

Of course I could only hope it wasn't the Baron flying the plane. It wasn't red so that caused me a bit of relief.

I looked at Tallis who was already running over to me. He pulled me to my feet as he searched the landscape directly around us.

"That plane will be back," he announced. "We moost take shelter wherever we can find it." He glanced to his right where, about fifty feet in the distance, a one-story and halfway intact building stood. One half was blown away but the other half was large enough to house us all until we figured out a better plan.

"We move there," Tallis said as he gestured to the building. I nodded as my hearing gradually returned and I heard someone say over and over again: "All my fault... all my fault..."

I looked at Bill and realized he was the one talking. He seemed well beyond shell-shocked as he sat upright and stared straight ahead. The expression on his face was wide-eyed but not seeing. It was as though he were staring at something horrible that only he could see. His eyes brimmed with tears that overflowed onto his cheeks.

"Bill!" I yelled. "Get moving towards that building!" I said and pointed to the structure in question. Meanwhile the rest of our group overheard me and started for the blown out building.

Once we reached it, I noticed my guardian angel still looking as shell-shocked as he had a second ago. He collapsed in a pile of rubble once we reached the shelter of the building and then stared at one of the intact walls as if he were watching a movie.

I crouched down beside him but when he wouldn't look at me, I turned his face in my direction. His eyes blinked with recognition and that blank expression on his face blanched into one of relief.

"You're alive..." he started.

I was surprised but figured he was just shocked and the shock hadn't quite worn off yet. "Yeah, thanks to you."

Bill started shaking his head as he pulled away from me. "Thanks ta me, you nearly died again. This was all my fault." His jaw got tighter as the tears in his eyes came doubly hard. He pushed to his feet and after swaying for a second or two, began walking away from us. Jeanne caught up to him and touched his shoulder.

"*Un instant, s'il vous plait, mon petit ami.*"

He threw her hand off his shoulder and looked up at her. "*Laissez-moi etre!*"

By then, Tallis and the Flamels were standing in his way, blocking the only opening in the building. Perenelle squatted down to his eye level and placed a

251

concerned hand on his shoulder. "That, we cannot do. Leaving you will only subject you to the Underground City's untender mercies."

Bill glared at her. "Don't you get it? I'm no good to anyone! An' this time I really fucked things up! All I ever do is screw up... again an' again an' again."

Harry peered at Bill like he was a rare archeological find he'd just sifted from the sand. "Hey, what's this really about, Shorty? 'Cause as far as I can tell, you told us to get our asses outta that building before it went up."

My little guardian angel appeared torn—like he wanted to answer Harry's question but he also wanted to hold onto... I didn't know, his dignity, maybe?

Addie got right into his face. "Stop talking shit about yourself and tell us what the hell just happened."

Bill took a deep breath. He looked beyond the opening and at the flaming pit that had been the Flamels stronghold like it had all the answers. "That sat phone I grabbed... Blondie put a tracker on it. That's how he knew where to hit us."

Tallis rolled his eyes to the cloud cover. "Sweet Bran, stookie angel!"

Kay whacked one of Tallis' muscular arms. "He feels bad already. Don't rub it in, all right?"

I approached Bill and wrapped my arm around his shoulders. "This isn't on you, Bill," I started as I eyed everyone apprehensively. "But we also don't have time to discuss this now."

Perenelle nodded. "Regardless of where we go, we cannot remain here much longer."

"There's a direct route tae the Dark Wood a short distance from here..." Tallis started.

"How far?" I asked.

Tallis shrugged. "Mayhap a mile or so."

Addie raised her hand. "Sign me up."

252

I nodded. "If Alaire knows where we are, it's just a matter of time before that plane returns with a legion of its best friends."

Harry swallowed hard and asked, "Alaire?"

"Aye," Tallis said with a nod. "Bastard's been supplyin' both sides with the means tae kill each other an' now we're caught smack in the middle."

"But why would he be playing both sides?" Harry asked.

Nicolas got a glum expression on his face. "For the purpose of obtaining Pandora's Urn."

Kay pulled her well-muscled head back a little. "Don't you mean 'Pandora's Box'?"

Wanting to avoid that conversation, I interrupted. "What makes you think the Urn is down here?"

Nicolas and Perenelle exchanged a glance between them. Then Perenelle answered my question. "Because we know the urn was once in the custody of Malecoda himself."

Nicolas took up the tale from there. "From what little we pieced together, the Urn was in the Lord of the Malebranche's possession since at least the fall of Rome. Many of Malecoda's most hardened soldiers were killed when the Spites broke free of the urn, forcing him to call upon his liege, Alaire, for aid."

"Spites broke free," I repeated, wondering if the Spites really had broken free...

Tallis's face grew darker. "An' push folks such as yerselves intae indentured servitude."

I could see where this story was going. "And because Alaire never does anything for free, he wanted Malecoda to hand over the Urn as the price for his help?"

Jeanne frowned. "Yet, as Alaire was Malecoda's sovereign and liege, could not Alaire have just ordered Malecoda to hand over this urn without all this fuss?"

253

Bill grunted. "Not if Blondie didn't know Maleyoda had it in the first place."

Addie slapped her right thigh hard. "And when the Spites broke free, *everyone* knew Malecoda had it."

"Including Alaire which was why he demanded the urn in return for helping Malecoda," I finished.

Harry was back to shaking his head. "So why do the Spites stay down here nayway? I mean, they can fly, so you'd figure they could go wherever they choose."

Nicolas nodded at him. "Logically, you would think so, *jeune homme*. But every last spirit in that Urn is intimately tied to the vessel that contains it. While they can go a fair distance from the Urn, they can never leave it behind completely."

The gears in my head began spinning. If it was true that Donnchadh really was a Spite... Hmm, if I could somehow get Donnchadh out of me and put him back into the Urn, it might work out for everyone but Alaire. But first I had to know if that was even possible.

I looked at Nicolas then at Perenelle. "Is there any way to get the Spites back into the Urn?"

Nicolas tapped his chin with his fingers as he considered my question. "As it happens, there is a certain ritual which may accomplish such a task."

Tallis's frown grew deeper. "O' course, the big problem is that we need tae find the Urn first, aye?"

I sighed. "And there lies the rub."

The moment I said the words, I felt a buzzing starting within my sword that began to travel up the blade, the pommel and inside me.

All of a sudden, it was like a projector screen dropped in front of my eyes. I could suddenly see an elaborately detailed Grecian urn as clearly as if it were sitting right in front of me. It bore some type of ritual markings around the base. A man suddenly appeared

254

beside the urn and as I watched, he began scratching a copy of the runes into the battered dirt beside the urn, next to a copse of trees.

Just as quickly as the vision came, it left. And then I was left with this intense desire to leave the structure we were currently hiding within and travel east. When I closed my eyes, the feeling only intensified and even though I couldn't see it, I had the definite understanding that the urn was calling to me, pulling me towards it. My sword continued to buzz.

Bill caught the look in my eyes first. "Nips, why you got that weird expression on yer face?"

I looked down at my guardian angel. "I think... I think I just got a vision."

"A vision?" Jeanne repeated, suddenly extremely interested.

I nodded. "It felt like... the urn was reaching out to me... maybe through my sword? Either way, I think we're meant to travel east."

Tallis shook his head. "Even with proper rest, we're nae in any shape tae take the Urn."

As though right on cue, Bill's phone emitted a ringtone and a buzz. He looked at it like it was an alien artifact. "Yo, since when did I git cell tower receptionary?"

Glancing over his shoulder, I saw a text of the picture of an urn. It was the same urn I'd just witnessed in my vision, right down to the weird markings on the ground and the trees in the background. In addition to man who was sketching out the runes in the dirt, this picture also revealed a bunch of worm demons and armed humans who were standing around the urn and protecting it, for lack of a better description.

I quickly waved Nicolas over and pointed at the picture. "Is this *the* Urn?"

Nicolas gaped at the sight of it. "*Mais oui*, it most certainly is."

Tallis looked over our shoulders. "Who in the name o' the Morrigan sent that picture?"

While the sender was marked "Unknown", Bill scrolled up until I saw a signature on the bottom. "Ain't Nothing But A G Thing?" he asked.

Tallis groaned in annoyance. "Gwydion... only makes sense the miscreant would know how tae use a cell phone in this place."

"Who is this Gwydion guy and what's his deal?" I asked, shaking my head. "First, he lures us into not one but two ambushes in his private, little Eden. Then he helps Bill and Jeanne escape the second ambush with his Tree twins. And now he's sending us useful info about an Urn we just happened to be discussing?" I swallowed hard as I wondered if the vision I'd just seen was from Gwydion as well? Somehow I didn't think so. No, there was a sureness within me that the vision had come from my sword.

Tallis frowned in resignation. "Gwydion spoke the truth when he said the only side he takes is his own. Sae while he may have nae love fer oos, he'll nae necessarily be the ruin o' oos either."

Bill spread his hands out. "Still leaves a lot of real-deal estate between those two spots, Tido."

By this point, Perenelle joined us. She tapped her index finger on the picture. "I can tell you those runes the man is drawing in the dirt have all the proper markings for the ritual we mentioned before. And if someone has control of the Spites through the Urn, it would be catastrophic."

Harry shook his head hard. "But Tallis just said we haven't got the numbers to take the urn. So maybe we need a plan B?"

"The shortcut to the Dark Wood?" Addie reminded everyone.

Tallis frowned. "Would that we could…"

"We can't just leave!" I insisted. "If we allow Alaire to take control of the Spites, that means his power just increased a hundredfold."

"Aye," Tallis nodded. And then he shook his head. "It jist sae happens that particular plot o' land that would lead tae the Dark Wood is the same location of the urn and Alaire's men."

"You mean the picture Gwydion sent," I started and Tallis nodded.

"Is the exact location o' the exit intae the Dark Wood."

"So we could attack, take the urn and retreat through the shortcut?" I asked.

"If the tides o' loock favor oos, aye," Tallis said as he looked at me with an expression of worry.

"Lo! The fell monster with the deadly sting!"
-Dante's Inferno

TWENTY-SIX
TALLIS

"We're fucked," Harry said.

Kay shook her head as she faced me. "There's got to be another way to at least get up to the next Circle to get out of here?"

Addie took a step back. "And then what? Even if we're able to get up to next level, that would leave us with what? Seven more Circles we'd have to get through before we'd make it to the Dark Wood?"

"Hey, there ain't no point in leavin' if we ain't got that urn with us," the angel started.

"Fuck the urn!" Addie yelled back at him. "I'm at the point where all I care about is surviving this place."

"If Alaire takes control of the Spites, your survival will be limited regardless," Besom said. Then she shook her head. "Our number one goal is taking that urn. Escaping needs to be number two."

"Sounds impossible to me," Harry said.

"And you can count on that blonde asshole who nearly annihilated us trying to do it again," Addie continued.

A droning racket in the sky reached me ears. Judging from the frightened looks upon each face, I knew it wasnae just me what heard it. The angel looked up to see where the noise came from and squinted hard. Though I saw naught but clouds, he

258

began sucking in his breath which told me he saw something more.

"Got an antiquified propeller plane kamikazing us, yo! We gotta duck fer cover!"

"Get as far away from the opening of this building as you can and crouch down," Nicolas said as everyone scattered to the far corners that were still intact.

"We're going to die if they bomb this place!" Harry yelled.

"They dinnae know we are in here fer certain," I responded. "As far as they're concerned, we could be anywhere."

"This place is a pretty good guess though," Kay said.

The droning grew louder. After another few seconds, the sounds of explosions ensued but though they were loud, the building 'round us remained. But 'twould nae remain as such for long.

At the sound of the propellers retreating, I stood up from me hiding place and approached the opening in the building. It took a moment for the dust from the explosion which was mayhap thirty feet from us, to clear. But when it did, I saw a brown plane flying low in the sky. 'Twas close enough that I could make out its markings.

Harry stared up with fear as he came alongside me, "It's retreating?"

The plane gradually soared out of sight.

"Nae, lad. They'll be passin' through here agin soon enow."

Kay frowned so intensely, I feared she'd be saddled with a permanent scowl. "Now what? There's no way we could survive all seven Circles to get out of this place so where does that leave us?"

"That jist leaves one way oot..."

Everyone but Jeanne looked at me with a stunned expression. Jeanne's nod and answer revealed she understood exactly what me plan entailed.

"Obstacles or no, the camp contains the only immediate exit from this Circle, *n'est-ce pas*?" Once I nodded, Jeanne looked upon the others. "Although it is less than ideal that we should have to face additional danger in order to make our escape, we can surely agree that any better way is presently beyond our reach."

"Then we're going to attempt to make it to the short cut to the Dark Wood?" Addie asked. "Which means getting by all Alaire's men and Gwydion?"

"Yes, you all are going to attempt to get to the short cut," Besom said with a quick nod. "But I'm not letting that urn go without a fight."

Nicolas nodded. "Me too."

Jeanne grinned at him with angelic sweetness. "Indeed, it is in our best interest to frustrate the designs of those who would gain control of the Spites."

Perenelle appeared less than certain. "But are we, who have so few resources and suffer from terrible exhaustion, up to such a formidable task?"

Jeanne touched her arm with genuine care and tenderness. "I am as sure of our ability to manage such a feat as I am certain we shall depart from this horrible realm very shortly. I can think of no one else I would rather attempt either task with than Tallis Black. I trust him and I believe all of you should, as well."

I had to admit, the lass had the gift of oratory. The way she spoke encouraged each person within our tribe and I was honored to know she placed such stock in me abilities. I said as much. Then the stookie angel broke the spell by flapping his arms while he squinted.

"Shh! It's comin' back 'round."

Everyone immediately returned to their crouched positions within our crude shelter. The plane drifted back into sight, once again, casually scouting the ground for any sign of us.

This time, the plane stayed close to the ground before flying back up into the sky and redoubling its efforts. Clearly whoever was flying the contraption was searching for us.

Jeanne kept her eyes focused upon me. "Is it possible this flying machine came from the camp we seek?"

"Anythin' is possible, lass."

"But is it probable?" Lily continued.

I thought about the question before I began to nod. "Aye, most probable." Me own eyes darted between the sky and the devastated landscape 'round us. "Follow the plane an' we'll most likely find the camp."

Jeanne stepped out of her hiding place, turning 'round to address us all. "Then let us embark."

Kay stepped up and put a sisterly hand on Jeanne's shoulder. "I'm in."

The stookie angel stood beside her. "Ditto."

Besom looked at all of us before joining Jeanne. "It's going to be tough, but then, what isn't tough down here?"

I stepped up next and one-by-one, all the others followed. As Jeanne and I agreed, there was truly no other way.

***

We began moving towards the opening of the building once more. The plane was circling overhead, thus it wasnae safe to venture forth.

Nicolas strode up to me position. "While I applaud your determination to make the best of this terrible situation, *Monsieur* Black, there is still the small

261

matter of trying to maintain the least number of casualties as possible."

I nodded at him. "Aye, be best if we could send a scout tae the camp tae determine the weak points in their defenses."

Jeanne was suddenly at me right shoulder. "Perhaps I can be of some assistance?" She hummed. "If I follow the plane's path, I have no doubt I shall arrive at our destination."

I hesitated. She gave me a shrewd look.

"But that is not your sole concern, *oui*?"

And I thought Besom the only woman who could see through me. "Aye, Ah seem tae recall that Cauchon takin' ye prisoner was how we first met."

She shrugged. "Only because I *permitted* Cauchon to imprison me. The voice of which I cannot speak informed me of two souls in grave peril. The only way to save them from certain doom was by allowing myself to be captured." She paused. "Can we both agree this observation was proven true?"

From anyone else, I'd have called her excuse a boastful way of preserving her honor. But from Jeanne, it made sense. Nae one wanders the Underground City for centuries without learning how to avoid those who would bring them harm. But, still, I wasnae willing to let her go. "It cannae jist be yerself doin' the scoutin', lass. Be best if ye had at least one other along with ye. Ah could…"

She smiled and touched me arm. "You are needed here to guide the others. In the meantime, Harry agreed to accompany me on this reconnaissance mission. With your blessing, we shall leave forthwith."

I felt a lurch in me heart. Whatever secrets she kept to herself, Jeanne was braver than many men. I only hoped her skills were equal to her courage. I put a concerned hand upon her shoulder. "Jist come back safe, aye?"

Putting her own slim hand over mine, she squeezed it. "*Oui.*" With a kiss on me cheek, she released me hand and fell back in line before talking to Harry in low tones.

I felt the eyes of Besom upon me and turned to find her watching me with a sly smile upon her face. I recalled the kiss Jeanne had placed upon me cheek and shrugged as though to say 'twas nae my doing. Besom laughed and waved me away with an unconcerned hand.

That woman was going to be me undoing.

Nicolas looked at me with an earnest expression. "My wife and I need to examine our remaining compounds. I have a hunch at least some of them will be immediately useful to us."

"Aye," I nodded.

Just as he fell back, Jeanne and Harry walked ahead in quick strides before lookin over their shoulders and waving. When I waved back, I noticed I was flanked by Besom at me right shoulder and her inept guardian angel at me left.

"Do you think she'll make it?" Besom asked, her voice low.

"Ah dinnae know, lass," I answered. "Boot if anyone can do it, Ah believe Joan of Arc has the best o' chances."

"Yep, her chances are as good as a two-headed-one-dicked monkey," the daft angel said.

"Does that mean her chances are good or bad?" Besom inquired.

"Good," the dunderheid replied.

"Leaves a question open," I said, choosing to ignore the angel's nonsensical conversation for the time being. "Who, exactly, does Jeanne hear that she cannae tell oos aboot?"

Lily shook her head and shrugged. "All I know about her are the basics... She was a French peasant

263

girl who started hearing voices. She believed the voices were those of the angels. Next thing you know, she's presented to the king, and ends up leading an army into Orleans. Then she was betrayed before being burned at the stake."

"Jeannie got seriously dealt a bad hand," the angel said as he shook his head.

"She believed the voices were angels?" I asked as I eyed the dunderheid with interest.

He backed away and shook his head. "Hey, don't look at me. I don't know nothin' 'bout any voices that Frenchie been hearin'! That ain't my department!"

Besom put a hand on the wee fellow's shoulder. "Someone's still talking to her, Bill. If you've got any ideas about who it might be, that'd help us a lot." Me Besom looked upon me with renewed tension on her lovely face. "I'm wondering if it's Gwydion she could be hearing?"

I gave the matter some thought before making me reply. "Tha's the sort o' dastardly deception the Welshman would indulge in, true, but Ah'm nae seein' it."

Besom frowned. "One thing we can all agree on is that we still don't know enough to figure any of this out and we also don't have the time."

"Aye... an' Ah surely wish we did."

***

Questions regarding Jeanne's true identity aside, there was naething to complain about when it came to her scouting skills. She caught up with us a mile from the camp. Then she led us to a low rise that was part of a vast wall of debris.

As Jeanne told us along the way, the entire camp was ringed by that nearly solid wall of rubble. 'Twas formed in the shape of a horseshoe. While our

264

scouting perch was easy enough to scale, she assured us it was nigh impossible to do the same on the far end—an area that happened to be next to the trees and the magic circle. The latter was still being worked upon by a distant, squatting figure. Since I lacked the angel's telescopic eyes, all I could make out were the black robes of the scribbler.

The sole entrance to the camp was guarded by a pair of machine gun nests that flanked either side. The Mephit worms were close by for backup. The activity in the camp seemed to be in preparation for another attack. Weapons were being uncrated and distributed, the troops were being drilled for hand-to-hand combat, and every person was coming and going between the dozen or so tents. I spotted the plane that had come after us next to an aerodrome. It was being refueled from its scouting flight.

The angel squinted in the direction of the circle of runes. Something he saw there made him grunt in disgust. "Well, dip me in honey sauce an' call me a Chicken McNugget... they got Crowley workin' on that artsy-fartsy project."

Addie's expression of alarm told me she recognized the name. "Crowley? As in Aleister Crowley, the occultist and magician?"

Nicolas sounded considerably less alarmed. "As in Edward Alexander Crowley, the son of a Christian Plymouth Brethren minister who spent his life pretending to possess great occult knowledge that he never, in fact, possessed. What he did not steal from his superiors, he created from a tapestry of falsehoods."

Me lips curled back in contempt. "Aye, Ah remember the silly sod well enough. 'The Great Beast', my arse... after all that nonsense he spouted in life, sendin' him down here was one o' the few public services AE ever did."

265

Harry nervously cleared his throat. "Hey, uh, this is fascinating stuff and all. But I'd kinda like to go back to the part where we figure out the ingenious plan that gets us outta here in one piece."

Jeanne gave him a reassuring pat on the back. "As a point of beginning, you will notice there are no lookouts atop these walls."

Kay shifted as the rocks underneath her made her slip. "Not to mention this pile of loose shit probably isn't the best place to be walking."

Jeanne pointed at our well-muscled compatriot. "Just so, *mon ami*, the enemy has enough troops to send out a scouting party in the event of anything untoward. Harry and I evaded one such party during our earlier reconnaissance."

Addie snorted. "With as hot as the Flamel's place was burning all they're gonna find is blackened stone and one hell of a bonfire."

The angel kept squinting at the camp with his eagle eyes. He suddenly began slapping me shoulder. "Shit, shit, shit!"

I grabbed his hand to make him stop. "Whit be the matter, stookie angel?"

He pointed with his other hand at someone who had just stepped out of a tent near the circle. "Tell me that's not who I think it is, Conan."

But it was. Even at a distance, there was nae mistaking the duster coat nor the rifle in his hand. The pack of wolves 'round him was the final confirmation. "Guess Jedidiah couldnae stay a pig fore'er."

I saw a little hope blossoming on Harry's face. "So that could mean Dahlia didn't stay a pig either, right?"

Addie smiled at him. "Dahlia may have gotten changed into something else, but she was never a pig." She pointed down at the slave hunter. "That asshole, on the other hand..."

266

Besom looked 'round at everyone with annoyance. "Look, character observations aside, this is going to make getting out here an even bigger problem."

Harry looked down at Jedidiah, who was walking towards the circle. "How d'you think we should handle it, boss lady?"

I saw a slight flush in Lily's cheeks at his respectful tone. "Let's just say I'm open to suggestions." Then she smiled at him. "And don't call me boss lady."

I found meself chuckling and me Besom turned tae look at me, giving me a wee smile jist atween the two of us. She mouthed the words "I love you" and I reached out to her, grabbing her hand as I pulled her into me.

"When we reach the Dark Wood, ye are mine fer the takin'," I whispered.

She glanced up at me and her left eyebrow arched. "Not unless I take you first," she whispered back.

"Um, the rest of us ain't gettin' no action soze save all that shit fer the bedroom!" the angel grunted.

Besom laughed with embarrassment and then nodded as Jeanne cleared her throat and gave the scene below a calculating look.

"I have a suggestion, but I doubt you shall deem it pleasant." She waved her index finger across the jagged top of the rubble around us.

I gave a disapproving grunt. "Nae, Jeanne. Even assumin' the rocks hold steady enough tae walk across 'em, every step we make would cause a sound an' stir that the dimmest guard would hear."

Jeanne was unfazed by me faulting her plan. "Only if the distraction I have in mind proves insufficient." She turned to Nicolas. "Can any of your remaining compounds create a great deal of noise and light?"

Perenelle answered for both of them. "As it happens, *Mademoiselle* Jeanne, I have a compound of which a few drops can produce quite an exciting explosion."

Jeanne's eyes lit up. "Would it require any special preparations for such an event to come to pass?"

Nicolas's wife pulled out the two vials from her apron. "Merely mix the two substances together and within a few moments, there will be enough noise and light to suit your purposes."

Jeanne gestured for the vials and Perenelle handed them to her. I took the latter by the shoulder. "Whit dae ye think yer doin', Jeanne?"

She gently but firmly pushed me hand away. "Providing the needed diversion... I shall rejoin you once I am finished."

Perenelle took her other shoulder. "I would advise you to mix the compounds then quickly remove yourself from them. The effect is a rather powerful blast."

I squeezed Jeanne's shoulder to keep her attention. "We cannae tarry long. Once they figure out the trick, they'll make sure that anyone who stays behind pays fer it."

The smile she gave me revealed a sad wisdom. "We will see each other soon. That, I promise."

With a quick *au revoir,* she slid down the slope and ran 'round the corner. Once she vanished behind the rubble, I stared at Harry. "Any idear where she's goin', lad?"

Harry stuck his tongue out and moved it from side-to-side. "There was this little spot where we were able to see the machine guns without getting noticed ourselves. Got no idea how Jeanne plans to get from there back to us afterwards, though."

Besom touched my arm. "You've got to admit, Tallis, the plan is workable."

268

Addie stretched her arms above her head. "Guess we'd better get ready for the go-ahead."

I still thought this plan was bloody balmy but I didnae have a better one on offer. As the lass said, there was naethin' to do but prepare for Jeanne's distraction.

"Who passes mountains, breaks through fenced walls and firm embattled spears, and with his filth taints all the world!"
-Dante's Inferno

TWENTY-SEVEN
TALLIS

It didnae take long.

An impressive boom followed the bright flash of light outside the gates. Then there was another... and another... and a fourth. Why Jeanne would set off so many at once I wasnae certain. Still, it did the trick of making nearly every demon and human trooper grab their weapons and rush out of the camp. Only the machine guns stayed manned by the Mephits.

The angel took the lead and we began running across the unsteady rubble. We slipped more than a few times, requiring us to grab the straggler in question and hoist them back up. Despite our starts and stops, we managed to cover enough ground to approach the circle and trees from the left.

Ignoring the blasts, Crowley never once looked up from his work upon the circle. Many of the signs and symbols that comprised it reminded me of what I had seen back at the Flamels' now-destroyed house.

In the center of it all, the Urn glowed with an eerie yellow light. The container was directly lined up to the tree that served as the hidden gate to the Dark Wood. I was about to go down when Perenelle put her hand in front of me and shook her head. To me raised eyebrow, she pointed down at the scratches upon which Crowley was working.

Nicolas was already giving the overall design a hard stare, his frown deepening by the second. Finally, he looked away from the circle and his eyes scanned all of us in turn. Then he slowly shook his head. Unless I misunderstood him, all the scratching Crowley had made was still short of the goal.

The angel hissed and began pointing to the front of the camp. Jedidiah was heading our way with his loyal pack of hell-wolves running at his heels. The scowl on Jedidiah's face told me he wasnae any happier than the rest of us.

The slave hunter slammed his boot down in front of Crowley's drawing hand. The pack took a cue from their master and snarled at the lowly magician from all sides.

"What is this?" Jedidiah demanded.

The little would-be wizard opened and closed his mouth several times, as though he was still figuring out how it worked. "Th-Th-The design... it just needs a few m-m-more touches."

In one motion, Jedidiah knelt down, pulled out his hunting knife, and stuck the point right between Crowley's eyes. "That's what you said an hour ago... The only result I have seen thus far is that the top of the Urn now glows."

The chattering of the little man's teeth became worse. "B-B-But that means it's working!"

The knife tip traveled from between Crowley's eyes to beneath his chin. "That means you have yet to do your job properly. If for any reason, this final hour does not yield the desired outcome, your usefulness will come to an end, as will you. Am I clearly understood?" Jedidiah insisted.

To emphasize his last point, he pushed upon the knife tip, making Crowley's head go back. As much as the knife would allow, Crowley nodded frantically until the blade left his throat. He eagerly returned to his work, his strokes even less careful and coherent than before.

Nicolas placed his hand over his eyes as if he couldnae bear to see how badly Crowley was making a mockery of the magical runes.

I stuck me tongue out to catch the direction of the breeze. Currently, we werenae downwind of the Fenrir, which was why they hadnae detected us. But that would change the instant the breeze switched direction. I began to wonder if abandoning the Urn, as appalling as it seemed, werenae the better option.

While Cauchon's lieutenant put his knife away, a buzzing came from his pocket. He quickly reached inside and pulled out a mobile phone. I looked upon the angel who was already ahead of me, pulling up the screen of his mobile. There were three reception bars at the top; and before, he couldnae get even one. The only explanation was the tent had its own signal booster that allowed mobiles to work down here.

Jedidiah put the mobile on speaker. Alaire's voice came through loud and clear.

"Report, Jedidiah."

The slave hunter cleared his throat. "There've been a series of explosions we cannot explain. These explosions occurred at the front of the camp."

Alaire sounded somewhere between worried and angry. "I trust they're currently being investigated?"

Jedidiah relaxed. "As we speak... we hope to know more shortly."

Alaire grunted before moving to his next question. "And what of the camp's sole purpose for existing?"

The wolf pack's master glowered at the old robed fraud at his feet. "There has only been incremental progress on the summoning circle for the Spites."

272

Alaire's voice grew hard and cold. "Define 'incremental'."

Jedidiah's face imitated my betrayer's voice. "If I may be blunt, I have no reason to believe the circle will be finished by the time the Spites pass through." He looked intently at the screen of his mobile. "And we have no more than ten minutes left to prepare."

Alaire hummed through the receiver. "I respect your bluntness, Jedidiah." He paused. "*However,* this report reminds me why I wanted you to lead the latest raid on the Flamels yourself."

Besom grew tense. Oblivious to us, Jedidiah frowned into the phone. "You may recall I was in the process of retrieving Beatrice from Cardinal Cauchon at the time, sir."

"Beatrice…" Besom whispered as she frowned at me. I shrugged for I didnae understand Jedidiah's reference.

Alaire's voice was unsympathetic. "Reciting your past failures won't make me inclined to forgive your present ones. Now that we've been reduced to relying on the likes of Crowley due to your—"

Pulling the mobile right beside his mouth, Jedidiah began yelling into it. "Had you given me more time, I would have been on that raid and you would have had your precious alchemists! But no, you wanted it immediately, which was why I was forced to rely on these ragtag, ill-experienced troops! Now they're dead and you have nothing!"

Alaire's laugh chilled me. "*Au contraire, mon bravo.* I have the one thing you care about more than anything else in this world. It would be such a shame to ruin it." Jedidiah's knuckles grew white as he gripped the mobile and his face turned a deep purple. After a few seconds, Alaire spoke again. "Do we have an understanding?"

The slave hunter's face showed pure hatred as he stared at the mobile. "We do."

"Excellent... then I shall leave you and Mr. Crowley to your work."

Jedidiah placed the mobile back into his pocket and started yelling incoherently at Crowley. Alaire had Jedidiah over some type of barrel. While I was fairly certain the rune circle was Cauchon's idea, Alaire never failed to take advantage so he could be the one to profit in the end.

A familiar buzzing filled the air, heralding the promise of pain. The Spites. The dark dot coming through the clouds pushed me to make a quick decision. I drew me blade, stood up and leapt off the top of the pile. I heard a few startled gasps from behind me but naebody could catch me.

The nearest Fenrir received the pointy end of me blade a second before me feet hit the ground. I landed right next to Jedidiah. I kicked him in the back and he fell into the still-kneeling Crowley. Yanking out me blade again, I swung it into the throat of the next wolf lunging at me. It gurgled as it flew past me while one of its pack mates latched onto me left arm. Before it could get a fair bite, a good-sized rock struck it in the head, making it whine and release me.

I looked 'round just in time to see Jedidiah turning over to aim his rifle. It was pointed right at me head and way too far for me blade to reach him. A shower of rocks hit him in the head and arms, sending his shot wild. A quick glance up confirmed me comrades were doing their part to assist me.

Crowley moaned when he saw the scuffling was marring his drawings. I had nae time for his theatrics. "Ach, out o' me way, ye fraud!"

After I yelled, me foot sent Crowley flying out of the circle. More of his precious scribbles became smeared as he skittered across the ground. He fell and knocked his head against the rubble. He was dazed if not unconscious, and completely out of the fight.

That gave Jedidiah enough pause to take aim again. This time, I was closer than before. Me blade smacked his rifle aside just as me foot slammed under his chin. He sailed into the nearest tree, and his rifle dropped at me feet.

I heard the rubble shifting behind me, followed by frantic footsteps, more rocks striking the ground and the snarls of the Fenrir. The growls near drowned out the rapidly approaching Spites.

Perenelle's voice rose above the din. "Keep him away from the circle, *Monsieur* Black! We shall finish the design as it should be!"

Meanwhile, Jedidiah shook off me attack and rose to his feet. Once I came close, he pulled out his knife and assumed a fighting stance. Good size though the blade was, I sneered at it with contempt. "Ye think that wee tooth has enough span tae match the sword in me hands?"

Jedidiah glowered at me as he raised the knife to his head. "I think this is my fight."

I swung at his head, and he ducked. He attempted making a straight run at me guts, which I sidestepped at the last second. I aimed at his head with the hilt of me sword only for him to slip to the right and slice at me throat. I took a step back to avoid his blade, and punched him in the nose to knock him back. I felt the bridge of his nose snap beneath me fist. Unlike the rifle, he held onto the knife the whole way down. Grabbing the hilt of me sword, I used both hands to strike me blade over him. He rolled away to the left before me blade could impale his flesh.

Blood streamed down his broken nose as he tried to pick himself up. A kick to his chest knocked him flat on his back again but not before he plunged his

275

blade into me right calf. Me trousers sheared as the pain rippled through me and I bit down hard upon me lower lip. I felt blood running down me leg like a waterfall. I focused past the pain and called on me Druid magic to staunch the bleeding. While I did sae, I tried for another swing at him. But I was too off-balance from me wound. He evaded it with ease.

A sneer began forming on his lips as we circled one another. He shifted the grip upon his knife and held it with his thumb on the hilt. Another unwelcome surprise came in the form of a pair of gunshots that flew between us. Some of the returning troops spotted us and were providing cover for Jedidiah. Worse yet, everyone but the Flamels were struggling with the three surviving Fenrir.

Besom's blade was finishing what I started but she was slowing down and the wolves were relentless. Only the Urn seemed to reflect any serenity in the midst of the chaos, its steady glow growing brighter with each scratch the Flamels repaired.

Without warning, Gwydion stepped out of the ether and into the battle. Clearly he'd just appeared through the shortcut to the Dark Wood, smiling as he shook his head.

"No, no, no, no! This won't do at all. This was supposed to be an epic fight for the ages! Not a simple brawl."

The wall we had walked across suddenly exploded, splintering the rubble between us and the rest of Jedidiah's troops. The Welshman sighed and contentedly leaned back against one of the trees.

"Much better."

I felt a momentary sense of relief meself before I remembered the one we left behind. "Jeanne!"

Jedidiah took advantage of me temporary distraction to strike. I had just enough time to swat his cheek with the flat of me blade, throwing his

276

attack askew. As he stumbled forward, I rammed me knee right into his gut before slamming me forehead into his broken nose.

Stepping in just the right spot to avoid being hit by either of our attacks, Gwydion shook his head and tut-tutted me. "Now was that very sporting of you, Bladesmith?"

I snarled at him even as me bad leg made me miss me follow-up stroke.

Jedidiah took the opportunity of me missed swing to throw his knife right at me chest. I moved but was tae close to dodge it fully. It landed under me armpit, scoring a fresh slice of agony upon me body.

Gwydion reached into thin air and pulled out a perfectly crafted sword that was half the size of me own blade. He casually tossed it to the slave hunter, who caught it but didnae appear impressed. He lunged for his rifle but the Welshman kicked it behind him, well out of his reach. That barely gave him enough time to block me sword stroke aimed at his head.

I glanced 'round and saw me Lily slaying the last of the Fenrir. The angel was running towards the demolished wall, yelling "Jeannie!" at the top of his lungs. The Flamels continued their drawings while the Soul Retrievers collapsed on the ground outside them, exhausted from the struggle. The Spites were now close enough for me to make out their individual specks.

Mind, I was still aiming to cleave Jedidiah's head while I took all of this in. Only a careless warrior is unaware of the entire battlefield around him.

"Near to the stony causeway's utmost edge…"
-Dante's Inferno

TWENTY-EIGHT
TALLIS

Gwydion walked beside and between Jedidiah and myself as our blades clashed again and again. He took one look at the slave hunter's form and shook his head.

"And here I thought giving you a blade of your own would make this fight more fair. It's quite disappointing, Jedidiah, though not as disappointing as you were to your own children."

I watched Jedidiah flinch at Gwydion's words even if he tried covering it up. The Welshman's smirk told me he'd also caught Jedidiah's reaction and he looked at me.

"You, on the other hand, Bladesmith? Ohhh, I'm not certain your clansmen would say 'disappointment' even begins to cover your misdeeds."

"Shut yer geggie," I growled, knowing full well he wouldnae keep from talking. Jedidiah and I were now playing one of Gwydion's favorite games. While watching two men fight, he thrilled to bring to light each of their failures. Whoever broke their concentration first would be defeated.

The smirk upon Gwydion's face turned into a smug rictus. "Well, betraying your clan to the Romans on your mission to become Fergus Castle's new lord… If any of your dead relatives could have participated in your execution, I daresay they would have."

278

Those painfully true words hurt worse than me flesh wounds. I felt meself falling back more than I should have. Had me opponent been better trained on the sword than he was, this would have been the moment I lost the fight.

Besom came up behind the Welshman, her own bloodstained blade poised to end his life. Without turning 'round, he held up his palm before pointing towards the debris walls over me shoulder. "I do believe you have more immediate concerns at present, Lily Harper."

I circled Jedidiah and got a good glimpse of what was left of the wall. A small spray of sparks came from our blades while I saw Jeanne run quickly across the top with a Mephit and human pursuer at her heels. Two of the humans held guns and were trying to shoot the Maid of Orleans.

Me Besom nodded and ran in the direction of Jeanne, calling to the stookie angel who was doing the same.

"She is quite lovely, Bladesmith," Gwydion said though I failed to give him me attention. "I am surprised she finds you suitable as a mate. Surely she could do much better?" He paused. "As I understand it, the current Master of the Underground City has his eyesights set upon her? Is that true? If so, he could certainly offer her whatever she should want?"

An overwhelming flash of light that could only have come from the angel blazed into me eyes. Even when I slammed me eyelids shut, I could still feel the light's rays penetrating. Judging from his agonized cries, Jedidiah took a full blast of the same.

I opened me eyes, barely able to see, and began dragging meself towards the bewildered slave hunter. He popped his eyes open and made another swing at me. I felt the knife still lodged in me armpit quiver in sympathetic pain over the impact.

279

The Welshman stepped back into our view, unfazed by the blaze of light that hit the rest of us. "But let us not dwell entirely upon the Bladesmith's woes," Gwydion began again. "Of course, before you disappointed your children, Jedidiah, you disenchanted your wife irreparably."

The slave hunter swung at Gwydion. "Don't you dare speak of her!"

The nasty, little trickster all but danced out of the way with a chuckle. "But that's always been the problem. You never did speak of her, not even when you allowed her to be taken to New Orleans against her will."

I saw a perfect opening to end this fight for good but I wouldnae take it for I respected only a fair fight. Gwydion's jibe allowed me to whack Jedidiah in the back with the flat of me blade to get his attention. "Don't play his game, man. We already got one fight as it is."

Our mutual jeerer raised his eyebrows in mock shock. "What? You don't like playing games, Bladesmith? I remember quite a few of them you instigated in order to hold onto your first beloved."

The jibe made me glance at Besom to see how she was faring. She was managing rather well against the worms and one of the humans who fell from the top of the wall.

Gwydion was suddenly right at my shoulder, smiling his toothy grin. "Quite an uncanny resemblance to your lost lass, eh?"

I tried elbowing his face only to hit naught but the empty air. I got me blade up in time to stop Jedidiah's head stroke but still felt a stinging cut on me cheek for me trouble.

Before Jedidiah could pull back his blade, the Welshman whispered into me opponent's ear. "Does Dahlia resemble your dearly departed, disenchanted wife, Jedidiah? She has the right skin tone but as for the other features..."

Jedidiah didnae take that well. "Enough!"

He made a great swing that would have separated Gwydion's head from his shoulders. But any fool could see it coming from a mile off and the Welshman was far more nimble than the average fool.

Once Jedidiah showed me his back, I decided the time for warnings was over. I made a clumsy jab into the slave hunter's shoulder blade that did little more than break the skin. He responded by making another overarching sweep that hit me hard enough to nearly drop me sword.

Och, how I missed the power of Donnchadh!

Gwydion was once more at my side. "And here your true nature is hidden under the guise of reticence and honor. Had your cousin, the rightful lord of Fergus Castle, been given the opportunity, perhaps he would have gifted you a far swifter death than the Romans did."

I could feel his words hacking away at me just as surely as if he were stabbing me flesh. He quickly sidestepped to Jedidiah, who was aiming his sword at me chest. The slave hunter glanced at Gwydion with less nonchalance than he intended.

"There is nothing to discuss, traitor."

Gwydion raised his pointer finger. "Almost exactly the same words you told Angie when you gave her up to Nathan Bedford Forrest's men in Murfreesboro... And all to save your own perfectly pale hide."

I could tell that one hit home judging by the way Jedidiah shook. His fighting instantly became more erratic and his defenses spottier. Only me leg kept me from finishing him proper.

The Welshman appeared at me side while I drove Jedidiah back. He continued to taunt the slave master.

"I wouldn't get too upset, Jedidiah. After all, you had several good years, a marriage and two children. It's far, far more than Tallis Black ever received for his pains. Why, his beloved didn't even survive the taking of Fergus."

Me attacks faltered at his words.

Damn him for knowing what he did of me and mine! And damn me for failing to focus past his cruel unmaskings to end this fight. Not that Jedidiah himself was having an easier time concentrating on me.

"So what are you saying, trickster?" Jedidiah insisted. "That I'm actually better than Tallis Black, the one-time Master of the Underground City?"

Gwydion used his finger to tap his chin. "Well, let's see, you betrayed Jacob Fortlow so you could have his pretty slave for a wife, yet you gave her back under duress, and then you waited just long enough for the yellow fever to take her life. Does that sound better to you?"

That was more than the slave hunter could stand to hear. "Stop..."

Under me breath, I sighed heavily. Jedidiah had just uttered the one word that all but guaranteed the Welshman would do anything but.

Gwydion came closer, the rapidly approaching Spites a dark accompaniment to his words. "You left your children in the hotel... It's a good thing both of them could pass as white in a city like New Orleans."

Jedidiah's face grew tight again. "Stop..."

"And by degrees, you found yourself in front of your wife's hastily dug grave, a wooden branch barely marking the spot."

"Stop...!"

"And yet her body wasn't even there. It had floated out to sea nearly two weeks before you found her grave. Still, it was an appropriate spot for your subsequent suicide."

Jedidiah yelled out an incoherent howl as he tried vainly slashing at Gwydion. The strokes went everywhere, leaving his back once more turned toward me. I called his name and when he turned to face me, this time, me blade plunged in true. The slave hunter gasped another yell as the point came out the other side.

As he fell to his knees, Gwydion leaned over him with a triumphant smirk. "That isn't even the worst part, I'm afraid. No matter what he told you, Alaire never had your wife in his possession even though he promised you he did. I daresay she's forgotten you by now. You are utterly alone down here and you always have been. Your place in the Underground City was more than earned by your own hypocrisy."

Whatever fight was in Jedidiah's eyes died as the Welshman finished. Jedidiah looked up at me and I saw he was a broken man.

"Finish me."

Glancing up at the sky, those damnable Spites were nearly upon us, their infernal buzzing promising pain to anyone unfortunate enough to cross their path. I shifted me eyes over to the Flamels. "How much longer?"

Perenelle answered for both of them. "Nearly there, *monsieur*! Only a few more markings and—"

While she continued, I was distracted by Jedidiah's hand grabbing me by the pant-leg and yanking from where he wavered upon his knees. "I said, finish me, damn you!"

I pulled away and put a boot on his back. Try though I did, me blade remained in the slave hunter's body. The Spite cloud drawing closer made me redouble me efforts. Suddenly, something strong knocked me aside before tackling Jedidiah to the ground. It wasnae until she was sitting above me blade in me fallen foe's back that I realized 'twas Besom!

Her blade stayed sheathed as she used her hands to choke the life from Jedidiah. He didnae bother fighting her, but opened up his arms to welcome the second death that awaited him. I heard his neck crack but Besom kept right on squeezing. That was when I understood the brutal truth of what I was seeing.

Besom was possessed by Donnchadh.

I grabbed me beloved by the shoulders and pulled her back. "Off him, ye foul reaver!"

Donnchadh responded by slamming an elbow into me gut. The blow staggered me and I leaned down low enough for Besom's fist to strike me chin. The force of the blow scrambled me brains. I could do nae more than stare when she easily pulled out me sword from Jedidiah's cooling corpse. When she raised it over her head, the Welshman popped up at me side.

"Having a bit of a lover's quarrel?"

I sneered but kept me eyes fixed on the advancing Lily with me sword in hand. "Ah've won yer game, Welshman. So Ah'd thank ye tae leave me be whilst Ah deal with this."

He chuckled softly while patting me shoulder. "Oh, there's no need, my steadfast hermit. That problem is about to solve itself."

The Urn flared its golden light into a pillar, making the sound of a battle horn as it did. Besom's eyes went wide while her fingers suddenly dropped me blade and she clawed at her throat. She started swinging herself to and fro as the noise from the Urn grew louder. Finally, she screamed a deep roar that ended when a red cloud suddenly billowed out of her mouth. The cloud rapidly compressed into a small dot that vainly attempted to resist the force of the gravity exerted by Pandora's accursed gift.

But each struggle proved unsuccessful. The red dot that was Donnchadh was sucked straight into the Urn just a moment before the cloud of Spites drew near it. Every last speck of the cloud of Spites was similarly sucked down the same hole, though they too vainly fought for their freedom.

As the black was being consumed by the ubiquitous force that the Flamels had summoned, I snatched up me blade before kneeling at Besom's side. "Are ye all right?"

She coughed a few times before she replied. "Y-Y-Yeah, I'm fine."

I heard rapid footsteps coming from behind me. When I looked over me shoulder, I saw what was left of the opposing troops running away from the Urn as fast as their legs could carry them. Nae doubt they'd heard all the stories about the damage the Spites could do if they came too close to a living being.

I helped Besom to her feet. "Why'd ye do a fool thing like summonin' Donnchadh?"

Her breathing was still ragged but her eyes shone with steadfast conviction. "I had to be sure he went into the Urn with the rest of them. If he remained inside me, he might have found a way to eventually take over." She shrugged. "Or maybe the Urn would have pulled Donnchadh out of me anyway and damaged me during his extraction?" She tried for a grin as she slapped her right forearm. "At least I got a neat tatt outta the experience."

From the downed rubble, something blue drifted towards the center of the circle. It wasnae very fast at first but it swirled faster and faster the closer it came to the Urn.

When I saw who was inside the glow, I recoiled. Quickly sheathing me blade, I ran right at the blue figure and grabbed her by the arm.

Jeanne looked down at her arm before giving me another sad smile. "You have to release me. Only I can quell the malevolence inside that container." I knew in me heart she was right. But I shook me head and refused to release her. Tears fell from her eyes, rolling down her cheeks and I felt me stomach drop at the barbaric injustice I was witnessing.

Someone grabbed her other arm to fight against the tide... 'twas Besom. "We need you! We need Beatrice!"

I tightened me grip again. Jeanne shook her head at me Lily. "I was never Beatrice."

Besom shook her head. "But... I heard her name... I heard *your* name!"

Jeanne smiled. "You heard the name for the spirit of Hope; that was the true Beatrice. In life and in death, Beatrice was merely Hope's vessel and its mouth."

"Then why?" Lily started.

"I have taken on Beatrice's mantle," Jeanne explained. "Now Beatrice and I have grown so close together that I know not where she ends and I begin. Regardless, this is my fate."

"Then 'twas Beatrice's voice what guided ye?" I asked.

Jeanne nodded with a sad smile. "Yes, it was Beatrice's voice I heard for so long."

Tears came out of Besom's eyes at her words. "It's so unfair."

Jeanne looked between us. "It is inevitable. I shall always love you both for trying to save me. But that moment passed many long centuries ago. Let me do my duty to others one last time."

I gritted me teeth hard before I finally released Jeanne. Besom, to her credit, held on a bit longer until Jeanne shook her head and reached out, prying

Besom's fingers from around her arm. Then Jeanne's body shrank into a blue, glowing ball.

I thought I could hear whispers of the French prayer she had been reciting when the angel and I first met her. When the Urn sucked Jeanne in, the golden light and overwhelming vacuum suddenly ceased.

The cutoff was so sudden that nobody dared move for a minute. Then the stookie angel ran forward to grab Pandora's terrible wedding present, which he held over his head.

"Jeannie!"

His sudden outburst caused the troops to begin running and shooting at us. The liberated Soul Retrievers ran 'round the Fenrir corpses and headed for the trees. The Flamels pulled out more of their vials while Besom and I withdrew our swords to cover our group's escape.

The Flamels threw a few vials that landed behind us, conjuring up an impassible wall of fire. It blazed so high and hot that I feared 'twould burn the trees behind us.

I tried running for the gate but me wounded leg hobbled me to the point that I could barely limp. Yanking out Jedidiah's knife, Besom caught me under the shoulder and all but dragged me forward.

Gwydion stood in front of the tree that housed the opening to the gate leading to the Dark Wood, his usual smile back in place.

"Allow me to get the door for you."

With a flick of his wrist, the gate opened wide, allowing us entry. We ran forth and tumbled into the Dark Wood, barely ahead of the flames.

"His face the semblance of a just man's wore..."
-Dante's Inferno

TWENTY-NINE
LILY

Everything still felt wrong.

This was supposed to be a happy occasion. We'd finally escaped the Underground City with Pandora's Urn. We'd completely destroyed the gate that led from the morgue to the Dark Wood to ensure that nothing from the Underground City ever escaped. We'd even gotten Donnchadh sealed away in Pandora's Urn with the rest of the Spites.

We'd accomplished so much and yet everything rang so... hollow.

Two minutes after we arrived in the Dark Wood, Bill dialed up his friends, Sally and Polly, at AE. He didn't stop holding his breath until he got an answer at the other end of the line. He filled them in on the situation and warned them about Alaire. There was a lot of back and forth before he hung up.

Tallis looked down at him with concern. "Are they all right, stookie angel?"

Bill nodded shakily. "Yeah, for now, Tido. But that don't mean much."

Harry drew up to his full height. "Any way we can help 'em out, Shorty?"

Bill looked up at him with a solemnity I didn't think he had. "They want you all ta rememberize a phone number to reach them in case you ever need to.

288

Don't put it in your cell... *rememberize it*, like I said. Use it ta git in touch with them when ya git home."

Addie gave Bill a thoughtful look. "This isn't over, is it?"

Tallis chose that moment to speak up. "Nae, lass... there'll be plenty more Retrievers what needs retrievin' themselves from down there."

By the time Tallis guided our group to the portals that would lead them back to their respective homes, they'd all memorized the phone number to Polly and Sally.

I offered to put the Flamels up at my place in Edinburgh. I had the room and they definitely needed a place to stay. However, they politely declined, saying they preferred to find their own way and they had something they needed to do first.

Tallis wasn't crazy about their idea. "That's a fool's errand. The moment ye set foot in AE, ye'll be at the mercy o' Alaire."

Bill pointed at his favorite verbal sparring partner. "What he said."

I stepped forward. "What kind of bodyguard would I be if I allowed you to fall into the clutches of the most dangerous person in the Underground City?"

Nicolas held up his hands and patted the air. "*Mes amis, mes amis...* we thank you for your concern. But as with Jeanne, this unpleasantness is an ordeal we too must face."

Perenelle put one of her motherly hands on my shoulder. "Besides, do not Polyhymnia and Thalia deserve the help of two nearby allies upon which they can depend?"

My ex-guardian angel chuckled unhappily. "They're pencil-pushers, yer lab rats. What the hell good does that do either of ya when the whip comes down?"

289

I winced at Bill's metaphor, envisioning all the scars on Tallis's back. But the Flamels took his comments in stride and they shrugged as one. Nicolas looked up at Tallis with a fatherly gaze.

"I know this seems as though my wife and I have taken leave of our senses but we face desperate and uncertain times, which call for unusual and creative measures."

Perenelle squeezed my shoulder with a smile. "Should we need you, we shall call upon you. Your conduct in the Underground City, *Mademoiselle* Harper, gives me every confidence that you shall continue to be our trusted ally."

Tallis sighed. "An' is there naethin' Ah can say tae change yer minds?"

They didn't reply but judging from Tallis' nod and sigh of resignation, he must have seen their answer in their eyes. Reluctantly, he guided them to the portal opening that would take them to AE. Our goodbyes with the Flamels over, it was now just Tallis, Bill and I.

And we had a good day's hike to reach Tallis' cabin.

Even though he didn't say it out loud, I sensed Tallis was hurting from losing Jeanne. And why not? If I'd worked out the story correctly, Jeanne had been a regular source of hope for centuries down there.

And her reward was being sealed in for all eternity with the most hateful spirits in existence. I glanced down at the Urn I carried in my arms and suddenly wanted nothing more than to smash it into a million pieces.

***

As we approached Tallis' cabin, I immediately knew something was wrong.

290

On the outside, the place looked the same as it always did. But there was something missing that I couldn't put my finger on. Then I realized what it was: way too quiet.

Tallis took in a sharp breath as he poked something at his feet. Turning it over with his blade revealed one of the Grevels—monstrous demon beasts Tallis kept as pets. Glancing around, I noticed more of the same bodies littering the area. A sense of foreboding overcame me when suddenly the door to the cabin flew open.

Alaire strolled out as casually as if he'd been housesitting and wanted to welcome us back.

He was wearing a frilly, white shirt and red, velvet pants that would have looked ridiculous no matter what, but against Tallis' cabin in the background, Alaire appeared beyond out of place.

"You have something that belongs to me!" he said to me and pointed at the Urn in my arms.

"It doesn't belong to you," I growled at him.

"It's from the Underground City," Alaire responded with a slight smile that made little sense, given the situation. "Thus, it belongs to me and I want it back."

I handed the Urn to Bill as I readied myself for a fight. Tallis attempted to hobble forward but I put my arm in front of him. I was the only one in any kind of shape to take on Alaire.

Slowly walking up to Alaire, I slid my blade free. "You want it so bad? Come and get it."

"Gladly," he said and glared at me.

Two axes appeared in either of Alaire's hands. He aimed the axes at my head and chest, blows which I blocked with my sword. That led to two minutes of us trading blows which only resulted in the clashing of our weapons.

"You know, Lily, you could have been happy with me," Alaire said with a shrug as he stepped back, presumably to take a small rest from our melee.

"Happy?" I repeated as my eyebrows reached for the black sky. "As your prisoner?"

"I would have given you whatever you wanted."

"How about freedom?"

Alaire came at me again, his strikes were well planned but there was a recklessness to them that made them easy to avoid. I amazed myself with my own swordsmanship, keeping up with my nemesis like it was no more than a sparring session with Tallis.

"Freedom is overrated," he said with little interest. "What I could have offered you was worth far more."

He blocked another of my blows and I, in turn, blocked his.

"The offer still stands, by the way," he continued.

"And my answer is still no way in fucking hell," I responded.

Alaire took a step back and dropped both of the axes to the ground as he smiled. "I see we are quite well matched and I have no interest in continuing this tedious game ad infinitem."

"So what does that mean?"

"It means that you should hand over the Urn to me forthwith and spare yourself and your fellow travelers my anger if you do not."

"Um, yeah, I have zero interest in giving you the Urn," I said.

Alaire grew frustrated and intoned something as he reached for his axes again. It sounded like a bad impersonation of a Lovecraft cultist but there was nothing funny about the increased speed he suddenly developed. Suddenly his blows became harder to fend off.

"You could have learned to love me," he announced, his eyes narrowed and hateful.

"I would never love you," I spat back.

As the tide began to turn, and Alaire's attacks began to weaken me, a tingle from my blade tickled the inside of my chest. It felt like Donnchadh when he wanted to emerge but less insistent.

"And now that decision will be the reason you die... once and for all," Alaire said but there appeared a sadness in his eyes that made little sense to me.

I grew calm right before a blaze of blue light washed over me. The light felt cooling at the same time that my wearied muscles suddenly felt reinvigorated. I realized it was my Self taking over, echoing through me and dousing me with an energy that hadn't been there before.

It quickly became a fair fight again.

Before long, I drove Alaire into retreat. Finally, one of my strokes disarmed him of his left axe, which flew through the air and embedded itself in the cabin wall.

I walked up to Alaire. Meanwhile the blue light that surrounded me continued to glow brightly.

Touch him, a voice within my head suddenly announced.

I reached out and grabbed Alaire's wrist, and the light of my skin made his skin hiss and burn.

While I tightened my grip, he yelled out, "Malecoda!"

A familiar black portal opened up behind Alaire. Nothing but darkness appeared on the other side of the portal but I could feel an incredible power coming from it. It was as though a giant wind began pulling and sucking at Alaire's clothing as though trying to pull him into the void of the portal. I continued to grip his wrist but soon I felt myself being dragged forward, towards the portal through the dirt.

My blue light flared brightly in response and I realized I'd have to release Alaire or we both would end up sucked into who knew where. I instantly let go of his wrist at the same moment that he was pulled into the darkness and disappeared. A second later the portal vanished and the blue light that danced on my skin evaporated just as quickly.

I turned around and caught Tallis and Bill staring at me. "I couldn't hold him," I said in defeat.

Neither of them responded. Instead, they both just stood there, staring at me. Tallis wore a strange smile.

"What?" I asked, not understanding the reason for their reactions. "We could still go after Alaire…"

"Nae," Tallis said.

Bill pointed at me and finally spoke. "Umm, Nips… you kinda like changed into a different person there for a second."

"I did?" I asked.

Bill nodded. "And ya might wanna look at yerself now."

I glanced down at my naked arms and immediately saw the difference. My skin was a different color, no longer flawless alabaster, a feature of the supermodel package I'd signed up for. Now, my skin had darkened a little, like I'd gotten a tan after a day in the sun.

Tallis walked up to me and ran his fingers down the length of my arm. "This is the first time Ah've seen anyone soonburnt by spiritual light."

I looked at him with uneasy eyes. "What does that mean?"

Bill answered my question. "If I had ta guess, Lils, I'd say yer submergin' with that thing that lives in yer sword."

"It doesn't live in my sword," I answered. "It lives in me."

Bill didn't respond but suddenly glanced down at his cell. "Hey, I missed a text in all the excitementation."

Bill sucked in a tight breath through his teeth. "Fuck."

That statement made me curious and I walked over to see who was texting him. I saw a picture of a man with bright white wings being held by chains in a dungeon. The smarmy signature of "Ain't Nothing But A G Thing" told me at once who the text had came from.

Gwydion.

But this time, there was an actual message with it: *Meet Jeanne's guardian angel.*

Bill choked out a whisper as he stroked the screen and looked up at us with wide and scared eyes.

"It's the archangel, Uriel."

TO BE CONTINUED IN
DEVIL IN DISGUISE
NOW AVAILABLE!

Get FREE E-BOOKS!

It's as easy as:

Visit my website www.hpmallory.com

Sign up with your email address

Download your e-books!

About the Author:

H. P. Mallory is a New York Times and USA
Today Bestselling author!

She lives in Southern California with her son and
two cranky cats, where she's at work on her next
book.

Made in the USA
Monee, IL
07 November 2022